I Repent

I Repent

Renea Collins

www.urbanchristianonline.com

Urban Books, LLC
78 East Industry Court
Deer Park, NY 11729

ISBN 13: 978-1-60162-750-6
ISBN 10: 1-60162-750-5

First Printing March 2013
Printed in the United States of America

10 9 8 7 6 5 4 3 2 1

Distributed by Kensington Corp.
Submit Wholesale Orders to:
Kensington Publishing Corp.
C/O Penguin Group (USA) Inc.
Attention: Order Processing
405 Murray Hill Parkway
East Rutherford, NJ 07073-2316
Phone: 1-800-526-0275
Fax: 1-800-227-9604

I Repent

Renea Collins

Joyce Elizabeth Goff
January 5, 1940–May 5, 2012

To my momma, Joyce Elizabeth Goff,

I love you more than I could have ever imagined. Miss you. I never could have thought life without you was life without my legs and arms. You were my biggest supporter, my backbone, and it took you leaving for me to realize you equipped me, you taught me, you loved me . . . All the other stuff I thought was so important wasn't, it was you!

I love you, Momma . . . Beautiful!

Leigh LaCour Belyn
June 6, 1993–August 11, 2011

Repent: to feel sorry or self-reproachful for what one has done or failed to do, be conscience-stricken or contrite: often with. To feel such regret or dissatisfaction over some past action, intention, as to change one's mind about or direction for good. To feel so contrite over one's sins as to change, or decide to change one's ways. To feel sorry, contrite, or self-reproachful over an error, sin, etc. to feel such regret or dissatisfaction over as to change one's mind about and one's heart. To turn around and go a complete and different direction; opposite.

—Webster New World College Dictionary, fourth edition.

Thank You

I want to thank Jesus Christ, who I love so much and who I thank for His blood! Thank You, Lord, for allowing me the mistakes, the love, and the forgiveness that you have sustained in me and allowed to flow out my life. Thank you, Jesus, for forgiving me and for giving me a new life every time I repent to You. Your grace is sufficient enough!

To my mother, I love you so much. Thank you for allowing me to tell my stories with no interruption. People don't often understand things, but you have sacrificed by allowing so many things from our lives to be told, and I thank you for thinking of others and allowing people to be healed and made whole through Jesus Christ. I love you, Momma, forever!

I'd like to thank my family for all the support, prayers, and dedication they have shown. Momma, Aunt Yvonne, Uncle Bobby, Aunt Mary, Aunt Linda, and Krissy: you all have sown life into me continually, and when nobody else was there to support me, you all have been there. Thank you to all my cousins, Toni, especially, for helping me and being a true friend and for the new laptop. I truly love you all.

To my wonderful daughters, there are really no words to express the love I have for you two. You two are my all; understand that, Brittany and Brooke. I would not be anything if I didn't have your beautiful eyes staring up at me, depending on me and loving me.

My son-in-law, Dana, I truly love you. I am so happy that God made you for my daughter. You are truly a part of us, and I could not ask for a better son.

I want to thank Apostle Maurice Broomfield for teaching me holiness and righteousness. Thank you for being a true example of a man of God and telling me the truth no matter what.

I want to thank Pastor Sherry Broomfield for loving me and praying for me. I thank you for your smile and for always being there whenever I need you and even when I think I don't. Thank you both for being my spiritual parents.

To Nikki Ajan, thank you for everything you are. You are a blessing. To have you on my team is like having a priceless jewel. Your humbleness of what you do and the encouragement and truth you sent when I wasn't able to open this book and deliver has literally helped me get up and continue! Thanks Nik and I love you☺!

And Shatoya Wilson. Thank you Toya for always being here and never letting anything or anyone come between our friendship. Thank you for never turning your back on me, never stabbing me in the back and always telling me the truth no matter if it hurts or not. You have cried with me, laughed with me, and held me up when I could not stand at all. I thank you for that and thank you for listening to every story, listening to me read and listening to my plans. I could never have found a friend (sister) like you. You truly were sent from God! Love you, sis!

Thank you to Prophetess Cynthia Roberson for all of your prayers and love over the years. I thank you and your husband, Scott Roberson (John boy), for believing in me. (Sorry, I didn't come to see you). I love y'all.

Thanks, Elder Bean, for pushing me so hard and not accepting anything but excellence from me. I love you.

Also, a special thank-you to Joylynn Reese for expecting the best and always teaching, leading and displaying the best to me as an author.

To everyone who listened as I read that day at my house: Gina, Big E, Lesha, Brittany, Brooke, Malonda, Joni, Toya, Jesse, Jeannette, Niaja', Phermin, Toni, and Saundra. Thanks so much. I love y'all.

And to The Original Cast of *I Repent, the Urban Stage Play,* thank you all. You all brought forth this novel into a live drama that brought the house down! Thank you Taniesha (Money) Frazier, Hermon (Flyboy) Noble, William Hicks, Capresha Hicks, Jackie Stone, Courtney Short, John Lipkins, Princess Price, Tammy Hampton, Justin Kee, Hope Evans, Kasper and Jodi Harris, Brittany and Dana Bradley, Sinatra Coleman, Ronald Lyles Jr., Jonathon Lyles, Gerald Lyles, and my li'l Brother , Sawaun Blakely.

To everyone else, God bless you and I love you,

Renea

Chapter 1

Where's my money?

"No, Jason! Please don't shoot me!" Reese screamed from the top of her lungs. She was standing upstairs, trembling in her hallway.

As shaken as she was, she was still beautiful. Her sandy-brown locks curled up instantly from the perspiration of all the action going on. Her light brown skin was flawless. She had the most hypnotizing hazel eyes a person ever wanted to see, and her body was carved out to perfection from God Himself.

She was holding on to Kev, her live-in boyfriend's best friend, tight, so tight that her freshly done fake fingernails were digging into Kev's flesh as he stood in front of her while Jason followed, aiming the .357 magnum at her head. She was terrified! She hid behind and had wrapped herself around Kev while he tried so desperately to pull her into the bathroom that was between the two bedrooms and away from Jason's rage. That was the quickest room to get her in and out of Jason's sight.

Reese's mouth was so close to Kev's ear that he could hear her whispering repeatedly, "Jesus, Jesus, Jesus."

Kev shook his head and couldn't help but think about how everything had happened so fast: the argument, then the fight. His thought was quickly interrupted with Jason yelling.

"Man, Kev, I'm tellin' you." Jason charged Kev, and looking him right in the eyes. "You better back up, son! I ain't playin'. I'ma do this broad!" Jason's eyes were glassy, big and red from all of the weed he, Kev, and Reese had smoked earlier that day.

Reese was screaming and hollering, trying to get away from Jason as he cocked and pointed the hollow barrow of the gun in her face. He was waving it back and forth, trying to get a steady aim at Reese's head.

"Jesus! Jesus!" Reese screamed out.

Jason laughed and gave Reese the evil eye while yelling out at her, "Don't call on Him now! You got it twisted, Reese! Nobody's coming to save you!"

Kev stood there speechless, watching the whole thing play out as if he were in the front row of some sold-out movie theater. He couldn't believe this was happening. He knew about Jason's fighting in the past, but this . . . this was something else.

Kev thought, then yelled out at Jason, "Jason, man, listen to me." He pushed Jason back softly but Kev stayed in front of Reese, making sure she was in the bathroom safely. She balled up into a corner behind him in the tiny bathroom. The door stood open with Kev and Reese on one side and Jason standing in the hallway, pointing the gun at them.

There fell a dead silence before Kev spoke again. Kev took a big swallow, then tried to reason with Jason. "Jay, think about this, man. You know it ain't worth all of this." Kev flung his arms up, smiled, and looked around, as if to say, "This is small potatoes compared to where we lived in New York."

Jason and Kev were from the Bronx. They were in Columbus, Ohio strictly for the dope game. The plan was to make money in Ohio, establish a drug cartel to stay there, run their business, and monopolize the city with their product. They figured if everything went according to plan, they would be leaving Columbus and heading back to the Bronx permanently within five years, and they were now on their fourth year in the city. It took time to gain the respect on the streets to take over a city.

Kev was trying to get Jason to see that there was no time for this foolishness, and with Kev being the mastermind behind their operation, he knew that they were close to having the city on lock. They could be headed home to New York for good in twelve months. In other words, Kev was saying, "Stop messin' up!"

Jason listened to Kev for a moment, then looked over into the bathroom at Reese and got a little angrier. "Man, move!" Jason demanded, walking up on Kev but never crossing over into the bathroom. Jason stood there with his shadow from the wall bigger than life itself. He was six foot five and 240 pounds of pure muscle. He was gorgeous; from top to bottom he was beautiful. He kept himself well groomed with his double-dipped dark chocolate skin and his bald head. He had a pair of four-carat diamond earrings in his ears gleaming brightly, and plenty of heavy platinum around his neck and wrist.

"Kev, man move! I'm tellin' you, she deserves it!" Jason ordered. "I ain't gonna let that broad talk to me like I'm stupid. Now come on, Kev, you know me! I know she's takin' my money. How else is it disappearing? Huh? Who else could be takin' it, Kev?" He looked a terrified Reese in the eyes. "Where's the money you took, Reese?" He hit the wall. "Where is it? I know you got it!"

Reese covered her head and squirmed around a little as if she were trying to disappear, but she never responded to Jason's question.

Kev shook his head and then intervened. "Jay, man, let it go," Kev said as he walked into the hallway, closing the bathroom door behind him.

Reese stayed on the floor in the bathroom, balled up in the corner. She never said a word. She could hear Jason and Kev talking through the door, but she never moved. She stayed there trembling and crying, wondering how she had gotten herself into this mess and realized something had to change in her life. She knew she couldn't go on like this. She cried on the floor and whispered softly, "Jesus."

She thought how foolish she must sound to the Lord after walking away from Him years ago when she was a teen. She shook her head back and forth, feeling so unworthy to even ask Jesus for help. She was for certain that He would never hear her cry unto Him. So, she held herself and rocked back and forth on the floor, believing she didn't have the right to ever call on Jesus again. She silenced herself and listened to Kev trying to convince Jason it was time to leave.

"Let's go, man! We need to get out of here. Forget her, Jay. Besides, you need to think 'bout this, you ain't find da money," Kev reasoned. "Man, if you kill her and you think she took money, how you gonna find it if she dead?" Kev asked. "Think, man, use yo' head! You don't need this." Kev put his hands on his head as if he was thinking and mumbled, "I don't need this. Man, we don't need this! We got too much to lose."

Kev looked over to the duffle bag full of money on the floor by Reese's bedroom door.

They kept their money there because they figured it was safe there and nobody knew where she lived besides the two of them. Not even their crew knew where she lived or where they kept their money. That made it less likely that they would get robbed. . . or so they thought.

Jason followed Kev's eyes and looked over where the money was on the floor in the duffle bag. He knew that Kev was right. He was just mad.

Kev walked up to Jason and reached for the gun that Jason was holding, trying to get him to let it go, but Jason wouldn't. He was too consumed by anger to back down, so he raised the gun and aimed it at Kev, as if he was going to shoot him.

"Put the gun down, Jay," Kev hollered, but Jason didn't, he kept pointing it at Kev. Kev gave him a grim look, then challenged Jason. "You gonna shoot me?"

Kev was huge too, with solid muscles. Even though Jason had a gun, Kev wasn't scared. Kev was trying to hold it together, but he was tired of Jason and all the drama he kept getting in while they'd been in Columbus. Kev was way past frustrated with it.

Kev was all about his business, so Jason's antics were really starting to distract them from their plans, and money. Kev knew there was a possibility that Jason could have blown some of the money without even knowing it because he knew Jason splurged a lot on foolishness, meaning other women. Kev knew Jason was possibly accusing Reese of taking some money to take the heat off of himself. For all Kev knew, this could have been a front.

Kev's family was in New York and he didn't get into any extra activities while in Ohio. He wanted to get money. His concentration was on building an empire, a cartel, not being a womanizer like his best friend had been. Getting involved with chicks had been the last thing on Kev's mind, not that plenty of women in the CO hadn't tried to get at him.

Kev's complexion was light and he had beautiful gray eyes. He had a perfectly trimmed and crisped edge up on his facial hair and he sported waves. His daddy was Italian and his momma was black. So when looking at him, one could see his beautiful heritage from both of his parents.

Jason and Kev had been best friends since they were eight years old. "Friends for life" was their slogan. Meeting at the school one day, Kev heard a big commotion and ran over to a group of boys who were jumping Jason. When Kev saw what was going on he decided to jump into the fight and help. Kev hadn't known Jason up until that point, but hoped that if it had been him getting jumped on, someone would have helped him.

They whooped the other boys together and became fearless in school and that behavior followed them to the streets of New York. That was the beginning of their twenty-eight-year friendship.

Therefore, Jason knew Kev wasn't going to back down because Jason knew Kev didn't play.

"Let's do this then, man." Kev grabbed the open end of the gun and pointed it into his own chest. "Shoot me, Jay." His voice got louder. "Shoot me! But I am not gonna let you hurt her!" Kev clearly stated.

Jason hesitated for a minute. He watched Kev's chest move in and out from him breathing so hard; and then Jason grinned, showing his dimples. "Naw, man, you know I ain't gonna shoot you," Jason's raspy, deep, slow voice said, and he lowered the gun, put the safety on, and tucked it away. He then reached his hand out to Kev and waited for Kev to cool down and grab it.

Kev looked at him, then smiled and took Jason's hand and laughed. "You a piece of work, man!" Kev grabbed the bag of money; then they gave each other pound and a brotherly hug as Jason followed Kev down the steps.

Jason looked around to make sure he wasn't forgetting anything before he left. He looked over at Kev and said, "Man, I ain't ever comin' back here!"

"Look at me real good when I say this." Kev pointed at Jason and said, "Don't!"

Kev opened the front door and went out, while Jason grabbed his jacket out of the living room closet and smirked. He went toward the door to leave, then stopped and laughed. "Oh yeah." He turned around and yelled up the steps, "Jesus got you out of this one. You better be glad!" He laughed and slammed the front door.

Reese jumped when she heard them slam her front door, but stayed there on the soft, plush carpet, whimpering. She lifted her head and said, "Jesus, how did I end up here?" as her mind journeyed back to exactly how she had ended up there. . . .

Chapter 2

The Beginning

I went to live with my grandma and grandpa when I was eleven years old. Actually, me and Momma had lived with them off and on pretty much my entire childhood. But I went to live with them without Momma this time. Momma couldn't come this time. Her boyfriend, Yellow, murdered her. I was there when it happened, heard the whole thing take place, but I couldn't do nothin' about it. I remembered it as if it were yesterday.

Momma had taken twenty dollars out of Yellow's pants pocket the night before without him knowing. She did it so she could give me some money for my field trip to the Dayton Art Institute the next day. To be honest, I didn't think I was going. I knew she didn't have any money. It was the end of the month and her welfare check didn't come until the first.

I went to her bedroom door the night before the trip and knocked. I was holding the letter from my teacher, Ms. Armstrong, in my hand. I figured the letter would explain how important it was to go. I knocked; and then I put my ear to her door to make sure she was alone.

"Ma, you in there?" I didn't know why I asked that. I knew she was in there. I just didn't know if she was alone.

She replied with her sweet, soft voice, “Hold on, baby, I’m coming.”

I could hear her talking to someone. Then I knew it was Yellow when he said, “Where you goin’?” I heard her telling him she’d be right back, to hold tight and to watch TV for a sec. I rolled my eyes to the back of my head when I knew he was in there.

I never liked Yellow because whenever he came around he would keep my mother high on that stuff that would make her turn into a zombie, never noticing me or what was going on. Not even caring if we ate, had lights or food, or if I had clean clothes or nothing; a zombie. Besides that my mother was too beautiful for that fool!

Yellow was notorious and known to be scandalous throughout our neighborhood. There were rumors about him committing murders and rumors that he came up on money and dope by robbing people a few years back. He was now known as the neighborhood dope man and whatever anyone in the hood wanted, from marijuana to crack cocaine, he could get his grimy hands on and into theirs; for the right price that was.

I didn’t like him coming around our house. I was afraid when he was at our house and I would think someone he backstabbed was gonna catch him one night while he was laid up with Momma. I knew from hearing people talk that in the hood, when they came to get even, they killed everything in their way, which meant everybody in the house.

Momma came out the door with her bathrobe on. She had her beautiful, long, black, curly hair wrapped up in a bun and her face was radiant. She was a beautiful woman. She was tall and slender like a model, with blue eyes, a very fair complexion, and skin smoother than butter.

She closed the door behind herself. Then, she smiled at me and said, "What is it, Reese?"

"Momma, did you remember I needed twenty dollars for tomorrow's field trip?" I held up the letter while I asked, hoping she had miraculously saved some money for me to go. After all, I told her at the beginning of the month, so just maybe?

"I told you I wouldn't forget, li'l girl. Now didn't I?" She opened my hand and put the twenty in it. She gave me a kiss on my forehead, smiled, and started to open her bedroom door.

"Momma, I'm sorry," I blurted out. I felt so bad because I didn't think she remembered or had the money, and it made me feel guilty for all the stuff I said to myself under my breath before I got to her door.

She laughed at me, tilted her head and walked back over to me. She put her arms around me and gave me a big, warm hug. She whispered in my ear and told me how much I was growing into a beautiful young woman.

"Reese, you will accomplish anything you want in life, baby. I know you have been through a lot of difficult things, but our lives are going to get better, I promise." She continued to hug me. Then, without letting me go, she looked at me and said, "No more drugs, Reese baby, I promise you. But more important, I promised God. Reese, I am so proud of you. You keep up the good work at school. You deserve to go on this trip."

I nodded my head and whispered, "Yes, ma'am." I wanted so desperately to believe things were gonna change, but it was a hard thing to do, and with Yellow being there I knew it was closer to impossible than possible.

Momma interrupted my thoughts. "Reese, I want you to believe me. Do you believe me? Do you believe things are gonna change, baby?"

I smiled and nodded yes. I didn't want to lie to my mother, but I knew it wasn't gonna change. We had been here with her empty promises so many times. I felt as though I was the parent and she was the little girl. I had to bathe her, feed her, and sit with her when she was high. I had seen too much too often, and frankly, at eleven years old, I was numb to the promises that my mother frequently uttered.

My mother was a drug addict. She was addicted to cocaine by the time I was five and that led her to prostituting when I was seven. I remembered hearing her and her friends in the living room partying every night. I would beat on the wall, loud as I could, and yell, "Stop!"

I hated it! Hated hearing what was going on in the next room while I was in my room trying to get my homework done. I imagined getting good enough grades to get us both out the hood when I got older. However, it was just a dream that faded into a nightmare.

I ran back to my bedroom and laid the money on the dresser. I was hype. I went to my closet and looked for something decent to wear for the trip. I found my blue jean mini skirt and decided to wear that with my pink sweatshirt that hung off one shoulder, and my Nikes with the fat pink shoelaces in them. I smiled at myself in my dresser mirror after laying the clothes on my bed. I was so happy to be going.

I decided to turn in early that night so morning would come faster for my field trip. I couldn't wait! I was so excited to see the different art pieces and whatever else the institute held in there. I opened my bedroom door and went to the bathroom to run me a bath. As I passed Momma's room I could hear Yellow hollering at her.

"Yellow, please, lower your voice. My baby is here," I heard Momma reply.

"Listen, Sophia, I don't give a care who in here, you better get my money! I had more than this in my pocket, woman!" Yellow proclaimed.

I didn't think much about them arguing, 'cause he always had something negative to say. It wasn't that serious. Yellow raved on, pouted, and complained about everything, so I went in the bathroom and took my bath. I put the Mr. Bubbles bubble bath, which my grandma brought me, in the tub. I got in the tub, closed my eyes, and laid my neck on the rim of the back part of the tub. I was relaxing and excited to be going somewhere new.

I finally got out the tub after being in there so long that my fingertips were numb and white. I dried off, still hearing Momma and Yellow arguing, and went to my bedroom.

"Sophia, where is my stuff? Huh? Why you always taken somethin' that don't belong to you?" Yellow yelled. I could hear him hitting the walls and throwing stuff around. To top it all off, he was calling Momma out of her name. "You want me to leave now? You so stupid!" he spat.

I heard Momma say, "Yeah, get out!"

Then he replied, "I don't know why I keep foolin' wit' you! You ain't nothin' but a dope head and that's all you gonna ever be!"

Yellow flung open Momma's bedroom door to me standing right there. I rolled my eyes and passed him in the hallway. He didn't want to look at me but had no choice, seeing we were both in the tiny hallway. We didn't talk to each other, look at each other, or acknowledge each other. He probably hated me just as much as I hated him to tell the truth.

The hatred between Yellow and me started the end of the summer. Yellow had stopped by while Momma had gone to the grocery store. He pulled up, blasting his music in his ghetto-fabulous car. I knew it was him 'cause he was playing that same ol' song he always played, "Bump N' Grind": "I don't see nothing wrong with a little bump and grind."

(Ugh, I despised him, and after that day, I wished he were dead!)

I was in the bathroom putting my hair in a ponytail because my hair hanging down my back was making me hot. That day had to be the hottest day of the summer. I was gonna ignore Yellow when he knocked, but it seemed like he beat and knocked harder and louder as I ignored him.

"Come on, Reese baby, I know you in there!" He laughed.

I went to the door, looked out the peephole, and said, "What? What do you want, Yellow? She ain't here!"

"Little girl, I know she ain't. She sent me over here to leave somethin' for her in her room. Open the door, girl. Stop playin' wit' me!" He huffed.

I wrinkled my nose, rolled my eyes, and then opened the door. I walked away, back toward the bathroom, and that's when Yellow grabbed me.

"Ooowee, Reese, you shouldn't wear shorts like that." He pulled me close to him and started kissing me on the neck. I pushed him and tried to get him off of me but I couldn't. I was powerless against him. Yellow was a big man with prison muscles. You know, the kind of body that looks like all he did was stay on the weight bench lifting weights.

"Yellow, stop it! I'm gonna tell my momma if you don't," I screamed.

"Um, Reese, you so tender and young. Umm, you need to let me take care of you. Yo' momma don't have to know nothin'. Come on, Reese. You smell so sweet, you so young."

"No! Get off of me, you pervert!" He was touching my legs and my bottom, rubbing his big yellow hand up and down my thigh. He started backing me into my bedroom fast. My eyes were big and my heart was beating a mile a minute.

"You gonna be a woman today, little girl. I'ma break you all the way in, let you see what a woman is." I begin to scratch his face, and I spat on him. I tried everything I could to get away. I cried and screamed but nobody came to help me; nobody could hear. I was so afraid he was going to rape me. Oh God, no! Don't let him do this to me! I want my momma! Momma, please hurry home! I cried to myself.

He started whispering and he laid me on the bed and was on top of me. "Come on, Reese." He kissed me on my lips.

I was so angry that if I had a knife I would have killed him, but I didn't. All I had was my teeth. So, as he forced his tongue in my mouth, I closed my eyes and tried to bite his tongue off!

"Ouch, you li'l . . ." He jumped up off me; then he bent down and smacked me in the face. My face turned fast from the hit. I grabbed the side of my face and looked him in his eyes. But I didn't care. I didn't even flinch from the hit. I just wanted him out of there. He touched his mouth and looked at the blood from his tongue on his hand. "Okay, little girl, all I wanted to do is make you a woman. Show you how a man takes care of a woman." He was out of breath.

I stared him in the eyes and watched the blood drip from his mouth. I was so glad I hurt him, but I wished I had bit it off!

"You could have had anything, Reese, anything you wanted, but it's cool. One day, li'l girl, one day." He turned and walked out my room.

From that day until this one, he'd never looked at me again.

After he stood at the door a few seconds longer he finally left, then Momma came out of her room. I figured she was trying to see if I was all right with all of the arguing they had been doing.

"Reese, I see you walking in that kitchen. You need to go to bed. You have that field trip in the morning, baby," Momma said.

"I'm getting somethin' to drink first. Then I'm going to bed, Momma." I smiled, leaving the kitchen with a big cup full of grape Kool-Aid. When I got down the hall the curiosity hit me.

"Hey, Momma? Did you take the twenty dollars you gave me from Yellow? I heard him say he was missing money."

"He gave it to me, and you don't worry about that! You stay in a little girl's place . . . Silent! Now, good night." She stood there, grinning, with her hands on her hips. I shook my head and smiled; and then I walked in my bedroom and shut the door.

About an hour later I was awakened abruptly by what sounded like furniture being thrown. Someone was yelling and screaming and it startled me. I jumped out my bed, opened my bedroom door, and went to the living room where the noise was coming from. Momma was in there sitting on the couch, smoking her cigarettes, and Yellow was standing over her, hollering. He hadn't noticed me but Momma did. She looked over at me and waved her hand for me to go back in my room, but I stood there.

"Sophia, you think this some kinda game? I told you before don't touch my money, didn't I?"

He was high. I could tell because I knew the actions that came with him getting high, and he had no problem snorting that stuff whenever he sat in the living room and watched TV. He would take some of the cocaine out of a little plastic tube, lay it on the coffee table, lean his head down, and sniff. Every time he did, it wouldn't be long before he would turn into this monster, acting invincible. That's how he was acting now. Yellow was out of control.

I looked around the living room and saw that the front door was wide open. I could see the television that usually sat in the living room now outside on the sidewalk, busted. Glass was everywhere! The front window was broken out, too, and there was a big hole in the living room wall.

My mother couldn't take her eyes off me. She waved for me to go back in my room again, but I didn't. She sat there so calm, not even blinking from Yellow jumping up in her face. Her eyes shifted from looking at me to looking at that fool. She lay back on the couch, crossed her legs, then puffed on her cigarette. She leaned her head back, closed her eyes, and blew out the smoke. "I know you don't think I'ma give you any money now. Look at this place!" She flung her hand in the air. They both looked around at all the damage.

She shook her head, then continued, "I put you out, and you come back in here through the window? And to top it all off you bust it out! I'ma have to pay for that, Yellow! Oh please, get out of my face!"

She waved him off, put her cigarette out in the ashtray on the table, and then she crossed her legs and began to shake one on top of the other. I hadn't ever heard her talk to him like that before. I covered my mouth from giggling, thinking, *that's what he gets!* "Yellow, it's over. I can't stay in this relationship!" She closed her eyes before she said anything else and he watched her, waiting for her next word. "I'm off the drugs, tryin'a do right by me and my daughter, and this"—she pointed back and forth to herself and then him—"is not healthy. Then you come here and break everything up." She took a big sigh of frustration. "I start my job tomorrow; Reese has school in a couple of hours . . . It's over. It's time for you to go, Yellow."

She got up off the couch and walked to the front door, which already stood open, waiting for him to leave. He walked over to her as if he was going to leave. He paused, and then grabbed her face with his hands and squeezed. "Who you think you talkin' to? Huh?"

His face turned grim and his pupils looked black. He yelled and pulled her down to the floor. "You must be out of yo' mind! Don't forget who I am! I may be a li'l high on this coke, but I ain't no dope head!" Yellow demanded, and pulled out his gun.

I was scared. I ran back to my room and called 911. "Hello, my momma and her boyfriend are fighting, can you please send someone around here? He has a gun!" I said to the 911 operator.

I was pacing my bedroom floor back and forth. My hands were shaking and my heart was beating faster than ever before. I could hear Momma trying to get away from him. The commotion in there was extremely loud.

"Don't be scared now. You talkin' all that mess! Say somethin' now, Sophia! What you got to say now? Huh?" He was yelling at the top of his lungs. I was surprised none of our nosy neighbors didn't come out. I knew they were listening.

"Yellow! Put that gun away 'fore somebody gets hurt. Please, baby, my baby is in the next room!" I heard Momma pleading.

I was sure he couldn't hear anything she was saying by now. He was in a full rage. The monster was out.

"You shouldn't have took my money! Why would you go in my pockets like that? Huh?"

I couldn't move. All I could do was listen. I heard Momma in the living room begging for her life. She was pleading for him to put the gun away before somebody got hurt, but he was high, hype, and completely out of his mind.

Momma was crying and pleading. "Yellow, please let's just go to bed. It's late. We can talk about this in the morning. I took the money 'cause you told me to get it out of your pocket, please remember. I wouldn't go in your pockets. I wouldn't disrespect you, baby. Please remember."

It got very quiet in the house, almost as if he was thinking and contemplating going to bed. Then I heard him speak again. "Naw, Sophia, I heard you; you said you was leavin' me. You know . . ." He laughed. "That's what you said. Now you got yo'self together you wanna leave me?" Then the wrestling between them started again.

"No, baby, that's not true. I won't ever leave you. Please, put the gun down and let's go to bed. Just put the gun away, baby," she cried, her voice trembling something awful. "Please . . . I love you," she whispered.

This eerie feeling was in the air. It got quiet throughout the whole house. I hoped he would listen to her and just go to bed. I heard him mumbling something to Momma. He had to have been very close to her. Then I heard her cry out very loud and that's when I heard her start praying as if she knew her life would be over soon.

"Jesus, please forgive me of my sins. Please, Lord, forgive me." As she prayed she cried. "Please! Forgive me."

I covered my ears with my hands and tried to forget that this was going on. I felt like I was losing my life, my breath; my breath had left my body for a second.

I was lost, but no matter how hard I tried to ignore what was happening, I could hear Momma. "Lord, please send your angels to protect my Reese."

That was the last time I ever heard my momma's voice. Even though I heard her cry out to God, all I could ever hear for years on were Yellow's words.

"If I can't have you, nobody will!"

I couldn't see what was happening, but from what I could hear, I knew what was next. I closed my eyes and prayed. I asked God to come into my house and save her. I pondered whether he would stop if I ran in there, but I was too frightened. I couldn't move.

"Please, Jesus! I don't know what to do without my momma. Please don't take her." Then I dropped to my knees and begged God to save my momma.

Next I heard the gun fire. I lay on my floor, dead; I felt dead anyway.

Then I heard another shot. I jumped. I stayed in my room a few more seconds, looking at the thread that twined the carpet fiber together. I looked at my hands, took them and pushed myself off the carpet. I staggered to my feet, opened my bedroom door, and went in the living room.

I could hardly breathe. I felt like I was suffocating. Momma was lying there, lifeless; then I saw the one shot to her chest.

"Momma!" I screamed. "Momma! No!" I cried and grabbed her. I put my arms around her. I was trying to get her to wake up. “Momma. Please. You gonna be okay. Wake up, Momma, please wake up.”

Tears continued to flow from my eyes. There was blood everywhere and all over me. It was on my hands, in my hair, and all over my legs. I felt like I was in a nightmare. All of this for twenty dollars, I thought.

I realized she was gone. There was nothing I could do. There was nothing I could say to bring my momma back; she was gone. Just that quick, she was gone.

I had just laughed with her, just joked with her, just was mad at her for something I couldn’t even remember? Now she was gone.

I sat there beside her in a trance; and then I noticed Yellow’s body lying there on the other side of the living room floor. He had shot himself in the head.

All I could hear in my ears was his voice saying to Momma, “If I can’t have you nobody will.”

It’s funny how I never thought about my father before Momma died. I never saw him before in my life until Momma’s funeral. He was a dark man and his eyes were as red as fire from all the liquor he must have drunk before the funeral. He came in the place hollering for Momma to get up out of the casket. It was a mess.

I couldn’t believe it. Here it was, my mother had just been murdered, my grandparents and aunts and uncles were arguing about who was gonna take care of me, and to top it all off, here came this fool in the place tripping! I hated that day.

After putting on a show down at Momma’s casket, my father turned around to me, bent down to eye level, and said, “Little Sophia,” calling me my momma’s name. He picked me up and hugged me, and whispered in my ear, "Don't be like yo' momma." He kissed my cheek, put me down, and walked out of church.

He was never to be seen or heard from by me again.

The drive from the burial site was quiet. I sat in the back seat, slumped into the window with my arm against the glass, covering my face. I still couldn't believe Momma was gone. Grandpa was driving and Grandma sat on the passenger's side silently, with the radio on the gospel music channel. I uncovered my face for a second and glanced at them. I knew Grandma and Grandpa were dealing with the loss just like I was; after all, it was their baby girl. Grandpa was holding Grandma's hand and massaging it.

None of us said a word in the car. We just listened to the radio playing "Moving Forward" by Israel Houghton. I felt like going somewhere and crawling into a corner and disappearing. I didn't feel like being bothered with all the relatives and friends who would be pulling up to my grandparents' house shortly after we did. I was still in shock after seeing and finding Momma lying on the floor. My heart was broken.

The car stopped and I looked over at the big white house and its beautiful wraparound porch. "136 Anna Street," I said.

"Hum? You say somethin', baby?" Grandma asked.

I didn't answer. I just sat in the car and thought about what my father said to me at the funeral. *Don't be like yo' momma.* I said aloud, "Don't be like yo' father." I continued to sit in the car well after I watched Grandma and Grandpa vanish into the house.

Chapter 3

The Invitation

"Reese, honey, you will settle in here just fine," my grandma said, trying to make me comfortable. She rubbed my back while she talked. She was sure to assure me that everything would be all right, but at the time I couldn't imagine it ever would.

The first few months after the funeral were the hardest for me. I could still see Momma and still hear her voice. I could even smell her perfume. I was lost.

I didn't want anyone telling me that "things will get better," "you will be okay," "sometimes in life . . ." or "well, God makes a decision to take some home." All of that, those words, were for the birds as far as I was concerned. My momma was gone and nobody, I meant nobody, could take her place. Even with her lacks, flaws, and mistakes she was still mine and nobody could tell me to move on.

Yellow had taken the one person I needed here, the one person I wanted to make things better for when I got older, the one person who believed in me.

My heart was bitter and I was mean to everyone who tried to say a kind word to me. One day my grandma got tired of it.

"Reese, how you doin' today?" she asked me.

I had seen her coming in the bedroom before she said anything. I hurried and sat up on the bed and put my magazine down with an attitude. I didn't feel like talking to her. I couldn't understand why she just didn't get the fact that I wanted to be left alone.

"Now, Reese, we know you goin' through a lot with Sophia gone, but, baby, we need you to get it together. I sympathize with you and I understand how you feel." She touched my shoulder.

"She was my child." She began to cry. "Now, baby, it's time for you to get focused back in school. It's been five months since your mother's been gone and . . ."

I heard nothing else she said. *What do you mean five months? I was with my momma my whole life and five months ain't long enough for me to mourn. Old lady, you better go 'head.*

"You know yo' momma would want you to. You can't sit around here and die with her, Reese." She lifted my chin to look at her and tears were forming in my eyes. I heard what she was saying.

"You said yo' momma spoke to God last, Reese. I want you to understand what that meant. Before she went on she asked for forgiveness, baby. That means she is numbered among the saints."

I smiled a little, thinking of her sitting in heaven.

"I need you to know that your mother would want you to continue yo' life. Don't lose it at an early age. Your momma's in a better place." She smiled, kissed my cheek, and left my bedroom, humming.

I sat there for a while, thinking; then I realized that I had to go on. I did believe that Jesus was real and that Momma was in good hands. I got up off my bed, shut the door, and went back over to my bed. I got down on my knees, folded my hands, and began to pray.

"Jesus?" I opened my eyes and looked at my pink wall that Grandpa painted for me when I moved in. It felt funny praying and talking to Him, but it felt real.

There was this presence that came in my room, as if someone were standing behind me. I closed my eyes again. "Jesus, hi, um, I need you. I'm only eleven and a half, but my mother died and I need your help." The more I spoke to Him, the more comfortable I was.

"Jesus, I don't know what to do without my momma. Can you help me?"

I began to cry, but at the same time I felt this pressure leave me. A comfort came that allowed me to understand I would be okay as long as I continued to hold tight to Jesus. I trusted Him.

I stayed in my room the rest of the evening, getting prepared to go back to school the next day with a fresh outlook. I had decided the most important thing for me to do was succeed in school. If I wanted a better life, if I wanted my life to be different from my mother's, I knew I had to do some different things.

After I got my clothes ready and slicked my hair back into a ponytail with a pound of Ampro styling gel, I took my bath, got in bed, and decided to talk to Him one more time before turning in. This time I spoke while I was in the bed and I stared at the ceiling.

"Okay, Jesus, I am swearing to you that I am yours. My focus from this day forward will be you and my schoolwork. I am only yours and I won't have sex until I am married. That way I won't get a horrible man." Then I whispered, "Like Momma." I closed my eyes and went to sleep.

I'd kept my promise to Jesus and studied hard the next three years to maintain a 4.0 going into my freshman year in high school. Summer break had started and I was ready for the time off. Life for me was pretty good. I was on the honor roll, I played volleyball, where I was the most valuable player, and I was very popular. I didn't have a worry in the world heading to high school at the end of the summer. I had made plenty of friends. I was a typical teenager. My grandparents made sure I had every pair of tennis shoes I could have imagined, along with designer clothing.

"Reese, now, baby, I think today somethin' special is gonna happen to you," my grandma said.

I looked up at Grandma driving the car and admired her beauty. I loved her so much. She was a light-skinned woman with long, wavy black and gray hair. I smiled and remembered when it was all jet black and realized she was getting older. I thought how much Momma looked like her with the hair and the flawless skin, distinctive bone structure, and full lips they both had. I laughed to myself.

Grandma had distracted me by yelling to get my attention while I looked through a magazine on our way to church. The church was on a seven-day corporate fast. I wasn't, but Grandma, Grandpa, and some of the dedicated members were. We were headed to the sanctuary for a shut-in with some of the other members, including my grandpa, who was the pastor of the church.

I really loved spending the night in the church. It always made me feel secure and protected. I would always imagine the sanctuary filled with angels guarding and protecting all of us while we were there. I always thought the angels were there waiting patiently to take everybody's requests back to the Lord. I laughed as I let my imagination run wild as a fourteen-year-old child. "Huh, Grandma?" I questioned.

Grandma covered my hand with her own hand, looked over at me, and smiled. "Something special for you today, baby," she softly said. "I prayed earlier today and asked the Lord to fill you with Himself, Reese. I know your momma's death is still painful but I'm asking God to show you that, even through horrible circumstances, He can and will give you peace in the midst of a storm." She smiled. "And, baby, your momma's death was the hardest thing me and your grandpa ever had to deal with, but—God! Woo—child, Jesus has a way to carry you through!"

I sat there for a second and thought about Momma's murder, then answered, "I hear you, Grandma," and smiled.

Grandma never said anything else. She just started humming one of her favorite songs she would sing to Jesus. I went back to reading my magazine and fantasizing about meeting the movie stars who were in there.

"Okay, Reese, we're here. Get our stuff out the trunk and come on in," Grandma said while she walked into the church and I did what I was told.

As soon as I opened the door of the church I could hear the members praying and could smell the sweet aroma from the candles that were lit coming from the sanctuary. I closed my eyes and sniffed in the linen smell and smiled. *How beautiful it is to commune with God,* I thought while walking into the sanctuary. I looked for a spot to put down my blankets and pillows to sleep, claimed a spot, and continued to smile while listening to the cries from the members unto the Lord. I looked up at the cathedral ceilings and the chandeliers and noticed they were barely lit. I then realized the candles were the source of light in the sanctuary. It was so pretty in there with the lights turned down like that, and it really set the atmosphere for Jesus to come and visit.

I closed my eyes and whispered, "Breathtaking."

I heard prayer coming from the altar and turned to see Grandpa there on his knees, praying. I wanted to go to the altar and pray but I had never gone before.

However, this day I didn't care if the other kids would make fun of me. Today I felt a pulling to go to the altar and pray; it was as if Jesus were calling me there, sitting on the marble altar, waiting for me to come and talk to Him.

I grabbed my blanket and went, not caring who was looking at me. I just knew it was something I had to do. The pull from the Lord was greater than what some people would think.

As soon as my knees hit the ground I felt an overwhelming comfort and peace. I felt warmth in my heart and before I knew it my mouth was moving and words I couldn't understand were flowing out. I imagined I stayed on the altar for a while, crying and speaking in an unknown language to man, only known to God. I knew my Redeemer had saved me and made me free. Free in my heart and free in my mind; I was free. The knowing of this was too powerful for me to be quiet or deny that God had given me a gift. So I worshipped Him and loved on Him as the others in the sanctuary watched and celebrated what God had given me: Him.

Chapter 4

A Broken Promise

I was in the tenth grade when this cliché of a boy walked by. Tall, dark, and handsome were his qualifications. Quite well by far the cutest dude at our high school and to top it off he was the star athlete: Mr. Julius Logan. I believed I noticed him before he ever laid eyes on me that day.

"Hey, man, wait up."

This big ol' boy ran by me in the hall. He had to be a football player, seeing the way he was dressed. One cleat was on and the other was in his hand, not to mention those tight football pants he wore. His school jersey had all kind of grass and dirt stains on it. The bell had just rung for the last period of the day. "You gonna be late to the field if you don't come on, man. Get that chick's number later!"

He hollered at another boy dressed identical to him, besides the one shoe on, one off. "I'm comin'," he yelled back, but continued to walk and talk to Lan'. Lan' was a cheerleader; a beautiful girl mixed with African American and Asian features, she had hair down her back, red flawless skin, and was very shapely. She was popular at our school, but, then again, so was I.

"All right, Lan', I'll see you after practice, right?" He smiled at her, showing his pearly whites. He had the kind of smile that would paralyze a girl, make her stop in her tracks like a deer in the headlights of a semi. He had the kind of smile that belonged on a Wheaties box. He had the kind of smile that if he was telling a lie, his smile would make it seem like the truth.

From that very moment I wanted him to be my husband. I had done good so far keeping my promise to Jesus that I wouldn't have sex before I was married. I had managed to stay a virgin all the way up and through my ninth grade year and I wasn't about to let Jesus down now. I didn't think about Julius being my boyfriend; I wanted him to be my husband, of course when we got older.

I looked him up and down and thought how cute he was. He was six foot three, with muscles bulging out of his chest, back, and arms—OMG—like the Hulk! His skin was so beautiful and silky, like he had Indian in him. His hair was short and curly. I had to say this: he was dreamy!

He turned around to go in the gym and bumped straight into me, this big linebacker who carried the number eighty-five on the back of his jersey.

"I'm sorry, I didn't see you there." He smiled and grabbed my hand. "You all right?"

"Yeah, I'm fine." I smiled back. I felt like melting right before him. Here I was talking and holding hands with Julius Logan, the highly scouted, most popular superstar athlete in Dayton, Ohio. My heart was beating a mile a minute and I knew my hand was clammy from being so nervous.

"You're Reese, right?" he asked.

"I'm Reese. What's your name?" As if I didn't already know.

"I'm Julius, Reese." He raised my hand, and then kissed the back of it.

We were so caught up in each other that both of us forgot about poor Lan' standing there with her mouth hung open. I was sure she couldn't believe she had just gotten her boyfriend stolen away from her in front of her face.

"Julius!" she screamed. "You don't see me standing here?"

"Oh, Lan', yeah, I see you." He continued to look me in my eyes but he spoke to her. He never let my hand go until, finally, she walked off angry.

"Your girlfriend just left," I said, laughing.

"She's not my girlfriend. Not at all, but you on the other hand . . ."

He had me, caught in the headlights of love.

Julius and I were inseparable from that day forward. We finished high school and graduated side by side. The both of us headed to Columbus, Ohio for The Ohio State University with scholarships: his a football scholarship, and mine academic, studying electrical engineering.

My plan was working and God had gotten me out of tight spots without losing my virginity to Julius before we married. I was secure and happy, and we were headed for some great things.

It was when we were in our sophomore year of college that it happened. The football team was headed to the Rose Bowl and Julius was Ohio State's man. He had all kinds of people pumping him up with promises, giving him money, and even giving him and me a car. But Julius was blinded by it all, and, to be frank, I was too. Who gives two college students brand new cars, money in their bank accounts, and hooks them up with a decked out condo? Alumnis do, that's who! But there was no need for me to ask questions, I was just along for the ride. It was hard in school. My grandparents didn't have a lot of money to give me so I considered it a blessing.

"Reese, do you know where my headphones are?" Julius asked. "I need 'em for the plane."

I watched him, but continued to stay on the couch and study for my psychology test. He went through every drawer in the kitchen looking for them. Our place was pretty nice and we paid next to nothing in rent. It belonged to one of the alumni who moved away but didn't wanna get rid of their property. It was way out in the suburbs of Columbus in a small city called New Albany.

The day we moved in, it had been completely furnished by every piece of furniture that I had ever pointed out to Julius in magazines. Not to mention he had someone go out and get new linens, new pots and pans, and new dishes. I was so shocked. All I remembered was thinking, *this man loves me so much*. He made sure I had gotten everything I wanted and needed.

"Baby, you don't know what I did with my headphones? I just had 'em yesterday. If I don't find 'em, it's gonna be a long ride for me to Cal," Julius proclaimed.

"Okay, I will find them." I puffed. I needed to study, but Julius needed me. I hadn't studied all weekend. I needed to keep my 4.0 for my scholarships and because I promised myself.

I went into the bedroom, bent down and looked under the desk, and pulled out the earphones. I didn't know Julius was right behind me.

"Babe, come on," he pleaded.

I raised my eyebrow. I knew what he was thinking before he even said it, because Julius was tired of waiting and he tried often to convince me to have sex before we got married. We had argued lately about the fact that we lived under the same roof and I wasn't willing and ready to have sex. Julius would be so upset that he would leave and stay over at one of his boys' places until he cooled down. I did wonder if he was having sex with other women, but it never showed its head. Not one time did any chick ever say he was messing around with her. He either had them in check or really loved me.

"Come on, babe. You know I ain't goin' nowhere. I love you, but a brother has needs." He pulled me close.

I ignored his words. "Here's your headphones."

"Thanks, babe." He grabbed me and kissed my lips.

"But, Julius, I promised."

He began to kiss me. "Reese, I promise you I won't ever hurt you. You all I got, babe. I love you. You have to trust me. Come on," he whispered. "I'm leaving for two weeks in a hour. I'm gonna miss you and I want you to experience how much I love you." He let me go, backed up, and stared at me. Next he got on his knee, pulled out a blue box, and opened it up. "Marry me."

I didn't know what to say. I felt like I was gonna pass out right there. The ring was beautiful. It was a two-carat marquise cut diamond with clusters of diamonds all around it.

"Julius!" I screamed.

"Marry me. I swear I will keep you smiling. I want you to be the mother of my children. You have been here for me, Reese. I love you." I got on my knees with him, put my arms around his neck, and whispered in his ear, "Yes, yes, I will marry you." I closed my eyes and cried out, "I love you."

That was it. My promise to Jesus was out the window.

For a while I was bothered that I didn't keep the promise to Jesus to save my virginity until I was married. I began to psyche myself up to believe that as long as I asked the Lord to forgive me before I did it, while I did it, and when it was over, it was okay to do. I didn't realize it wasn't okay to break a vow to God, and I did.

A few years later, Julius and I were graduating from Ohio State. Our next plans were the wedding; then he would be off to football camp as the number-one draft pick in the country. I was headed to our new home in Cleveland, Ohio's suburbs.

Julius didn't want me to work yet. He wanted me to travel with him during off-seasons and be active with the team's wives during the season. So for me life was shopping, trips, clothes, jewelry, and dining.

I was happily married to the man of my dreams, and within a year of marriage we had a son. His name was Michael.

Life was pretty good for a while, until I found out he wasn't exactly the Prince Charming in the fairytale I was living.

"Babe, I'm headed out. You don't need anything before I leave do you?" he yelled from the bathroom.

I sat on the couch with our four-day-old baby Michael on my shoulder, rocking him. "Seriously, Julius, out where?" I was so frustrated with him. All he ever did anymore was go out and kick it with his boys. I was so tired of it.

"Yeah, I'm goin' out wit' the boys. You got a problem wit' it?" He came out of the bathroom and stood there looking at me like I did something wrong. I took a deep breath, closed my eyes, and said, "Babe, please, stay home with us. We need you and you promised me . . ." I didn't even think he heard me. He walked away, huffed a little, and mumbled under his breath. I put the baby in his swing and followed him. He was standing in the mirror of the bathroom, putting on some cologne.

"Where you goin'?" I asked.

"Out, Reese, I'm goin' out. Why?"

"What do you mean why? Where's this coming from, Julius? Huh?"

He put his shirt over his head, his diamonds in his ears, and his cross around his neck. "I wanna go hang out wit' the fellows, Reese. Can I do that? I'm tired of being here wit' you."

He looked down at me, and then walked away. I stood there for a second with my hands on my hips, speechless, watching him walk. I wanted to slap the taste out of his mouth for getting so smart with me, but I decided to do something else.

I walked to our bedroom, grabbed my suitcase out the closet, and began to pack my and the boy's stuff. I heard him coming down the hallway.

"What you in here doin'?" He smelled so good and looked so good. But I was mad. His sweet-talking and fineness weren't going to get him out of this one. Julius had been out all week long partying, leaving me here with the baby. He never got up in the middle of the night with the baby. This was for the birds as far as I was concerned. I could go back to Dayton and let my grandma spoil the baby and me!

"Uh? Reese, you leavin' me, babe? Fo' real?"

"Yes, I'm out of here! Michael is only four days old and you think you gonna keep leaving me here alone and not help at all. Hum, bet you don't. I'm out of here!"

He grabbed me around my waist and started laughing. "Come on, girl, quit all that. You know we belong together."

"I'm not so sure anymore, Julius. All you do is hang out with the fellows. There's females calling the house phone asking for you!" His eyes got big when I confessed that women had been calling the house for him. He looked puzzled, like he was trying to figure out what they may have told me.

"Who called here? What women, Reese?"

I ignored his question and kept right on talking. "You come back in here drunk and want me to be here, stuck in this big ol' house all by myself! I'm tired of this!" I flung my arms up and started crying.

"Aw, baby, I didn't know it was that serious to you. I won't go. I'll stay here with you and the baby. Okay? Just don't cry. You know I hate to see you cry."

He took off his shirt, picked me up, and walked back to the family room with me in his arms. "Let's watch movies, or you wanna go out? We can do whatever you want, babe. I can't lose you." He put me on the couch and began to rub my feet. His cell began to ring over and over. He looked at it each time and started acting a little nervous, but never answered it.

"You gonna answer that? Who is it and why they keep calling so much?" I questioned.

"It's the fellows, they probably wondering where I am," he responded.

We stayed hugged up all night. We were okay . . . I thought.

Julius began to take our son everywhere he went. He was a great father. He loved Michael so much. Julius didn't have any family besides me and the baby. His mother had abandoned him from birth. He lived with different family members until he was in high school, then the coach at our high school and his wife took him in to stay with them.

Being faithful and loyal was a huge thing to him. He never wanted to feel betrayed or lost. The problem was Julius didn't know how to be that to his family, meaning me.

I began to sink myself deeper and deeper into the things of God. I was afraid that I was going to lose him. So like I did when my mother died, I called on Jesus and allowed Him to keep this boat afloat.

Two more years went by and marriage was getting harder. I found myself with another baby. We named him Gabriel.

Julius never wanted to name his sons after himself. His mother had named him and he hated her. He didn't want her to have anything to do with a name for his seed.

At this time things were pretty come and go between us. When I came in, he left, and when he came in the house, I left. We only saw each other at night when it was time for bed, because I was out all day shopping or with some of the other players' wives goofin' off somewhere and Julius was in training season.

Julius's football career was booming. He had just signed a contract with Nike and done a couple of commercials. He had also signed a new contract with the Browns. Money wasn't a problem, but his lack of loyalty and faithfulness seemed to finally catch up with him.

I was out one day alone. The boys were with the nanny when I get a phone call from Julius telling me to meet him at one of our favorite Italian restaurants.

"Babe, where you at?" He sounded so sad when he called.

"I'm downtown, why?" He knew I didn't have anything to say to him because of his behavior as of late. Julius had been turning out. Not only neglecting me, but drinking, smoking weed, and using cocaine. He knew I didn't approve of it. I always thought he was so much more than a superstar athlete. Julius was incredible to me. His mind was brilliant and I always wanted and saw so much more in him than I think he even saw in himself.

"We need to meet now. Reese, I love you. I promise I do."

"Okay, you are scaring me. What's wrong?" Tears started coming out of my eyes and my stomach felt sick because I knew something had gone wrong.

"Babe, it's okay. We gonna get through this, just meet me there. I'm pullin' up now. How long before you get here?"

I was walking down the street, going into another retail store when he called. I had gotten used to shopping. That's all I did to pacify me and fill the time I spent alone. "I'm headed to my car now. I should be there in ten minutes."

I wasn't being as polite or nice to him as he was to me. I was tired of Julius. All he did was party like a rock star. The most time I spent with him was late night and early mornings when he came in smelling of alcohol and weed, thinking he was bionic from the coke. He would force himself on me, and, as he called it, make passionate, heated love to me. I often lay there thinking of the seed I had sown by losing my virginity to him. *I will never vow to you again, God, and not hold to it.*

Remembering his voice softly whispering in my ear all those years ago, "Reese, I will always cherish you," now I laughed as I thought how foolish I was to listen to his sweet-talk and invisible dreams that had turned to disaster.

I walked up to the nice restaurant and smiled back at the waitresses and waiters who frequently had waited on us.

"Your seats," the host said, guiding me to the seat with her arm and hand. I smiled back but wondered what I was walking into. Nowadays who knew when it came to Julius? He was so unpredictable. He lied so much and by now had had so many affairs with different women I lost count.

"He's back here in you guys' favorite seats." She smiled. "Haven't seen you in a while, Mrs. Logan."

I grinned and continued to walk. I turned the corner and saw Julius sitting there. It didn't matter what that man did, what drugs he was hooked on, he was still gorgeous. The wild life hadn't lain in the bed with him yet and impregnated him with the drug or alcohol look.

He was sitting there with his elbows on the table and his hand on his forehead as if he was deep in thought. He never saw me walk up.

"Hey, what's goin' on?" I said softly, and then sat down.

He got up from the table and let me in my seat. I noticed he had put his wedding ring back on. He hadn't worn it in over four months so that was a surprise to see.

I figured he was going to tell me how sorry he was for all he had done—all the embarrassment, all the affairs—and how he was ready to clean himself up and be a great husband. Yeah, yeah, yeah. I had heard that one a time or two.

"Reese, I'm so glad you came." His eyes were bloodshot, and before he could say a word, tears began to fall from his eyes.

I sat there and waited. My heart was already speaking to me and telling me this was going to be bad.

"Baby, please don't leave me. Please." He held his head down while he spoke to me.

What has he done? He can't even look me in my eyes. Oh, Jesus, please don't let him have a disease! Please! I thought.

"Reese, I messed up. Somebody is pregnant."

I looked away. I could see the waitress smiling and coming over to take our order. I waved her away, then looked at him, speechless. I didn't know what to do. I was stuck for a moment, in between thoughts of what to do next. *Should I punch him in his head? Spit on him? Should I just get up and walk out of here, never to see him again? What should I do, Jesus?*

I could see Julius's lips moving, crying and trying to tell me what happened, but I couldn't hear him. I grabbed my heart and began to cry too.

"Baby, baby, please say somethin'. I am so sorry."

I couldn't say a word. It felt like someone had stuck a knife in my heart. I sat across from him and watched him try to explain.

"She couldn't have been any older than twenty. She was walking, carrying a newborn baby. I drove by her and thought about approaching her, then I turned around. I offered her a ride home and it started from there." I'm sure the expression on my face let him know I was ready to ask him questions about this. He reached his hand over the table to touch mine, but I pulled my hand back when he touched me. He then hit the table as if he was upset.

I couldn't just leave it alone. I wanted to hear it all. I gave him a mean look and told him to finish the story. He took a deep breath and continued. "Babe, please, I don't wanna tell you anymore. Please don't ask, just leave it alone."

"Within a few days I was meetin' up with her at motels." He said it so quick, so easy. I knew then his love for me was not equal to the love I had for him. He continued, "It was just sex. I am so sorry I did this." He held his head down and blurted into a hysterical cry. "She had a newborn already so I didn't think . . ." He grabbed the top of his head like he was deep in thought. "I was going to end it with her, Reese, I swear. I texted her and had her meet me at the motel, but when I got there, it was gonna be the last time."

He then whispered, "I had sex with her again thinking that would be it. That was two months ago and I haven't seen her or had any contact with her since. She called me today and said she was pregnant."

I couldn't hold my peace for another second. "You are an idiot. You're a professional athlete, and you don't even think enough about yourself, your wife, and family to protect yourself? Really? What if you have a STD?" I sat back in my seat.

To be honest I wasn't surprised. I sat there watching the other people in the restaurant while they talked to each other, held hands, and ordered their food. I watched the waitress take orders and I even looked at one lady's shoes as she dangled them while talking to her date. Then I looked back over at him. His eyes were bloodshot red, a little snot was coming down his nose, and such desperation was on his face. However, even though he displayed all of this, I was not moved, not at all. I put my hand on my chin and tuned him back in.

"I told her to get an abortion, I would pay for it and give her some money but she won't, babe. She won't do it."

I was disgusted by him.

"Reese, before you say anything, please . . ." He reached his hand out to take mine across the table. I looked down at what he was doing. I was motionless. "Baby, please tell me you won't leave me. Please don't take my family away from me, don't take my boys. I need you, Reese."

I didn't deserve a man like this. I had given him me. I'd been faithful and loyal. I had his back, even when he made me look foolish and this was what I finally got: him having a bastard baby with some chick? And to top it all off, he put me in danger! He didn't know that chick or any of the others he had been with. He was out there unprotected, doing him, not ever once thinking of me. This was not a marriage. It was a joke! I could've caught a disease believing him.

I had to decide what I was going to do about this marriage. Was I going to continue going through all this heartbreak that Julius was causing me? Or was it time to leave him? I sat there and thought back to better times with him, and then I thought about how many years I had been crying from something he had done to hurt me.

I blurted out, "Three years of marriage and this is what I get? What's done in the dark comes to the light." I covered my mouth with my hand and realized I had cried almost every day for the last year. Every day there had been some type of problem, infidelity, and issue. Either he was caught cheating, or he was putting me down. Not to mention he had become a control freak. He was never pleased with anything I did. I was always incompetent in his eyes. Nothing I did was good enough for him. I felt like I was in a prison cell in my own house when he was there. I couldn't cook right, I had a funny look on my face, something was always wrong in Julius's eyes. We could never just be at peace.

"What you say that for?" he asked, but I never answered.

I realized our life together must come to an end. Julius was not my problem. It was time to get my boys and begin a new life without him.

"Baby? Baby? Answer me. Say something."

I looked at him, grabbed the water I was drinking from the table, and threw it in his face. "See you in court!"

Chapter 5

In His Arms After All

From the moment I got up to leave the restaurant I was planning my next move. I got in my car and sat there a few minutes, replaying everything Julius had confessed and remembering him crying and hollering my name as I ran out of there. Everyone in the place watched and, I was sure, wondered what happened to the nice young couple we used to be. I caught a glimpse of a couple of the waitresses standing near the entrance whispering. It was awful. I felt so humiliated.

What happened? All I wanted was a happy marriage, a strong bond that nobody could break. I wanted us to trust in each other, and that would make us a force to reckon with. But, after years of trying, praying, and forgiving it was over. I thought Julius and I would conquer the world one day, but I guessed not. I didn't understand it.

I reached in my purse and grabbed my cell and called my girlfriend from college, Eva. Eva lived in Columbus and she was my best friend. We became best friends in school when Julius and her ex-boyfriend played ball together.

She came from California with her boyfriend. She was a pretty and very smart girl. Tall, brown skin tone, flawless, and always, and I did mean always, wore a good weave. She stayed modeled up, meaning she wore every brand there was that was expensive. From her clothes to her car to her jewelry and accessories, she had it all and never was she seen without makeup, eyelashes. She never had a man who didn't have a big-bank account and who didn't spend that bank on her. Material Girl should've been her name!

Eva married some big-time attorney. When I heard it, I was not surprised. Any and every guy in college had proclaimed their love for that girl so it was no surprise she had finally been caught. We talked frequently but hadn't seen each other for about a year.

"Eva, what's going on with you?" I sadly stated.

"Hey, Reese. What's goin' on? Haven't heard your voice in a few days. Girl, I've been calling you, but no luck! Where you been?" She chuckled.

I was silent for a second.

"Reese? What's wrong? I can tell something's wrong. What is it?"

I couldn't pretend anymore. "Eva, I'm divorcing him! He has a baby on the way."

I heard her sigh out a long, saddened cry for me and what I was going through. "I am so sorry, Reese. Oh, honey, what happened?"

I thought for a minute and remembered something I heard Bishop Jakes say one time; then I blurted it out. "The wedding has run out of wine." That was it; that's exactly what happened.

"Huh? What you mean?" she questioned.

I didn't have any answer for her. All I knew was I was getting my boys and leaving Cleveland today. "I will be in Columbus in a few hours. I have got to get out of here."

"I understand. Well I'm here. You and my god babies come stay with me," she demanded.

I could tell she was trying to make me feel better. "I'm okay. Really, I knew something was going to happen. It had to. He has been living so carelessly for a long time." I looked in my rearview mirror at myself and touched the bags under my eyes with my finger, shaking my head. "It was bound to bite him on the behind."

"Yeah, you right about that, girl. I just don't think you need to be alone, Reese. Come to my house. There's plenty of room."

I didn't wanna stay with anybody. I just wanted to go to a nice hotel, order room service, and relax with my boys. Just love on them and hold them. She must have felt me because she didn't mention it again.

"You got a lawyer? We gonna take that Negro for everything he got!" She screamed through the phone. "I can't believe him! I'm so mad. I told you not to marry that fool!"

"I know you did, I know," I agreed.

"Reese, my husband is in the car with me. I'ma put you on speaker so he can advise you," she said.

I wasn't ready for that. I had made up my mind to divorce him, but, I didn't feel like talking to an attorney right then. Eva, however, stayed above it, meaning she was always finding a way to get an increase in revenue. And I knew she knew I was going to get paid! I believed her intentions were good. She didn't want anything. She just wanted to get him.

Julius and Eva didn't care for each other. Ever since college they had a problem with each other. Julius would say, "Don't trust that skank! She will stab you in your back if she could." Then Eva would come back with some statement about Julius being a dog and how I deserved better. There was a rumor when we were all in college that Julius and Eva had messed around before. I asked both of them and they both denied it. I recalled driving to one of Julius's practices and waiting outside until they finished.

When he came over to my car I smacked him in the face in front of all his boys.

"You been messing around with my best friend? Huh? Have you?"

All his boys laughed and some hollered out, "Man, you grimy if you did that!"

"Come on now, man," he answered them. "I ain't do nothin' like that!" He looked at me. "Reese, I'm tellin' you the truth. That never happened and never will! I love you too much to do somethin' so grimy to you." He picked me up and said, "Baby, I love you. I would never mess with one of yo' girls. You got my word on that."

He put me down, stared me in the eyes, and said, "Reese, for real, yo' girl grimy. She tried me, babe."

I smacked his face again. "You're a liar!" I got in my car and left.

So word got around that Julius called Eva a skank. I wasn't surprised to find out that she was ready to help me get all of Julius's money.

"Give me a few days and we can talk, but for the next couple of days I just want some quiet time with my boys. You understand don't you?" I told her, "I will look for a place and—"

She interrupted. "Say no more. I understand, but we gonna hit him in the head before he can see what's comin'! Ol' dog! Ugh! I told you you were too good for that fool!" We laughed, said our good-byes, and hung up the phone.

Julius had been blowing up my cell ever since I left him sitting there wet, and that had been well over four hours ago. I never answered the phone when he called.

I hurried home and packed up some of my things and the boys. I knew he wouldn't come home right away because he'd said on one of his texts how embarrassed and ashamed he was, and how he didn't wanna face me. I put them in the car and headed toward the freeway. It was over! I had debated leaving him over and over in my head for at least eight months, so the new development was the straw that broke the camel's back. Besides, all he wanted to do was sit on the phone and manipulate me with his fast talking, double talking, and confusing questions. I wasn't having it. I was done, finished, through with it and him!

I listened and jammed to Canton Jones "Hater Today" while I zoomed down the freeway. The boys slept in their car seats in the back. I frequently looked at them through the mirror and wished things were different, but they weren't. Julius had made his choices and that was that. Yes, my heart was broken into tiny pieces but at the moment I couldn't feel it. All I felt was anger.

I tried to listen to some of my favorite worship music and release the pain, anger, and inability to forgive however, I needed time for this right here. If the truth be told, I wanted him to hurt; hurt like I had been all those years I invested in his raggedy butt! That's what I wanted.

As soon as I arrived in Columbus, we settled in our new home, the Hyatt at Easton. I picked up my cell to call my grandpa, but Julius was texting me like crazy. One text read: Bring my boys home! Next one: I'ma take 'em away from you!

I looked at the cell, laughed, and began to talk back to his text as if he could hear me. "Please, ain't no judge in his right mind gonna give you my sons! You wanna fight? That's what you gonna get!" I picked up the cell and started typing him back, then thought about it. "That's what he wants: communication. I will not say a word. I'll just see him in court like I said."

My text went off again. This time it read: Reese, please come home. I need you. Please don't do this, babe. I need you.

I sat on the edge of my bed staring at that one for a few moments. I wanted him so bad. I loved that man. He was my one and only true love. Oh, how I wished Julius would have repented before now for the way he treated me. Moreover, as much as I wanted him to be telling the truth, I had no place in my mind that believed him or in him anymore. All Julius would be good for was paying me!

I set the cell on the bed and went into the bathroom to get ready for bed. I was going to turn in and get up early enough to find a daycare for the boys, find us a new home, and go shopping (on Julius) for everything new. Then the pictures started coming. He sent pictures of us getting married, pictures of the boys when they were born, pictures of us in high school at prom, at homecoming, at games, and at interviews. I took my cell and placed it on my heart and cried. I then erased them all. If I wanted to move forward, I couldn't stay there playing in my past.

Eventually I turned the cell off, realizing I would never get through to Grandpa with this going on. I eventually called Grandpa on the hotel phone. I knew by now Julius had called my grandparents, trying to plead his case and hope one of them would say something to me to make me come to my senses, in his words. *Yeah, right, not this time.*

Plenty of times he would call them, mostly Grandma, to convince me to let him back in the house. And a lot of times, it worked. Grandma would say, "Forgive him.

You were married young and that's what men do before they grow up."

I would sit there and look at Grandma like she was out of her mind. I would end up doing what she told me to do, miserably. I knew my grandpa wouldn't go for it but Grandma believed you stay with a man through hell and high water. I didn't believe that one. Maybe if it was the fifties I'd have thought differently, but it was 2008 and I was twenty-six years old. I didn't have time to waste on no man, not even one I was hopelessly in love with.

Grandpa was a wise man of God and I needed him. It was a perfect time to talk to him; the boys had eaten, had their baths, read books, and were tucked away in their bed, sound asleep.

I looked around the beautiful hotel suite, went to the desk, sat down, and called Grandpa. I hoped Grandma wouldn't answer. I didn't wanna bother her with this. Her blood pressure would go up; I just knew it would.

"Hello? Who callin' here this late? It's nine o'clock!" I smiled and giggled a little when I heard Grandpa fussing. It reminded me of old times when Julius or one of my friends would call the house after eight. They would get told off foolin' with him.

"Grandpa? Grandpa, it's me, Reesie-cup!" That's what he called me.

"Oh, it's my baby girl on da phone. What a surprise. Where you at anyway? That boy done called here a million times lookin' fo' you and them boys!" He fussed again.

"Grandpa, we're okay. I'm in Columbus." I took a deep breath then said it. "I left him for good, Grandpa." I could hear him moving around in his leather recliner. It was almost like I could see him sitting there in it with a Coca-Cola bottle on the side of him, the radio on the other side, with him listening to some sports game on AM radio while at the same time watching every sporting event imaginable on his seventy-inch flat screen with surround sound, which Julius got him for Christmas. He was so funny!

"Left him, hon? What he do? Vonnie, Reesie-cup on da phone." I could hear him telling Grandma what was going on. "Yeah, she sound okay. Done left him. You was right."

"Grandpa, I just wanted y'all to know what was going on and where I was," I told him.

"You need somethin', Reesie? Grandpa and Grandma will come if you need us. Now what's goin' on, 'cause he called here cryin' and sayin' somethin' about a baby. You pregnant?"

Oh no! I can't believe he told them that. He is such a drama queen. "No, Grandpa, I'm not pregnant! Julius done got another woman pregnant though." I took in a deep breath and continued. "I just want out of this, Grandpa." I couldn't be strong any longer. Who I needed was on the phone: my dad. He was like my father, the only one I ever had. He raised me as if he were my daddy and I loved him as if he were just that.

"Oh, Reesie-cup, I'm so sorry, baby. I told that boy a few years ago to get his act together, that you wasn't gonna keep stayin' by him with all that mess he was doin'. Told him, you was too strong to keep puttin' up wit' nonsense. I just hate to see this day, and I hate that you in pain."

I could hear the pain he had for me in his voice. It got raspy and sounded dry, as if he was losing some of his words while they came out his mouth.

"I don't know what to do, Grandpa. I feel like I lost everything. What am I going to do without him?" I was going into hysterics on the phone. While my grandpa held the phone I could hear him breathing and turning pages; then I figured he was in the Word of God.

"Baby, you are not alone. You ain't gonna die. You haven't lost everything. Now Julius, he's the one who has lost. If he wanna stay bound to his flesh and continue to be married to lust, let him. It is an unfortunate thing but it happens. You, my darling, will pick up and become stronger from this. You are my baby and you have overcome some horrific tragedies in your young life, so you just know, this too shall pass!" Grandpa was preaching and I was listening!

"Trust me, everything that happens has to go by Jesus first. Understand you are safe in His arms and covered under the blood of Jesus! You gonna be all right. It may be a road you have to travel on, Reesiecup, but believe in your God and know He has you and them boys. Storms come, baby." He paused before saying, "This will not be the only one you face, but you have to hold on to Jesus while in a storm. Now, if you have made your decision to leave, you have to move on, pray, and forgive. Hold tight to the Lord, baby girl."

I knew he was right. As he spoke and continued to minister to me the peace of God came over me. I got on my knees and with my grandpa on the other end of the phone we cried, talked, and prayed. And I felt in my spirit that things really would be okay. *I mean, God hasn't brought me this far just to leave me . . . right?*

Chapter 6

Jay

Eva invited me to dinner at Brio, a popular upscale restaurant, to celebrate her thirtieth birthday. Plenty of people came and gathered that night for her dinner party. I was a different girl than the one who showed back up in Columbus three years ago. I was no longer a mess, no longer heartbroken, no longer married, and no longer a stay-at-home momma.

I had it going on. I was working in my field as an electrical engineer for the city of Columbus. I had my own home way out in the suburbs that I had purchased with the settlement money I received from my divorce. I worked out constantly, spent time with my boys, and had plenty of money in the bank. We were set financially for life.

I found myself and the boys a nice Holy Ghost–filled church that I loved and that was it for us. That's what we did: family, school, church, work, and exercise. I didn't have any time for men in my life. I did go on date here and there to the movies and maybe dinner, but no big deal. I knew I wasn't ready to be in a new relationship. Julius had hurt me bad, and to tell the truth, a piece of me was still broken from it all. I had been celibate since the divorce and promised God once again I would stay that way until marriage.

I thought I was scared to fall in love. It was safer for me to just pass men by when they tried to get a conversation going. I did pretty well until Eva's party.

I pulled in front of Brio to valet park my brand-new, shiny black S 550 sedan that Julius brought me a couple of weeks ago for my twenty-ninth birthday. He still showed love and proclaimed his heartbreak with gifts; I took them. I smiled at the attendant and threw him the keys. He smiled at me and watched as I walked across the brick street of the Easton Town shopping center into Brio. I did know I was looking good with my floor-length mink wrapped around me. My hair was weaved into an edgy black bob with Chinese bangs that lay just right on my forehead. My makeup and eyelashes were flawless. I kept myself together, always. I had on some cream wool pants and a cream sweater that overlapped and hung low in the front, with pearls that started as a choker and ended at the top of my waist.

I was clean, entering the place, looking like a million dollars. I looked around the restaurant and saw Eva standing up, telling one of her famous stories about the banks she had worked in. Eva was quite the storyteller, keeping her audience laughing and intrigued, wondering what she would say next out of her mouth. It was her gift. She was the district manager of over five banks in Columbus, and five in Dayton, Ohio.

I noticed her hair was different from the previous day when we celebrated her birthday privately as BFFs at her favorite place, Chicago Pizza. Her hair was weaved with Italian wave Indian Remy, which meant it was very, very expensive. Eva was getting a little heavy in the thighs, but had a small waist that made up for it. That's what men loved about her.

Eva loved to talk. She would talk and talk and talk. Everyone who had the opportunity of having a conversation with her listened and either nodded or said frequently, "Um, huh." Again, no one really minded because the stories she told were very funny. Just watching her explain things made people smile. Her eyes would light up as she told a story, as if she were reliving the incidents right then and there.

Eva's back was turned to me as I approached the dinner table but everyone else could see me coming. I put two fingers to my lips and mouthed, "Ssshhh." Everyone laughed as I walked up behind Eva and scared the daylights out of her. Eva jumped and turned around.

"Girl, you scared me," she screamed and grabbed her heart.

"Well, that's the only way we can get you to sit down and eat." I started laughing and had my hands on my hips, being sassy. We hugged each other and gave each other kisses on the cheek, and sat down; then we all ordered.

After an hour or so, two very attractive men came in and sat at the bar. I had seen them when they first walked in and so did Eva. Eva whispered in my ear so her husband wouldn't hear. "Girl, you see what just came in the door?" I looked at her sideways, knowing she knew what I was thinking: *stop!* I nodded and continued to sip on my iced tea, never saying a word. I wasn't that interested in them. Yeah, they were both fine, and I did mean fine, but then again, so was Julius. That thought right there stopped me frequently in my own tracks.

Now Eva, on the other hand, was always looking for trouble when it came to men. However, tonight she couldn't display her usual flirtatious behavior because her wealthy husband was there. She whispered to me,

"Girl, those two at the bar are fine, and lookin' our way. Dang, I wish Adam wasn't here with me."

I whispered back, "Girl, sit there with your hubby. Stop it, it's gonna get you in trouble one of these days." I laughed. Her husband, Adam, looked at us a few times, but he wasn't really paying any attention to us. He did get up all of a sudden and walk over toward the men at the bar. He gave them the "what's up" nod and then shook both men's hands.

Eva's mouth and mine hung wide open. How did he know them? I wondered if they were his collogues or maybe his clients or something. Whatever the case may have been he brought them back over to the table with him.

"Baby, a couple of colleagues of mine . . . Is it all right if they sit for a few? We need to discuss some things," Adam asked.

Eva was in shock. I had to kick her under the table so she would at least close her mouth. She got up and put her hand out to shake theirs and meet them. "Oh, okay, hello . . ." She put her professional on. She was so funny.

The men sat down and were in a conversation with Eva's husband. It seemed pretty serious but none of my business. I looked down at my watch and realized I needed to get home to my babies soon. Eva caught me.

"No, it's still early." She leaned into me with her drink in her hand and whispered, "Don't leave me alone with these fine men. I'm tellin' ya, I won't be accountable for what happens."

I laughed. "Girl, you have to go to church with me. Please let's make sure you give your life to Jesus!" She laughed and I stayed a little longer with her.

Soon the crowded dinner table became empty. I got up and put on my coat. I did see the men stare at me quite a bit. I had to admit, I liked it. I dramatized everything I did. While putting on my coat, for instance, I made sure my weave shook, knowing it would fall right back in place. I knew how to entertain when somebody was watching.

I kissed Eva good-bye on the cheek, went out the door, walked across the street, and gave the attendant the ticket for the car. While I waited for the valet to bring the car around, I noticed one of the men come out from Brio and walk toward me. I figured he was coming to talk to me. I had been told since the day I was born how beautiful I was, so it wasn't a big deal for any man, any color, age, or stature, to approach me. I didn't want him to see the big Kool-Aid smile on my face while he was running across the street over to where I was standing.

"Woo! *This is a fine brother,*" I said under my breath while biting down on my bottom lip. I managed to get a pretty good look at him. He was tall with a bald head, athletic build, and was very chocolate. He dressed as if he could pull out a million bucks and not blink. The brother was fine and I continued to admire him. He was all jeweled out. I noticed the nice platinum link around his wrist, not to mention the platinum Rolex I spotted on his left wrist. I had to admit I was getting interested. I could tell by the suit he was wearing that it was tailor made for his muscular frame.

"Hello, I'm Jason but you . . . you can call me Jay. I was at the birthday party inside." He nodded toward the entrance. "I couldn't help but notice you there. How are you tonight?" he asked, smiling with teeth that had to be bleached they were so white. He held out his hand to shake mine. I smiled and reached out and touched his. I stared at the platinum bracelet on his wrist, dangling as we shook hands.

"I'm fine thank you. Yes, I remember you from inside." I smiled, getting a quick glimpse of his handsome face.

"Two questions for you, what's your name and where's yo' man?" He rubbed my hand softly, still embracing it close to his heart.

"I'm Reese," I told him. "I don't have a man. I'm divorced."

He smiled; then he lifted my hand up as if we were dancing and he was going to spin me around then in his arms. "Well, that's what I wanted to hear. I didn't wanna steal some man's woman away, but believe me that's exactly what I was intending on doing tonight."

I loved his confidence in himself. Very humorous this one was. "I love the comedy." I laughed.

He still held on to my hand and replied, "What else could I say walkin' up on a fine woman like you? You standin' over here like you don't need anything from no one." He playfully pointed at my handbag.

I couldn't take my eyes off of him. He had the most amazing dimples on his face. When he moved his mouth they sunk so deep into his face, making him the sexiest man alive. I had to speak to God in my mind while I watched him and tell Him, *thank you!*

I was completely into this man. I almost felt like I was under a trance. No interruptions could bring me out of it, not even when the attendant was trying to give me the key to my car. I heard his deep voice speak again.

"Look at you, all together lovely, baby. You got the designer bag, the Red Bottoms, and jewelry. Your hair flowin', nails manicured, and I'm not even gonna say nothin' about yo' pedicure. I know you have on stilettos but I bet you got those toes done up too!" We both cracked up! He touched my ear and felt my diamond studs. "I have to respect that. I knew the valet was gonna pull up in somethin' fly and your fine self was gonna let him escort you right into it." I laughed. He was so funny and what I really liked about him was the fact he wasn't intimated by my success. I thought that made him even the more attractive if that was possible.

"I don't know what to say. I mean all of that is true but I'm not some diva. I work hard for everything I got."

"Yeah, I'm sure you do, Ms. Reese. I do too, and you have become number one on that list. Can I work hard for you?" He escorted me by my arm into my car. This one didn't miss a beat.

I felt like a schoolgirl. I hadn't felt like this in a long time. My heart was fluttering like I was going down a big hill in the car. Then I reached in my purse and handed him my business card.

"When can I see you again?" he said, leaning over in my car window. Before I could reply he continued talking. "Let me take you out tomorrow. We can do anything you like. What do you like to do for fun, Reese?"

I didn't know what to say. "Surprise me." I smiled, then pulled off.

I watched him stand out there and look at me drive 'til I couldn't see him anymore. I felt good about this one. It felt so right to me. I thought about the man all the way home and how he had me standing out there smiling, laughing, and giggling, like I was sixteen. "This is the one," I said aloud. "This one is real."

I was so happy with Jason in my life. Jason made sure he kept his word to me. He did everything he promised me that night we met. He made me number one on his list. This time around I had a man who did everything in the world to prove that he loved me. He treated my sons as if they were his and made sure I had everything I needed and more. I was wrapped up into him. We had become so close in such a short time, but like I said, it felt just right.

There was only one problem; I didn't keep my promise and commitment to God again.

I hadn't noticed I left someone out: Jesus. I had backslid right out of the will of the Lord for my life and I was sure for my son's lives. I was in trouble and didn't even know it. All I knew was I was enjoying my life. I was loved and protected by a fine man and didn't want or need anything else, including Jesus. I just didn't think about Him. I figured as long as I didn't acknowledge Him then I would be okay. I knew I would eventually go back to my first love, Jesus, but for now, I was happy doin' me! I had officially traded in my Holy Ghost for objects, affection, and greed.

After months, Jason figured it would be for the best if he moved in with me, seeing we spent so much time together anyhow. I agreed. It was such a good feeling having a strong, black, successful man—not to mention fine as all get-out—living with me. Woo, that man could take my breath away. Jason made everything about my sons and me. He even quit traveling so much to stay with us in Ohio. He sent his business partner in his place. He was wonderful to us.

"Baby, we need to go to the grocery store. I wanna cook for you and the boys when I bring them in from playin' football wit' me," he would say. I was finally living my fairytale.

He impressed me every time he opened his mouth, and the gifts he brought me frequently amazed me. Every time he left the house and went somewhere he made sure he came back with gifts.

After months of living together I stopped working and stayed home with the boys. Jason suggested it and thought it would be good for them until they were older. Jason was such a family man. He wanted a family so bad and did everything he could to make this life come true for the both of us. He frequently talked about the life he had back home in New York with his family. He didn't want the life he grew up in; he wanted better and a stable one for me as a woman and my boys as kids. He talked about how his mom had him and his brother at a young age and they moved from place to place and his mom from man to man. He hated it and did everything he could do to show me he wanted better.

I believed him and wanted it too. I had been through so much growing up. Our lives were so similar that our stories seemed to wrap around each other. I figured together we would be dynamic and I thought we would end up married, saved, and living the American dream.

Jason was wonderful. After a few months of us being secluded to just each other and my boys, Jason started going out. Unlike my ex-husband, Julius, he wanted me to go out with him and meet all his friends.

"Babe, you gotta meet Kev while he's in town this weekend. You'll love him," he said in reference to his best friend, who I'd heard a lot about but never met. Jason had pretty much just been under me and kept away from his business.

I playfully responded, "Not as much as I love you."

"Aw, babe, you know you wonderful, don't you, girl?" He grabbed me close and kissed me.

"You gonna make me go against my rules and marry you. That what you tryin'a get me to do? Fallin' all hard for you and stuff."

We both laughed.

"Seriously, Reese, Kev is golden. He has been my best friend since we were kids. I can trust him wit' my life."

He grabbed his cell and turned it on to call Kev and let him know we were coming out. Before I could say a word to Jason, he was fast down the stairs. He talked about Kev all the time so I was excited to finally be meeting him. Jason had told me he and Kev were inseparable and that they were more like brothers than friends. He told me they had been friends since they were kids and how they had gone into business with each other years back. He went on to tell me they came to Columbus to expand their business.

"Babe, you ready to go?" Jason hollered up the stairs.

I was in my mirror, putting the finishing touches on my hair. "Be down in a sec, babe!" I screamed.

"Okay, baby, hurry. We still have to drop some money off at the sitter's for the boys!"

I loved Jason for caring about my sons as much as he did. I believed he did because he didn't have any children of his own. He was such a loving man and my boys loved him just as much as he loved them. But I was in for a surprise from this point on.

Chapter 7

The Best Friend

I was finally ready to meet Jay's best friend, Kev, but for some reason I was nervous. I thought maybe it was 'cause of all of the good things Jay had said about him. Was I even worthy to meet the almighty Kev?

I gave myself one more glance in the mirror, then turned out the light and began to walk down the stairs. I could see Jay standing at the end of the stairs with his back turned away from me. He was talking to Kev on his cell. I knew this because he'd said his name while talking to him. I heard him ask Kev if he was playing pool. I stopped halfway down the steps and listened to what Jason was saying. He had his speaker on so I could hear their entire conversation.

"Man, you interruptin' my shot! I got two grand on this game," I heard Kev say.

"Where you at? I want you to meet somebody," Jason proclaimed.

I heard a long sigh come from Kev before he said anything else. "Who, Jay?" Kev sighed again. He sounded so frustrated with Jay, but I had no idea why. "We down here for money," Kev snapped. "Look, Jay, I know how you get around women and it ain't always good, so maybe I need to remind you why we in Columbus. We down here for the money, Jay, not some chicks!"

I continued to listen to their private conversation. I wanted to hear more so I stayed there on the steps and eavesdropped, hoping Jay didn't turn around and catch me.

"Jay, come on now; you know that Columbus is our ticket into making millions." Kev stopped talking for a second and I could tell he was taking his shot. I heard the stick hit the ball, then the other balls and down one of the pockets on the pool table.

"Yes!" he shouted with victory, then turned his attention back to his conversation with Jason. "Jason, I'm not tryin'a get into yo' business, man. I just don't want nothing to mess that up; after all, it's my business too."

Jason was getting angry at how Kev was talking to him. I could tell he was getting angry because the truth hurts, though, and from the tone of Kev's voice Kev was telling him the truth. True enough Jason was a little high-strung and would get involved with women. He'd told me a time or two. This sometimes created drama for himself, the crew, and the woman involved, but nobody had been bold enough to tell him but Kev. Everyone else who worked for them was afraid. Again, I'd been told a time or two.

"What you mean, Kev? You think I'm out of control or somethin'?"Jason questioned.

I watched Jason try to stay in control but it was obvious he was getting upset. I started walking slowly down the stairs when I heard Kev answer Jason calmly. "Naw, man, you not out of control. You do what you do. We at the Brownstone playin' pool."

It seemed as if Kev realized there was nothing he could say to Jason to get him to understand, so he let it go. I could sense the worry of him wondering if Jason was gonna bug out sooner or later. He would be more than likely the one responsible for picking up the pieces. Kev had always picked up Jason's pieces whenever Jason got himself in trouble. Kev was there to make the situation right.

Jason had a problem with his temper and had put his hands on more than a few of the women he dated in the past, but Kev would smooth out the problems by paying the women or sweet-talkin' them into just leaving Jason alone, for their own good that is.

"All right, man, I'll be there in a minute." Jason hung up, then turned around and noticed me coming down the steps. He smiled. "You ready to go?" He put his arm around my waist, then kissed my cheek.

"Yep, ready to go." I didn't tell him I heard his conversation, and I was pretty sure he didn't know. We left, headed to the sitter's first, then to the club.

After we stopped by Toya's and gave her money to take the boys to Magic Mountain, we went to meet Kev. Kev was still playing pool when he saw Jason coming through the door.

They locked eyes and raised their heads at each other to signify saying, "What's up." Next, Jason started talking to a few fellows in the room.

Kev turned around and continued to shoot pool. I knew who he was right away 'cause I remembered him from Eva's party. I couldn't help but watch him shoot, because the brother was so fine. I remembered that he and I had given each other the eye the whole while we were at the dinner party. To be real, I was a little surprised when Jason came out to get my number instead of him. I chalked it up that maybe I had imagined the connection that night or something.

After making his shot, Kev turned around again and looked at Jason. He did a double take, and that's when he noticed me. Kev looked surprised but still remained cool. When Jason saw Kev looking, he grabbed my hand and walked over to him.

"Here, baby, sit right here for a second." He pulled out a chair near to them. I could hear everything they were saying but I didn't know what they were talking about, nor did I care.

"Sorry, man, I beat you to it. Besides, Kev, you got a woman in New York." Jason smiled. "And you don't cheat." He either winked or had something in his eye. Jason laughed and walked away, saying to me, "Baby, baby, come and meet my best friend, Kev." He grabbed my hand and we walked over to Kev.

I could tell Jason thought the whole thing was funny, but I didn't know what the joke was then, only later. However, Kev didn't think anything was funny and he was wearing the stern look on his face to prove it.

"Kev, this right here is the love of my life." Jason was hugging me and he had his arm around my neck. I put my hand out to shake Kev's.

"How you doin'?" he greeted me.

I looked at him. "Hey, I heard so much about you," I replied and smiled. I stared back at Kev until Jason interrupted.

"Y'all want somethin' to sip on?" Jason asked.

"Yes, babe, you can bring me a diet drink back. Thank you." I touched Jason's hand.

Kev didn't say a word to his best friend. He just watched me as Jay walked away. He stood there as if he noticed everything about my appearance in less than five minutes. He pushed his bottom lip in and ran across it with his tongue, forgetting that I was there with Jason, it seemed.

I watched him and imagined what he could possibly be thinking about me. I had on a pretty red sundress with the back out and a pair of chanel sandals, and my toes were perfectly manicured with a French manicure design. He examined my frame from top to bottom. I stood there letting him admire me; after all, what could it possibly hurt? I knew what he was thinking, but to be brutally honest, I liked it. Kev was handsome, way beyond the good looks of Jason. Kev was beautiful. So, I stood there, letting him make me feel like I was the most beautiful woman he had ever laid his eyes on. And I wondered and imagined what he was thinking.

He looked at my ears and saw that I had diamonds in them. These diamonds weren't cheap.

Kev was so caught up in me and I was so caught up with my imagination that I didn't even see or hear Jason walk back over with the Diet Pepsi. "Kev, man, you okay? Why you lookin' like that?"Jason asked.

Kev tried to get it together real fast before answering Jason. "What? What you mean, man, I'm straight." He took one more look over at me and stared in my eyes, which were almost the same color of my skin, and then he said, "Breathtaking." He said in a mesmerized tone that let me know he hadn't meant to say the words out loud.

Jason wasn't really paying attention to how Kev was looking at me. Obviously he didn't think it was a big deal. I couldn't imagine those two could ever let some broad come in between them, but I may have been wrong.

"Kev, you sure you don't want somethin' to drink? I'm goin' back over to the bar." Jason nodded over to the bar.

"Naw, I'm cool," Kev said.

"Okay. I'll be right back," Jason said while he touched me on my back.

"Okay," I said softly, and smiled.

"So, where you from, Reese?" Kev asked.

"I'm from Dayton, it's about an hour away from here."

"Yeah, I know the place. I've been there on business a few times or two," Kev said, keeping his eyes on me.

I started moving to the beat of the jazz music that was playing in the restaurant. I stopped paying attention to Kev and shifted my eyes to Jason, who was at the bar talking to a couple of fellows.

"So, Reese, you work or are you in school?" Kev asked.

"I graduated from OSU a few years back and now I work."

"Okay, okay, that's cool. What do you do for a livin'?"

The music got louder so I moved closer to Kev to reply. I put my mouth to his ear to answer him: "I'm an electrical engineer." I was so close I just knew Kev had to have been able to smell the perfume on my skin. He closed his eyes and bent down toward my neck to get a better smell of my scent when Jason approached.

"What's up? What's goin' on over here? Y'all look like y'all havin' an intense conversation or somethin'." Jason laughed.

Kev backed away from me slowly with his hands behind his back, still staring into my eyes. My heart was fluttering because I knew I wasn't imagining what was going on between us. I knew we had just shared a moment. I didn't know what to think. Why would Jason's best friend be coming on to me? Better yet, why did I like it?

I started feeling guilty and uncomfortable and finally blurted out, "Jason, let's go. I need to get ready for work tomorrow so I need to get back to my house." I said, as I motioned my finger toward the steps and moved toward the stairs that led to the exit, "Come on, babe."

Jason caught me and grabbed me by the waist and pulled me close to himself, closing his eyes and smelling my neck. I looked over at Kev, wondering what he possibly was getting out of this. Jason interrupted our silent communication.

"Um, you smell so good. Stay wit' me and have a drink. Or let's get somethin' to eat. You hungry?"

"No, Jason, I'm not. I need to go." I rolled my eyes and pulled away from him. I was feeling uneasy, and all I could think about were Kev's gray eyes looking at me and me looking back into them. *What's wrong with me?*

After a few more minutes of Jason begging me to stay, he gave up. Jason grabbed my hand and said good-bye to his friends. He smiled all the way out of the place, not knowing anything had happened, but I, on the other hand, knew different.

I looked back as I walked up toward the exit and watched Kev watch me and smile as Jason and I left.

The next time I saw Kev was one night when Jason was away on business in New York. I still believed they were businessmen. And why wouldn't I? They had businesses. They owned properties all over the city and were in business with Eva's husband, so there was no reason to think anything differently or ask any questions.

Jason had called me but I didn't hear the phone until he hung up. I was busy with cleaning my house and listening to some music. I listened to his voice message, and Jason said he was concerned and had asked Kev to shoot by and check on the boys and me.

I went in the front room to water my flowers when I noticed someone standing and pacing across my front porch. I went to the window and peeked out. That's when I noticed Kev standing out there. I ran over to my "Louie" bag and grabbed my lip gloss to put some on my lips, and I turned down the music and listened to him through the window.

"Why am I doing this? He's my man's best friend." I threw the lip gloss back into my purse, never shining my lips. I went back over to the window, then the peephole, and watched him talk to himself.

"Okay, what if she asks me why I'm here?" He paced back and forth outside. "I don't wanna be here. This ain't a good idea."

He pulled out his cell and dialed, then appeared to think a minute. Kev's back was away from the door and the cell was still to his ear. It must have been ringing.

I opened the door and touched him on the shoulder. "Hey, Kev, what you doin' here?"

I believed I startled him a little. He turned around, still holding the cell to his ear. He put the phone down and away.

I was standing there in a T-shirt and pajama bottoms. My hair was pulled up in a ponytail, swinging back and forth while I moved.

"Hey, Reese. Jay asked me to come over here and check on you. He said he, um, been callin' you but you're not answering?" He motioned his hands like he didn't know. "He wanted me to come by and see if you needed anything."

"I'm sorry the music was too loud." I laughed.

He reached his hand in his pocket and grabbed some money. He handed it to me.

"What's this for?" I asked, looking down at the money.

"I don't know. I'm just tryin' to be a good friend and do what I was asked. Jason wanted me to bring it to you."

"Well thank you for being a good friend but I don't need it. I'm okay," I said calmly.

"Look, Reese, all I know is I'm to leave this with you, so take it." He pushed it toward me.

I looked at the stack rolled up in his palm. I thought about it a few seconds, then took the money and walked back in the house. "Come on in, Kev. Want something to drink?"

Kev followed, I was sure wondering what kind of game I was playing. He walked behind me, following me into the plush living room filled with nice African American artwork.

"Uh, naw, not right now. I'm not thirsty. Nice place," Kev said as he sat down on the chocolate suede sectional. He sat back and got comfortable, putting both his arms across the back of the couch.

"Thanks," I said while picking up my cell to call Jason. "Hold on a sec, Kev. Let me call this man so he won't worry 'bout me." I touched him on his knee, and stood there waiting for Jason to pick up the phone. "Hey, baby." Kev watched, looking at my smile and eyes light up when I heard Jason's voice. "Baby, I didn't know you were calling me. I was in here dancing and blasting my music." I laughed.

Kev sat on the couch, watching and smiling every few minutes when I glanced over at him.

"Okay, baby, I'm going to talk to Kev for a little bit and wait for you to call me back. Hope everything is going well and hurry back!" I ended the call. I sat down on the other end of the couch and we began to talk until Kev saw a picture of my mom.

"Who is this? She looks just like you."

I paused before answering, knowing the pain of losing my mom was still there. I thought for a minute on how it took God to get me through her death. I took a deep breath and then I whispered aloud, “Thank you, Jesus.” As simple as I was acting, I could never forget Him or what He had done for me even if He never did another thing.

I got up and then sat beside him on the couch. I took the picture from him gently and looked at it. “This is my momma.”

“Yo’ momma is fine, girl. Where she at?” he playfully stated.

I chuckled, then covered my mouth, and I got off the couch and went over to my patio window and looked out. “My momma passed when I was younger.”

Kev got up and followed me. “Oh, Reese, I’m sorry, I didn’t know. Jason never said anything to me about that.”

“It’s okay. I know you didn’t mean anything by it. It’s still very hard for me at times.”

“Reese, I understand. I lost my mom a few months ago.”

I heard the pain in his voice. He spoke slowly, almost as if it hurt to say the words. I imagined it did, knowing the pain of losing my own momma. I turned away from the window and walked over to Kev. “I’m sorry, Kev. I know what you’re going through.”

“I came back to Ohio right after her funeral, but I wonder sometimes if I should have just stayed up there.” He gazed out the window a few seconds then said, “I got to get myself together.”

I wondered what he was referring to, but didn’t ask any questions. I walked up to Kev and hugged him. Kev embraced my hug. “You know this is the first time since my mom’s passing that I felt some type of warmth.”

We both closed our eyes and held the embrace a few seconds longer. I could smell his cologne and felt myself melting from his touch. While Kev held on, I imagined being his. There was something about him that attracted me to him. It was uncontrollable and felt completely right, even though I knew it was wrong.

I opened my eyes and realized this wasn't appropriate, and let him go. I could feel that he felt the same way, as he had slightly resisted releasing me.

"Thanks, Reese. Sometimes that's all you need is a hug," Kev told me.

"Oh, yeah, that's what you need sometimes is just a hug," I agreed. *Oh my God! What just happened?* I said to myself. *We had another moment, that's what happened.*

We sat back down and talked for hours and realized how much we had in common. That became the beginning of our friendship.

Shortly after that day we started spending a lot of time together, but nobody thought anything of it. We were close, inseparable, and told each other everything. Kev told me about him and his woman back in New York and I told Kev all about the troubles Jason and I were starting to have. We comforted one another and never thought anything more of our relationship than just that: two people with a lot in common comforting one another. Well, that's what we told ourselves anyway, but I knew Kev had feelings for me.

I, on the other hand, felt something for Kev too, but I was loyal to Jason and knew he had been there for me and the boys. So I drowned out my feelings for him with loyalty to Jason, even though Jason's true colors were starting to show.

Chapter 8

The Truth Hurts

A year into the relationship and Jason had started changing. He was not the loving, caring man I met; he had become mean and he didn't care who felt his wrath when he became upset. If he was angry because of something he would come in and take it out on me. He frequently verbally abused me with insults. I often asked myself where the Jay I knew went. I could feel it was only a matter of time before Jason would act a complete fool and explode. I felt it coming.

It all started one day when the boys were in their bedroom, playing with toys. I went upstairs to get them to quiet down and get ready for bed. When I reached their room my older boy, Michael, had a gun to my younger son's head. I screamed and cried out unto my son. "Michael! Put that down!" I was so afraid, tears immediately filled my eyes.

"Mommy, it's for play, see?" Michael held the gun out to me. "Don't cry, Mommy. I wouldn't hurt my baby brother. Okay, Mommy?"

I stood there in their doorway in shock, then ran in and took the gun. "Michael," I questioned, "where did you get this from? Huh?" I walked away from him with the gun in hand and put my hand to my head and began to cry. "I can't believe this!"

I walked over to my six-year-old son, Michael, and bent down beside him. Both boys were crying by now and scared. "Where did you get this, baby, huh? Tell Mommy."

Michael pointed to my room. I closed my eyes. I knew then that Jason had brought that gun in the house. I whispered and looked toward my room. "Show me; show Mommy."

Michael got up and took me by the hand and led me to my closet. He went way in the back and pointed. "Mommy, that's where it was, right there."

I noticed a small box I had never noticed before. When I picked up the box and opened it, it had guns in it. Then I noticed plastic Baggies filled with a white substance. I bent down and examined it. That's when I realized there was cocaine in my house: not just in my house, but my boys had found it!

I grabbed them each by their little faces and made them open their mouths. I looked inside to make sure they hadn't swallowed any of it. "You boys didn't mess with this stuff did you?" I held up one of the Baggies. My emotions were everywhere when I realized how much danger I had allowed my sons to be in. I thought about what could've happened if they had swallowed some of the dope or one of them would have been shot and I screamed out.

"Oh my God! Jesus!" I cried in relief. I fell to my knees and began to scream out to Jesus. I looked at how upset my babies were getting and I knew I had to be strong for them. I had to get up and comfort them and take control of this situation. I covered my mouth and held my boys and cried.

I put the boys to bed and waited for Jason to get home. While waiting I took the dope and flushed it all down my toilet. I was so angry and I wanted him to understand I wasn't playing with him. Bringing drugs into my home was unacceptable.

"Bet you don't bring no more of this stuff in here!" I declared. He had gone too far.

I kept calling his cell the entire time I waited but he didn't answer. I started leaving him voice mails.

"Jason! When you get this call me! Please!" I hung up and paced back and forth to the bedrooms then I sat on my bed and boohooed. "Jesus, if you just give me a sign, I will leave him alone, please."

But I knew I wasn't ready for it to be over between us. I knew it was probably for the best but I wasn't ready to let him go, not yet. What more of a sign did I need? He brought drugs and guns in my house.

I sat there on my bed and stared at the closet door, then jumped up and went over and opened it back up. I found a storage closet inside my closet and opened it up. That's where I found a briefcase, sitting there. I pulled out the silver briefcase and tried to open it but it was locked. It didn't have a key. It was the kind that had to be opened by a code. I sat on the bed and thought and played around with a few numbers.

"Zero-five-two-three! That's it, Jason's birthday! That's the code!" I said. I had tried numerous numbers, such as the house address number. *Why not his birthday?*

Once I entered it, the briefcase opened.

"Oh my God!" I shouted after seeing the contents. I looked toward my boys' room, got up off the bed, and closed the door quietly. I didn't want to disturb them while they slept.

I flipped through the cash I'd stumbled upon. " It has to be at least fifty grand!" I went to my bedroom window and looked out before I began to count it.

I thought about how Jason never invited any of his friends to my home except Kev. I started to panic and get paranoid. Realizing how much money, dope, and guns were in my possession was frightening. "He has put us in danger!"

I wasn't a dope dealer. Somebody could run up in here or, worse yet, the police could be watching my house. Since Jason wasn't returning my calls I picked the phone back up and called Kev this time.

"What's up, Reese?" Kev answered.

"Kev! Where the heck is Jason? I've been calling his cell for about an hour and he's not answering me. He needs to get here fast. I found his stuff!"

"Oh, uh, I'ma have him call you, Reese. You all right?"

"No! I'm mad as heck! I can't believe this . . . My boys found that mess. Tell him to come get his stuff out my house now, Kev."

"Okay, okay, Reese, calm down. I will have him call you."

I hung up the phone, but the craziest thing happened. Kev's cell had dialed me back up, and I heard everything that was said. From the background sounds, apparently Kev was sitting at a bar somewhere with Jason discussing their next move when I called. I could hear Jason running his mouth. I pictured him flashin' his money and touchin' up on some young thing.

"Jay! We got a problem, we need to go now, man!" I heard Kev holler. "I told you, Jay! I told you!" I could hear Kev yell.

I heard their doors shut once they were inside the vehicle.

"Man, what happened? Just tell me everything she said! What's goin' on?"

I felt weird listening in on them, but how ironic was it that Kev's cell had dialed me? So you bet I was gonna listen.

"Reese found that stash you left at her place! I told you don't do it!" I heard Kev say.

I pictured Jason probably reclined in his seat and leaned way back, acting all smooth. "It's cool. I needed to tell her the truth anyway. I'm tired of actin' like somebody I'll never be. I'm a killa, that's what she needs to know!"

I couldn't believe I was finding all this out this way. I was so angry at Jason for the deceit that he had done, and to act all concerned about me and my boys and do this made me know he was playing games with my mind and my heart.

"Man, you a fool, that's what you are! Don't put yo' hands on that girl, man, she cool people," Kev told him.

"What?" Jason sounded surprised by his best friend's statement and, frankly, I was too. Jason had never raised his hand to me before. "I ain't, man, no reason for that wit' her. She'll be all right once I get there. Just take me to my truck. You ain't gotta come wit' me. We straight."

"I don't mind goin'. Just in case it gets out of hand, man. Jay, I know you. You get there, flip out, then it's all bad," Kev reasoned with Jay.

I was speechless. I felt so betrayed by the both of them. First of all, Jason was my man and he had deceived me and brought trash in my house. Then there was Kev, Mr. Innocent himself, I had thought. I had felt we were connected and he had my back. *Yeah, right!*

"Naw, man, I got it. Stop right here," I heard Jason order. I could hear Jason get out the truck. Kev must have sat there because next I heard an engine start and a car pull off. It became silent on the phone for a few seconds, and then Kev said my name.

"Dang, Reese, I'm sorry. Just can't get in the middle of that." A few seconds later the phone went dead. I'd heard enough anyway.

***

When Jason pulled up to the house, I was still upset. I got off the couch in the family room and looked out the window at him walking toward the house. He was so cool and calm, talking on his cell and laughing. I heard him turn the key; then the door opened up and I went back over to the couch and sat down. I looked at the time on the cable box; it was well past midnight when he finally got there. The boys were upstairs in their room, sleeping.

I couldn't contain my mouth. I couldn't just let him get this one off without telling him to get that mess out of here.

I watched him come in, then hang his coat up in the closet. He grabbed himself a soda, kissed me on the forehead, then sat down beside me. I had to ask myself, *Is this idiot for real?* I couldn't believe him. I couldn't believe he was acting like nothing had happened. All along this man had been telling me he owned a business and he's nothing more than a dope dealer. *Really?*

I watched him sit and flick through the channels on the TV. "So, Jay? I mean, you not going to say nothing? I know Kev told you." I got up off the couch and stood in front of him with my hands on my hips.

"Where the boys, Reese? They in the bed?" He leaned back on the couch and pulled out a blunt. "Come sit down and smoke wit' me." He patted the couch beside where he sat.

I frowned at him then continued to talk. "Unbelievable! What? Smoke with you? Are you serious? Jason! You have been lying to me since day one and you want me to sit down and smoke? Naw, that's not gonna happen. See that dope you had hid all in my bedroom? It's down the toilet!" He didn't respond so I kept going.

"And those guns you got all in the closet, you need to grab them up and get them out of here now! I'm not playing, Jay. That's foul what you did! You know how dangerous that is? Leaving dope, money, and guns up in here? The boys were playing with those guns you left in here!" I began pacing. "What if they would have gotten hurt, huh? You didn't think about that!"

I stared at him, waiting patiently for him to give me an answer or explanation or something, but he didn't. He just sat there. Eventually then Jason put the blunt down and looked at me.

"You flushed my product down the what? You must be out yo' mind. You know how much money you just wasted? Huh?" He laughed. "Wait 'til I tell Kev this one! You flushed it." He picked up the weed, puffed, and watched the smoke go in the air and shook his head.

I walked away and mumbled under my breath, "This doesn't make any sense. You so stupid."

Up to this point of the conversation I had never seen Jason flip all the way out. He didn't react while I was fussing. He just sat listening to me and smoking his blunt. But when Jason heard me call him stupid, it must have made something in him snap.

He got up off the couch and grabbed me as I went by him. He pulled me on to the couch by my arms. I tried to fight him back but it was useless. He was too strong for me. He then threw me down and got on top of me. It happened so fast and he was so big and powerful. I couldn't move or get out of his grip. He was squeezing my arms tightly.

"Stop, Jason! Stop!" I screamed as loud as I could and then he put his hand over my mouth to quiet me. Next he did the unthinkable. He pulled a gun out by where his ankle was and put it to my temple. He took his hand and uncovered my mouth. I gasped for air and began to cough.

"You see this? This is dangerous." Jason was serious as he stared in my eyes, letting me know not to disrespect him again.

I never opened my mouth. I understood what he was saying. Tears began to well up in my eyes and then fell down my cheeks as I felt the cold, hard metal against my flesh. I realized I was in a situation I didn't know how to get out of. Even though I hadn't called on my Heavenly Father in quite some time, I began to because that was all I knew to do, given the circumstance.

Jesus, please help me! I prayed. My heart was racing and I thought about my sons up the stairs, sleeping. I prayed to God that they wouldn't come down and see what was happening. *Jesus, I am begging you to please cover my sons in the blood of Jesus!* I screamed in my head; then all of a sudden I felt a peace come in the room, and I knew that after walking away from God, He was still there when I needed Him.

"You understand me, Reese? I know what dangerous is and this is dangerous." He repositioned the gun to my temple and cocked the gun. I closed my eyes, thinking he was going to pull the trigger.

"Don't worry about nothin' I bring in this house. I won't let it hurt you or yo' sons. You understand me?" His voice was deep and cold with no love in it. All I could do was hope I would live to see another day.

"And I should smack you for flushin' that coke! That was twenty grand! What's wrong wit' you? " He pushed me to the floor and I lay there crying, and shivering.

Jason sat on the couch and smoked his blunt while he watched me cry on the floor 'til he finished his blunt. He got up and put the gun back where it was, went to the closet, grabbed his coat, and went out the front door. I heard him turn his car alarm off, then shut the door and pull off.

I stayed on the floor, balled up, crying, but could hear my son Michael coming down the stairs. I hurried and wiped my eyes so he wouldn't see me cry.

"Mommy, where did Jason go?" Michael asked.

"Out, he will be right back." I sniffed.

I had decided right then to send the boys to their father's. I wanted them to be out of my home until I knew what to do about Jay.

When Jason and I first started dating Jason was their hero.

Up until now I had no idea that Jason would ever harm me, but now, as I had to pick myself up off the floor, I realized I was so wrong about him. I tried to reason with myself that he was just demonstrating what dangerous was, but it wasn't working. There was no reason for him to ever put a gun to my head. I knew better than that. I knew he was indeed dangerous. People didn't just put guns to others' heads to show how dangerous it was. That didn't happen unless you were indeed dangerous.

I put Michael on my lap and kissed him on his cheek. "I love you, baby. You know Mommy loves you don't you?" I said, smiling at him.

"Yes, Mommy. I love you too." He grabbed my cheeks softly and kissed my lips. My heart melted when he did that.

"It's time for you to go to bed, Michael, you have to go to school in the morning."

"Okay, Mommy," he replied, putting his arms out so I could pick him up.

I did and took him to his room to lay him in his bed, and I was still trembling from what Jason had done.

I looked around the room my sons shared, which was filled with every kind of toy and game imaginable for children. I looked at the SpongeBob décor, smiled, and laid Michael in his bed. I gave him another kiss, this time on the cheek, then went over to the baby's bed and kissed him and covered him up.

Michael whispered, "Mommy?"

I turned around. "Yes, son?"

"You forgot to pray with me."

Even though I didn't pray like I should have, I still made sure my babies talked to God every night before going to bed. I walked over to his bed and got on my knees and begin to pray with my son.

"Jesus, we love you, Lord, and no matter how far we seem to get from you in our lives, please cover us, love us, and protect us always, in Jesus' name."

I rose off the ground and Michael sat up with all smiles. "Michael, you have to go to sleep, you have school tomorrow, baby."

"Mommy, you forgot to say amen. That's all, Mommy, just amen."

I chuckled. "Amen."

I laughed, turned off their light and watched the nightlight glow on their wall. I then closed the door behind me.

As soon as I walked out of the room, I saw Jason standing right there in the hallway, watching. When I noticed him, I stopped in my tracks. My heart was beating a mile a minute, wondering what he was going to do to me next.

He walked up to me and I tried to back away, then I put my hands over my face for protection, thinking he was going to hurt me, but he didn't. He grabbed me, put both his hands around my upper arms and pulled me close. He hugged me and kissed me on my lips.

Tears streamed down my face. I was so confused. Not even an hour ago this man had a Ruger, to my temple.

"Reese, we all right? You wit' me?" Jason said.

I closed my eyes and wept as I prayed that everything would be all right.

Chapter 9

Another One Just Like You

From the day I had discovered the truth about Jason, our relationship was never the same.

Jason was the Midwest's biggest drug supplier and I was way over my head to think I could handle being a hustler's wifey. With all that I dealt with, all I could think about was him flirting and frequently cheating on me. I knew I had problems. How in the world could that be all that was on my mind?

Jason was out of control. He did what he wanted. He would often flaunt his other women in my face and put the drug dealing out in the open too. I was tired of it and him and I was ready to say good-bye to Jason once and for all.

So Jason calling me to go out to lunch so we could talk was right on time.

"Babe, I don't have a lot of time for this, but I know you've been upset about everything. I can meet you for lunch. I don't have a lot of time for this, Reese. So we gonna discuss it and that's gonna be it."

"Okay, I'll be there in a few, Jay."

I knew he didn't wanna lose me so I would sit at this lunch and put it all on the line. I would demand that he respect me and stop with all the nonsense.

I got myself together and headed to the restaurant downtown he suggested we meet at. Jason was already there when I arrived. The whole encounter reminded me of when I was meeting up with Julius, my ex, and ending that marriage. I hoped this wasn't gonna go like that, with me giving him a bath with my glass of water, like I did Julius.

Jason was sitting down drinking a glass of water and talking on his cell when I came in. He saw me and stood up and got off the phone. He pulled my chair out, waited for me to sit, then kissed me on the cheek.

"Babe, you look nice today. You got your hair done?" he complimented me.

I smiled. Jason could be quite a gentleman at times. He knew how to make me feel on top of the world sometimes. Then there were other times when he made me feel at the bottom of the hill after falling down it. I wondered which one it would be today.

"Listen, babe, no more secrets," he said. "No more lies."

"Jason, I just don't know if I can handle all of this. "Every time—"

Before I could finish he leaned over the table in the restaurant, looked around, then back at me. "If you can't handle my lifestyle, tell me now. There's plenty of women who can right here in Columbus."

I sat there looking at him with my mouth hung open. He motioned his hands and shrugged his shoulders as if to say, "So what."

"Listen, I'm just bein' honest. There's females right now who wanna sit in that seat you sittin' in." He pointed at my chair. "Listen, just let me know wha' you wanna do 'bout this, Reese. Either you wit' me, or not."

He got up and walked out the restaurant, leaving me sitting there alone. I was crushed and my feelings were hurt. *This can't be the same man who was so caring. Where did he go?* I wondered while I sat there, looking like a plum fool. Then I thought, *today I'm at the bottom of the hill.*

After that conversation he wasn't even going to get it together. I was certain it was time to go!

I sat there a few more minutes and thought about my relationship with Jesus and how so many times in my life He came to my rescue. I thought about that, and then picked up my cell to call Grandpa. I dialed his cell then hung up. "Why bother him with this? I know what to do: pray."

I left the restaurant and decided to go by Toya's house. Toya gave good advice and was a woman of God. She wasn't only my sitter for the boys, but a good friend. I picked up my cell and called her while I drove.

"Hey, T, what you up to?"

"Oh, not too much. When my boys comin' back from their dad's in Cleveland? I miss them."

"They'll be back soon, T. Promise you that. I miss my boys so much!"

"Good! Can't wait to hear 'bout their trip," she said.

"I wanted to stop by and talk awhile. Kinda going through some more drama with Jason. I need to talk, girl. Jason is headed out with Kev and some more friends so I can hang out tonight."

"Okay, that's fine. I'm here for you Reese" she said.

"I'm pulling up. I'll be in there in a second." I saw her open the door while she was hanging up the phone. I got out my car and walked to her door. Toya stood in the doorway, smiling at me.

"Come on in here, girl, it's gonna be all right!" Toya said.

"Yeah, I imagine it gets better," I replied. "Pour me a cup of that good ol' coffee you make."

"Gotcha." She smiled and then we went inside to her kitchen. "Reese, you are too good for that man. You and your sons deserve better than that."

"I know, Toya, really I do, but he does love the boys. He spends time with them and makes sure they have the best." I was so confused about my feelings, in one breathe I knew I needed to leave Jason and in the other breathe, I was defending him and staying in the mess.

"Come on, Reese. How much could he care about them if he treats their mother with so much disrespect? You need to think about that. Reese, I'm tellin' you, get out of this."

I sat there at the kitchen table staring out the window. I heard everything Toya was saying and I knew in my heart she was right.

"Reese!"

"Huh? I answered, still while I was thinking how bad this relationship was. I glanced over at Toya.

She rolled her eyes in what seemed to be frustration. "You see that coffee in front of you?"

I looked down into my cup of coffee.

"You better smell it, 'cause you already awoke!"

We both began to laugh. My laughing was to keep from crying.

"For real, Reese, though, on a serious tip, you should give this to Jesus. You already know what He can do for you."

I fiddled with my hands to show Toya I didn't wanna hear it. This was something bigger than me getting it together with Jesus. But deep down, I did know that she was right. "I know, I know! I do wanna get my relationship right with Jesus and I know that's the only way I can get my life." I put my head down and sipped my coffee.

"I'm not gonna beat you wit' it. But He got you and those boys. Walk away, babe, before you get hurt. It's only a matter of time before he starts getting physical. Jason is a time bomb!"

I looked out the window, then said, "Waiting to explode."

Chapter 10

The Money Is Safe

Jason did agree to take his dope somewhere else, but he kept the money at my house. That was the only place he and Kev agreed it would be safe. The money was safe, but I was miserable. I knew I had made a mistake by getting in this relationship this fast and I was looking for a way out. It seemed as though every time I was ready to walk away, Jason would pull me back into it with his gifts, trips, or fear tactics. Eventually, I gave up hope and thought this is what my life would be about. I figured I might as well accept it. That was until the day Jason and Kev got into a fight.

Jason and Kev were out enjoying the night with a few members of their crew. They went out to celebrate because Shy, the youngest member of their crew, was going off to college. They went to the strip club to celebrate. Before the night ended, the two of them were fighting.

Jason was very close with Shy. He didn't really have him selling; he more or less had him following him around, like a protégé, to take over or be a key player one day. He took Shy everywhere he went, bought him clothes, and kept him geared up. He took Shy out of town with him and treated him like he was his son.

So the night was supposed to be all about Shy, but it wasn't. It ended up being all about me.

After I left Toya's house feeling so refreshed and renewed and believing I could change I was awakened by my cell ringing. I looked down at it and saw that it was Kev. He was pumped when I answered.

"Hello?" I yawned. "Kev, it's after one o'clock in the morning. What's wrong?" I sat up in the bed and turned on my light. I was a bit nervous and didn't like late night calls because it made me think something was wrong.

"I'm sorry to call you this late, Reese."

" Is everything all right?" I wondered what was going on. Kev didn't call me at one in the morning.

"Jason needs to get it right." I could tell Kev had been drinking. He would never call me and say all of this, but I decided to listen. I knew he needed an ear. And as many times as I leaned on his shoulder and cried it was time for me to return the favor.

He began to tell me that he and Jason had fought. He told me what happened earlier that night, word for word:

"So, Jay, how everything workin' out between you and Reese now?" Kev asked.

"Man, that crazy woman flushed that stuff down the toilet!"

Everybody in their crew laughed.

"What?" Kev laughed more. "What you do?"

"I wasn't mad. I figured it was understandable, her being mad and flushin' it, but then she started actin' crazy. She slipped up and called me stupid!"

Their whole crew was listening and laughing as he displayed what he did next.

"I jumped off that couch and tried to wring her neck!"

He walked up to Shy and put him in a chokehold as demonstration.

Kev got uncomfortable in his seat, like he wanted to say somethin' else about what Jay did.

"Bro, you shouldn't do that girl like that. She cool," Kev said.

Jason looked at him. "Are you serious? Naw, man, she ain't getting away wit' that. I gave her a pass on da dope!" He shook his head and continued to look at Kev. "That was twenty grand she flushed. Crazy chick!" Jason yelled.

Kev sat there and put his head down like he was deep in thought as he moved his head to the music. "'Nothing Even Matters,' that's the jam!" Kev said, moving his head some more to the Lauryn Hill and D'angelo duet."Naw, bro, you wrong for that. You should have never had that in her house, you know that. I told you not to do that but you don't listen," Kev said.

"Bro, why you on this tonight? That's yesterdays news . . . Come on. We suppose to be celebratin'. You over there on that Lauryn Hill mess! Man up!" Jason laughed, then got distracted by one of the strippers.

"Come here, baby, what yo' name is?" Jason joked. He was pullin' her close to him, whispering in her ear and smilin'.

Jason watched Kev getting upset, shaking his head like he was displeased at Jason and what he was doing."Kev, what's up? Why you so worried about what I do to Reese? She ain't your concern." Jason was tired of Kev always reminding him about the good woman he had. "You act like I'm cheatin' on you or somethin'." Jason chuckled and blew out the smoke from the weed then passed it to Kev.

"Naw, man. I'm just sayin'. Reese is a good woman. What more do you want from a woman? That's all, man," Kev reasoned.

Jason started smiling. "You see that right there?" He pointed at the stripper he was talkin' to; then he handed her some money. "That's what I want right now, and when I'm finished wit' her, I'll go see Reese."

Everybody in their crew laughed at Jason; everybody but Kev.

"Man, you wrong. Reese is fine. She has a college degree and a good job," Kev stated, shaking his head as if Jason had to be the most stupid man in the world for playing a woman like Reese.

"Since you feel like that, bro, why don't you get wit' her then?" Jason was getting upset. "You talk about her like you want her. Huh, you want Reese, Kev?" Jason got up off the stool and stood in front of Kev.

Kev smirked and got off the stool too, still with his drink in his hand. "I tell you what, Jay. If I had gone after her instead of you, she would be mine. You don't want her."

Kev and Jason were drunk and getting loud. The rest of the crew was watching and getting nervous that this was going to turn into something real bad.

Kev put his glass down and stood face to face with Jason. "I said it: she deserves to be treated better than what you treat her man, that's all. That woman is fine!" He smiled, flung his hands in the air, and turned to sit back down when Jay punched him in his jaw.

They started fighting after that and everybody tried to break it up, but it was bad, and when it was all over, Jason had a black eye and Kev had a busted lip. Kev left the club after that, leaving Jason in the club without a ride because no one else knew where he and Reese lived.

The other line clicked, interrupting Kev's story. I told Kev to hold on while I answered the call. I closed my eyes, took a deep breath, and said, "Hello."

"Aey get up, come get me! Kev left!" he yelled.

I held the phone a second; then I answered him. "Where?"

"Club Traffic, downtown. Hurry up, I'm ready to go!" he demanded.

"Okay. I'm on my way." I clicked over. "Kev, you still there?"

"Yeah. That him?" he replied.

"Yes, I'm going to go pick him up. I'll call you tomorrow okay?"

"Yeah, all right." He was about to hang up and then said, "Reese, be careful, he was pretty upset. But I wanted you to know what went down."

"Okay, talk to you later." As soon as we said bye my cell was ringing again. It was Jay calling back. "Hello."

"You left yet?"

"I'm about to."

"Hurry up, woman! I'm ready to go!"

"I'm on my way, Jason. I'll be there in a few."

He had hung up before I finished my sentence. I was glad Kev called because it gave me a feel of what I was walking into.

I put on my clothes, grabbed my keys, and left. While I drove I thought of how tired I was of him and I wanted to tell him. Things weren't going to get better. I needed to end this.

"Okay, Jesus." I sighed. "I want out of this mess. I'm ready, please help me!"

Jason was already out there waiting when I pulled up to the club. He ran over to the car, then took a beer bottle and threw it into the driver side window, busting the glass all over my legs.

I screamed! I could not believe he did that! "What did I do?" That was my question. I didn't wait for an answer though. I tried to put the car in reverse and pull off but I couldn't fast enough.

He then walked up to the car and yanked me out of the window by my neck. He carried me by my throat over against the wall of the club as if I were a rag doll. I had my hands around his trying to loosen his grip some. I couldn't breathe. My neck hurt so bad and saliva was coming out the sides of my mouth, wetting up my face and shirt.

The bouncer ran over to him and yelled. "Aey, man! Aey, let her go!"

Jason acted like he didn't hear him; he kept on attacking me. "I'ma kill you, Reese!"

The bouncer tried to contain him and make him let me go. I got away for a second. I finally could get air. I began to scream as loud as I could and I tried to run away.

"Help me, somebody, help me! He's gonna kill me! Jason, what's wrong? What did I do? Please tell me," I begged him. He caught me again and put his hand back around my throat.

Some of Jason's crew finally came out from the club, and when they saw him out there clowin' they started laughing and made the bouncer go inside. Then they got Jason to let me go. They picked me up and threw me in the back of the car as I kicked and screamed.

I managed to get it together for a second and grabbed the top of the back seat with my right hand. I lifted my head and looked through the rear window at the bouncer standing there in shock with his hands on top of his head. He probably was wondering whether I was going to die that night.

When I realized I couldn't escape, I lay in the back seat of the car while it raced down the street with Jason in the front passenger seat.

"Ouch! Stop punching me, please," I pleaded. He was punching me every few minutes and spitting at me.

I covered myself the best I could with my hands over my legs and head. I jerked my hands back because they were wet with blood. Then I realized my legs were cut up pretty bad.

I was so scared. I remembered what Toya had said when I was at her house earlier about him getting physical. My hands were shaking and the car was movin' fast down the streets.

Shy had jumped in the driver's seat and sped off in case someone had called the police on Jason at the club. Jason was breathing hard. He turned around and looked at me.

"Reese," Jason calmly said. "You been messin' with my boy? Huh? You messin' wit' Kev?"

Shy looked over at Jay. "Come on now, Jay. Don't do her like that, man, don't spit on her. You know Reese ain't doin' nothin'."

Jay hollered, "Man, stay out of this! She don't mean nothing to me! Just drive da car 'til I tell you to stop!" Jason took his gun out and played with it. Shy didn't say anything else, he just drove.

"You gonna answer me, Reese? You been messin' around wit' Kev?"

"No, Jay, no! Please don't hurt me, please don't hurt me, Jay." I begged him to stop like I was a dog beggin' for food. I thought he was going to kill me. I began to pray quietly. "Jesus, please help me. Lord, I need you!"

Jason leaned in the back seat, put his gun to my thigh, and cocked it. "Look at me, Reese!"

I was trembling and shaking, I couldn't control it. I was terrified of him. I felt the gun against my skin like I had felt it against my temple the first time he pulled the gun out when the boys had found them in our house. I lifted my head and looked him in his eyes like he told me to.

"If I ever find out you messin' wit' my boy, I will kill you. I mean it!"

I cried on the floor of the car, threatened, abused, and tortured. You'd think after that I'd have stayed as far away from Kev that I could. You'd think . . .

Chapter 11

The Reality

I woke up the next morning in my bed. I didn't remember anything after Jason put the gun to my thigh and told me he would kill me if I messed with Kev. I didn't know where Jason went, but he wasn't there with me. I looked over on my wall at my beautiful crystal clock that was in my momma's house when I was a little girl. It was two-thirty in the afternoon and I must have been tired. I thought about how I felt: tired . . . Tired of all the drama that had begun. Tired of Jason and everything that came with him; just tired!

I didn't have a minute to think about my boys or myself anymore. Everything had started revolving around Jason and what he needed, wanted.

I looked for my cell and saw I had a few missed calls. Kev had called and texted. He told me to give him a call when I got his message. He said Shy called him and told him what Jason did to me and he was so sorry.

I was still a tad bit upset with Kev for not telling me about them being drug dealers, so I definitely wasn't gonna call him and tell him what was going on between me and Jason. Those days of leaning on him for support were over! The way I was thinking, if Jason thought I was messing with Kev, he might as well have been in the back of that car beating me too.

I got up slowly because my body was sore from the beating. I laid my clothes out for the day and decided to get out and go to the movies or something. I needed some space. I needed to get my mind clear and for me that meant dinner and a movie.

After I took my bath, got dressed, and was about to walk out the door, I heard Jason turning the key, coming in. I was a little nervous because I didn't know where his mind was after last night, but I was ready to face him.

He walked in the house and looked at me.

"Hey, babe. You okay?" He had bags from the mall in his hands. "I left you sleepin'. You looked so peaceful I didn't wanna wake you. Reese, fo' real, I am so sorry for what I did and wha' I been doin' to you. It's not cool. I owe you an apology, babe."

He walked over to me and hugged me, rubbing my back. He looked down at me and asked, "You forgive me, babe? You wit' me?"

I stood there. I didn't know what to say or do. I wanted to forgive him; after all, he was all I had known for quite some time. He hadn't always been that bad, just here lately.

I grabbed his face, closed my eyes, and kissed him. "I forgive you, Jay."

He let out a sigh of relief. "I love you, Reese, I do. I don't wanna lose you. I know I say a lot of foul things sometimes, but I know it won't be as simple as gettin' another pretty face. Babe, I'm sorry."

He threw his hands up and continued. "I've just been under all this pressure lately. We got these new shipments comin' in. I'm tryin' to flip the business and make it legit, and Kev sayin' he wanna walk away; he can't do it no mo'! He ain't the same since his moms died. No heart fo' it."

I thought about what he was saying about Kev. I wondered if he was gonna be okay and if him wanting to leave had anything to do with me. I hurried and fixed my face before Jay noticed any concern I was having. I didn't want a replay of the night before.

"Reese, go 'head, babe, and get dressed. We have a reservation."

"Okay, but can I open my gifts first?" I smiled and stood there in front of Jay like a little girl waiting patiently for the go-ahead as if it were Christmas or my birthday.

"Of course, baby." He nodded toward the bags. He sat on the couch, leaned back, and lit up his cigar and watched me.

I reached in the biggest bag and pulled out a shoebox. I looked over at Jay sittin' there, smilin' at me. It was a pair of Red Bottoms.

"Thanks, Jay, love 'em." I smiled and went to the next bag fast. He knew it took more than a pair of shoes to impress me; after all, I was married to an athlete at one time, with mad cash.

I went in the next bag and there was a small box from Tiffany's. I looked over at Jay and he laughed.

"Yeah, I bet that got yo' attention." He got off the couch, put his cigar in his ashtray, and came over to me. He took the bracelet out the box; then he put it on my wrist. "I love you, Reese," he whispered and held me tight.

"Jay, this is beautiful."

"It was made just fo' you, it better be. Seven carats enough for you, Miss Fancy?" he asked.

"I love it." I went to open another gift but he stopped me.

"Baby, come on. I got somethin' special for you a little later. But we have reservations now."

I smiled, took my new stuff, and went up the stairs to change. I grinned and looked at him.

"What? Why you lookin' at me like that?" he asked.

"This is the Jay I love. Where he been?"

We both laughed.

I was happy that Jason and I were back on track. We had an awesome time at dinner and now we were headed back to the house, when Jason got an important call. I didn't hear who was on the other end.

"Hello? Today, oh man." He looked over at me. "Hold on a second, baby. I gotta make a quick stop." He smiled.

I laid my head back against the headrest and closed my eyes. I was comfortable and didn't have a care in the world. Shoot, I was out on the town with my fine boo!

Jason drove to Miller Avenue. I didn't know who had called or what it was about. I was just glad to have my Jay back.

"I gotta handle this real quick. Just sit back and enjoy this ride." He smirked.

I looked up and asked Jason, "Where are we going?" I never got a response from him.

He pulled out his cell and dialed a number. "I'm here."

A minute later Shy came out of an apartment. He was all smiles when he saw me. He walked over to my side of the car and I rolled down the window for him and smiled.

"Boy, am I glad to see you! You okay?" I put my arms out the window and motioned him for a hug. I kissed him on the cheek.

"Okay, now, Shy, don't get hurt. Don't be kissin' on my baby like that!" Jay jokingly threatened.

We all laughed.

Shy looked at me. "You okay fo' real? Thought I was gonna have to pull my gat out on him! Out there trip-pin' like that!"

Shy was no older than nineteen. I was proud of him. He was getting out of the streets, and as stated earlier, on his way to Bowling Green University on a football scholarship. He was a good kid with so many great qualities, but he got hooked up with the wrong people. Jason had met him from going to the football games and seeing him tear up the other teams, scoring.

"What's good, Jay?"

"Where Kev at? Why y'all ain't get him to come do this?"

Shy listened; then he got serious. "Kev said call you. He had somethin' to take care of, so that's what I did."

Jason moved around in his seat a little like he was a little agitated that Kev didn't come. I wondered where Kev was but I dared not say a word. I kept my thoughts to myself.

"Hey, Jay, when you gonna let me drive this?" He pointed to Jason's shiny black Hummer, which was chromed out, with music blasting.

Jason never responded. He looked over at me. "Stay right here."

I obliged and Jason got out of the truck. He turned and grabbed his fitted baseball cap that sat on the dashboard and put it on his head. He shut the door and then walked off with Shy. I watched as they talked in the middle of the street.

Jason reached his hand out and gave him dap. Next Shy reached in his pocket and pulled out a key and pointed at a car that was parked behind the Hummer. Jason gave him a stack of money then came back to the truck.

"Let's go."

"Where we goin'?" I replied.

"Get out the truck, Reese. I got to be somewhere now, baby." Jason was still a little aggravated after hearing what Kev said.

I hurried out of the truck, trying to keep up with Jason. It was hard because I had on the Red Bottoms he'd just given me. I had both Jason's and Shy's attention as I walked.

Jason pointed to a brand-new dark blue Toyota Camry and told me to get in. I had to admit I was puzzled, but did what I was told so Jason wouldn't get mad. We got in the car and he drove off, speeding down the street.

"Where we goin' Jay?" I asked again.

"Why, Reese? You wit' me, you safe." He reached over and touched my knee as he sped down the freeway. "Baby, if I didn't tell you . . ." He looked over at me. "You look beautiful tonight." He smiled, took my hand and held it, then kissed it. I smiled at him, then reached over and kissed him on his cheek. Jason's cell began to ring.

"Hello," he answered it, then listened to what the caller had to say. "I know, I know. I'm pullin' up now."

Jason pulled up to the airport and got out of the car. "Stay right here, babe. I'll be right back."

He was still on the phone but had his hand over the receiver when he spoke to me. He shut the car door and looked down the busy sidewalk at all the people waiting for their rides.

"I see y'all. Come on." He waved his hand in the air and two females began to walk toward him.

Upon seeing the girls, I knew immediately what was going on. Jason hired young girls to travel with their product from New York to Columbus, inconspicuously dressed as college students going home for a weekend. Jason was always at the top of his game and he knew if he used them more than a couple of times, the possibility of them getting caught increased. So he always tried to find new girls who wanted some extra money and were willing to carry dope on an airplane to get it.

He usually found the girls who were rebellious to their parents, the ones who were in the clubs with fake IDs, or boosting clothes for a living and looking for anything to do to get money. Jason looked for the ones with the nothing-to-lose mentality, the hardcore young chicks who were already headed for a downfall.

He could pick them out in a crowd, the bad girl, that is. He liked the ones who were looking for love in all the wrong places, and Jason knew how to turn on the charm to get what he wanted. Jason would lie to the girls, give them hopes of a relationship with him and a fairytale lifestyle; that was all it took to seal the deal and make the ladies do whatever he wanted. He always found the ones who never thought twice about what would happen to them if they were caught, and would never tell if they were.

The females traveled by plane through JFK Airport in New York straight to the Columbus International Airport with no problem. They brought back to the CO anywhere from two to five kilos taped to their bodies; and no one noticed a thing. When I found out what they were doing and how, I wondered how in the world they got away with it with all the security at the airport since 9/11. But they did, and they got away with it plenty of times. Jason would always be nervous until the plane hit the ground and they got their dope off the females.

When the girls got to the car I was shocked. They looked like two of the most innocent girls to ever go to college. However, they weren't. They were young girls who were getting their hustle on.

They got in the car, but Jason didn't introduce them to me. He acted like I wasn't there. It made me a little mad to be ignored, but I understood that they were just doing business.

I pulled the mirror down on the visor, wanting to see what they looked like. When Jason got in he started talking to them. "So everything everything? No problems wit' that weight on?"

"No problems. I got two and a half kilos and she do too," one of the girls said to Jason. She nodded toward the other girl. "That's five! You ain't gonna find nobody like us, Jay. I don't know why you keep tryin'!"

Both the girls laughed.

I couldn't believe it. These chicks had just transported five kilos of cocaine on an airplane and were cool, calm, and laughing! *Don't they know how much trouble they would be in if they were caught? Then again, if the police pulled us over right now, I would be in for it too. Woo, God, help me!* I got nervous and started sweating and moving around in my seat.

I looked over at Jason and he appeared to be fine, asking them questions like, "How was your flight? Y'all hungry?" He told them that he had them a nice suite downtown and a couple of friends were gonna take them out on the town before they went back tomorrow.

This was unbelievable! My heart was beating so fast, yet everyone else seemed as cool as a cucumber. I looked out the window and listened, and then watched them in the back seat.

The two girls couldn't have been any older than eighteen. One was a heavyset Spanish girl with long black hair that she wore in one ponytail, which hung halfway down her back. It was probably her studious look that got her out of the airport.

The other female was a black girl, tall and slender. She was dressed in a pair of jeans and an Oxford shirt that matched her tights and a pair of black platform shoes. She wore micro braids in her hair and it was pulled up into one ponytail ball in the middle of her head. She also had some nice Vogue glasses on.

Yeah, they ain't gonna get caught, I thought, *not with that look.*

They were in the back seat laughing and talking. They paid no attention to me, so I stopped paying attention to them. I flipped the mirror back up and continued to look out the window the rest of the drive.

Once the car stopped, I realized we were back at the place on Miller Avenue. Jason and the girls got out of the car, but I stayed inside the car.

Jason turned around and came over to my side of the car. "Come on, babe." He opened the door.

I hesitated at first because I knew they were going to handle their business with the dope, and I didn't know if I wanted to be a part of that, not realizing I was already a part of it. I sat a second longer, and thought, *he really loves me if he's willing to show me his business like this. Aw, he really do trust me.* I smiled.

"Come on, Reese. I ain't gonna hold this door open forever." He smiled and my heart melted. I would feel warm inside every time Jason showed his dimples. I stepped out the car and took his hand. "I want you to see somethin'," he explained.

"What, Jay?" I knew not to ask too many questions. "No more secrets," I whispered.

As we walked toward the door, Kev pulled up in his truck. We all turned around because we could hear his music bangin'. Jason stopped and waited for him. Kev got out of the truck and was runnin' toward us. I watched Kev as he approached. He was dressed in a gray tailor-made suit with a burnt orange shirt and he had the nerves to have on shoes that matched the shirt to a tee. I had to admit, I was impressed. *He's so neat and clean,* I thought; then I sniffed in how good he smelled because the cologne lingered on. I tried to play it off and look uninterested; however, it was hard for any woman to ignore this man. Even the young ladies were batting their eyes.

I hoped nobody noticed me secretly admiring him. I couldn't help it, Lord knows I tried, but was hard to ignore and getting harder to control.

While I stood there waiting for him to catch up to us I found myself staring at him again. Finally I had to admit that it was impossible and he was too irresistible not to look at. I didn't know if it was 'cause he was so fine or if it was his personality that had me going crazy every time I saw him. *Whatever it is, I need to get control of it quick,* I reasoned.

Kev also wore a pair of Chanel glasses on his face, which made him look studious. His haircut was precise. His skin was radiant and the shadow on his face was trimmed with perfection, I noticed. I knew I had to make myself turn away before anyone noticed me staring 'cause if Jay saw me, he would kill me. He promised that! And after all the drama that had just happened no one needed anything else to transpire.

I noticed Kev's lip was swollen a little, then looked over at Jason and his black eye and shook my head.

"What's up, Reese?" Kev's eyes met mine.

"Hey, Kev. How are you?" I answered, trying to act like I wasn't paying him any attention, but I couldn't help it.

"What's up, Jay? You ready for this?" Kev said. They still had a little tension between them since their epic fight. Kev shook Jason's hand. "Let me holla at you for a minute, bro."

"Hold on, Reese," Jason said to me, holding up one finger and walking away with Kev.

Kev pulled Jason to the side to talk to him. "First is, last night is squashed? We too good for that," Kev tried to whisper but I could hear everything.

"Come on, man, you know I ain't gonna never let no chick come between you and me, Kev." They gave each other dap.

"Yeah, all right, Jay, but why you got her here? She don't need to be here, man," Kev questioned his boy. "That girl got kids. What if somethin' goes down up in here? This the biggest shipment we have done. Anything could happen," Kev explained as I looked on.

"Man, she straight, I got this. That's my woman, remember?" Jason said, looking at Kev seriously as if to remind him of the night before. "She all right as long as I'm here," Jason proclaimed. He used his hands to express his frustration with the questions Kev was asking him. "Bro, fo' real, I want you to quit worrying about her! I understand y'all friends but, bro, you startin' to trip!" Jason expressed while he walked back over to me; then he led me toward the apartment.

Kev decided to stay out of it, I guessed, because he didn't say another word. He just knew I didn't belong there.

I already missed talks with Kev that I knew we wouldn't be able to have anymore. His conversations with me were deeper than I had with Jason. I had expressed my love for God to Kev many times and how I wasn't in His will anymore.

I was looking around the outside of the apartments as I walked, stepping out of the way of trash and a dirty diaper in my path. I didn't want my new shoes to touch the dirt. It wasn't like I hadn't experienced this type of hood before, because before my mother was killed, we lived in a neighborhood in Dayton just like this one.

Once inside the apartment, my eyes took a quick glance around. I saw an old, dirty couch in the front room, and a big-screen television that was hooked up to a PlayStation 3 game system. Of course there were a few young dudes surrounding it, playing the game. The music in the place was so loud; I couldn't even hear the young dudes screaming from the excitement of the game. I could just see their lips moving.

I was tripping off the entire scene. It put me in a daze, so much so that Jason had to tap me to follow him upstairs into a bedroom. I followed, looking at the back of his hooded mink jacket as I walked.

I didn't know what to expect once I was inside the room. I saw Kev sitting on a bed, smoking a blunt. He passed it to me while I sat down beside him. I could still smell the fragrance of his cologne. I closed my eyes for a second time and sniffed in unnoticed. I took the weed and looked over at Jason as he watched me and Kev interact.

I couldn't help but wonder if he'd noticed the way I had been looking at Kev.

"So, Reese, you look nice today. Where y'all coming from?" Kev asked. Kev was just being himself, but it wasn't helping Jay stay cool. He was getting upset and let me know by the evil looks he was giving me.

I answered him quickly. "We went to Mitchell's for dinner." I said it so dry that Kev didn't say another word to me.

Jason looked at me and motioned for me to come and sit beside him, so I did.

The females we had picked up from the airport were taking off their clothes with some assistance from a couple of guys in Jason and Kev's crew. They were making sure the girls didn't put any dope aside to sell or use themselves. My mouth hung open as I watched the girls pull dope off. Some of the dope was strapped and taped to their body and other dope was placed securely in the heel of their shoes.

They first had to take off their regular street clothes, then a second set of clothing that was tight like workout clothes, which they wore underneath the first layer. They then pulled the tape off of them, unraveling the drugs from the Saran Wrap that was holding the dope in place on them.

This is a mess! I thought, never opening my mouth and saying a word to anyone else in the bedroom.

Kev and Jason weighed the dope, then told the females to get dressed. It was crazy to me; even with me being high I couldn't understand what kind of women would be comfortable with taking their clothes off and leaving them off in front of men, let alone women. It puzzled me.

I watched the girls as they flirted and talked to the other men in the room. I knew they had to be high off something besides weed because of their actions. They had no respect for themselves.

When they finished getting dressed, Jason had me give both the girls $5,000. I thought the women were stupid for taking such a risk for only five Gs. I giggled.

"Reese, what's so funny?" Jason asked.

"Nothing," I proclaimed and straightened my attitude up while Jason looked on at me.

He got up and came over where I was standing. "What, babe? Why you laughin'?"

"Nothin,' Jay, dang."

I was getting nervous because I knew all about Jason's explosive temper. He would snatch me up right there in front of everybody if he thought he needed to.

He grabbed me and pulled me to him. "I know what's wrong wit' you, you high," he said. "I forgot Kev gave you that blunt."

I looked over toward Kev as Jason held me. He turned his head away when I connected eye to eye with him, like he didn't care. I looked back at Jason into his eyes and smiled, never saying a word. He bent down and kissed me, not realizing the silent talking that was goin' on between me and Kev.

Then Jason reached in his pocket and pulled out the key to the Toyota. "Here." He held the key in the air and looked at the young girls. The slender girl grabbed it; then Jason said, "That's for you two. Work it out."

The girls smiled with excitement and argued about who was going to drive it back to New York. Me, I just sat there in awe. *Five grand plus a car. Now that right there could make a chick want to get in the game.*

Chapter 12

The Warehouse

Things had only changed a little since Jason apologized and took me to their dope house. He was still doing him, just with a li'l discretion now.

Jason had given me a few more beatings. If he thought I was gettin' out of hand or when he thought someone was interested in me, he found a reason to fight. I was so lonely and so afraid of him, felt like I was locked away in a dungeon and Jason had eaten the key! I was miserable.

Kev and I didn't talk anymore because of my decision to stay with Jason. He said he couldn't stay by as a friend and watch that, so he and Jay remained friends and he and I only ran across each other when we had to.

I was numb to everything and I even thought about snortin' coke with Jay a time or two just to have something in common with him and maybe ease the pain . . . I didn't though.

I had given up on anything and everything but staying next to Jason, like he wanted me to. I'd stopped working, the boys were with Toya the majority of the time, and I closed everyone out except Jason. All I did was shop, smoke weed, party like a rock star, then sleep.

One day the boys' father called and threatened to come get them if I didn't get my act together. While he fumed, I held the other end of the phone, smoking a blunt and uninterested in what he was talking about.

"Reese? I know you can hear me, girl. Are you listening to me?" Julius sympathetically asked after yelling at me. He took a deep sigh and blew it out into the phone loud. I could hear how frustrated he was at me but I was high and didn't really care.

"I'm tellin' you, if one more person in Columbus call me and tell me how you out in da clubs shakin' yo' butt and high, I swear I'm comin' to get my boys!"

"Chill out, Julius!" I flopped down on the couch. "I hear you, but it ain't that serious! I take care of my boys, and you . . . you can't tell me anything! If you would've had yourself together we would be there with you. So don't come calling me with this!" I hung up. He was getting me all upset, but deep down I knew he was right; I did need to get it together.

I watched my cell ring over and over. I knew it was Julius calling back and I wasn't about to answer so he could tell me how wrong I was about something or other. I went upstairs and looked in my bedroom closet, and I grabbed that same silver briefcase I had found. I opened it up and started counting the money in it.

I looked out my bedroom window to make sure Jay wasn't coming; then I sat down beside the briefcase and money. I had a thought run through my mind: *take the money . . . take it all!*

Everything was about to change for me later that day when Jason came storming in the house.

I was sitting on the couch in the front room watching *Diary of a Mad Black Woman* when he came in the house. I knew something was wrong with him because his nose was all flared out and he was breathing heavy. That always meant he was furious. I got a little uncomfortable thinking he was gonna fight with me. I thought back, trying to figure out if I had done something that he may have been mad at me for.

"Hey, Jay, is everything okay?" I hurried and got up and stood beside the front door in case he was gonna swing. I figured I could run out the door real fast.

He was on his cell ranting on and on about how he was gonna get Shy for something or other. He never even noticed me moving around, uneasy, or even heard me asking him if he was all right.

I gave a sigh of relief and sat back down and watched the movie because I knew he wasn't mad at me. I really didn't care what Jason was talking about or what he was mad at as long as he wasn't upset with me.

I was watching the movie, but every now and then my eyes would shift to Jason on the cell. He was going back and forth, up and down the stairs and whispering on his cell as he walked around the house like he was getting prepared to go out. I had no idea who he was talking to on the phone. I just let him be until out of nowhere he said, "Baby, you love me? Huh, baby? Drive me downtown real quick to take care of somethin'." He stood over me. "I need to go take care of somethin'."

I looked up at him. I didn't feel like going anywhere with him. I could feel in my gut he was up to no good.

He winked. "Okay, then, go for a ride wit' me. You know you my ride and die," he joked.

"Where?" I asked.

"Oh, just put on yo' shoes and ride. We'll be back in a few. You just stay in the car. Pause yo' movie."

He smiled. I did. I paused my movie and put my shoes on.

"You ready, babe?" Jason asked.

"Yep, I'm ready."'

"Where yo' keys? I'ma drive yo' car."

I handed him the keys, and we left the house and got in the car. He started the car and sped down the streets, jumped on the freeway for a few minutes, then got off downtown and went to Front Street.

"Why we over here, Jay?"

He was dialing a number but was irritated when I questioned him. "Reese, don't worry 'bout it. Just sit out here. I'll be right back!" He opened the car door and got out. His whole demeanor had changed. He looked serious. "Lock the doors. I'll be right back," he stated.

"Jay, is there a bathroom in there?" I really needed to go. I wanted him to tell me to come on in. I didn't care that it was a warehouse, I just had to go.

"Stay in the car, Reese! I gotta do somethin'. Just sit tight." He slammed the door, took his gun out and put it in the back of his jeans, and went in. I turned my nose up and wondered what the heck was going on. *He pulled me out the house for this . . . to sit in the car.* "This don't make no sense. He gets on my nerves."

We were at some warehouse that appeared to be vacant, but I noticed there were cars of some of the other guys who worked for Jason too. I looked for Kev's truck but it wasn't there. My stomach felt sick when I saw he wasn't there 'cause I really wanted to see him, even if it was through a window. I sat there for a few more minutes, then started looking in the mirror and playing with my hair. I was used to waiting for Jason to take care of business; it wasn't no big deal anymore. I just had to pee this particular day.

I laid my head back and patted my fingers against the window while I waited. "Oh my God, I have to use the restroom!" I screamed out, wondering what the heck was taking Jay so long. Even though I hadn't been waiting five minutes, it felt like an hour having to go the bathroom.

I looked at the warehouse again. I was thinking about going in, but didn't. I just sat there clapping my knees together and holding it in. I eventually dosed off. When I came to, I looked at my watch and I had been asleep for about forty-five minutes, waiting. I looked around and realized my car was the only one out there now. So I figured it would be okay to go in and use the bathroom.

I put my purse underneath my seat. I grabbed the keys out the ignition, opened the door, then got out. I took a few steps toward the entrance that I had watched Jay go in. I hit the remote to lock the car doors. I heard it beep so I knew my car would be secure. I'd seen on the news all the robberies in that area.

As I got closer to the door I could hear somebody hollering. I thought I was trippin'.

"Jay?" I said. But he didn't answer. So I walked into the warehouse and immediately I had to cover my nose from the horrible smell that was in the air.

"Jay!" I kept walking. It was a little dark in there so I walked slow and followed the light that was coming from the back of the warehouse. The light was dim and seemed as if it was moving slow back and forth. I put my hands on my arms to try to stay warm, 'cause it was cold, damp, and musty in there.

"Hello? Babe, where you at?" I asked, looking around the dirty place. "I can't hold it anymore. I gotta pee." Jason never answered but I could hear him talking from a distance. I stopped to get a clearer listen.

"Who is he hollerin' at?" I said aloud. I started walking again. As I got closer to Jason's yelling I could smell a horrible stench of urine. "Ugh! I'ma gag." Then I heard Jay again.

"You had to do it! Who else could it be? Come on, man, just tell me what you said," he demanded. He sounded very frustrated. I couldn't see who he was talking to but I did hear someone, and it sounded like they were crying.

I knew then that this was something bad, but never did I think I would see something like I would see.

I started walking slower, and I got quiet and even began to tiptoe through the puddles of water toward Jay's voice. I figured if he was already upset I needed to ease myself in here to use the bathroom. That's all I needed was for him to get angry with me, too.

I could see Jason's shadow flickering on the wall from the drop light that hung in the middle of the warehouse by a wire. I walked closer where I could see everything and then I peeked around the corner.

Jason's back was to me. He had on a pair of black leather gloves and he had plastic covering his boots. His white T-shirt had bloodstains on it and there was a man on the floor. I couldn't see who it was because Jason was standing over him. He only had a pair of boxers on—no socks, no shoes, no clothes—and he covered himself with his hands and arms, and was balled up as if he was protecting himself. His feet were covered in blood and as he moved on the ground he seemed to be soaking wet. I assumed it came from the puddles of water in the warehouse.

I glanced across the room and then, of course, I saw the bathroom, which was across the room from where I stood. I could clearly see the toilet because the bathroom door was wide open and Jason's jacket hung over the door. There was a wooden chair beside where Jason stood, fallen over on to the floor. It had blood and duct tape on the arms of it that looked as if someone had cut somebody loose.

I absolutely couldn't believe this. It was a nightmare! I felt like I was in a horror movie with too much suspense.

My eyes then went back to Jason. He had finally moved and that's when I saw that it was Shy on the ground. I stood there, heartbroken for him; he was too young to be here.

"Oh my God, it's Shy!" I said quietly. Instantly my hands started shaking and my heart started beating fast.

Shy was soaked with blood. He was shivering all over and breathing heavily. It was a horrific scene; I would never forget it as long as I lived. He was practically naked and bruises were all over his light body. He had a gash across his forehead, his nose was filled with dried blood, and both his eyes were black and almost shut. His lip was swollen with blood and saliva was on the side of his face; it was messy. He was lying there with his arms around his knees and duct tape on his wrists that looked like someone let him loose from being restrained at one time. He was crying softly, "Jesus." I heard him.

I wanted to turn around and leave. I was so afraid of being seen, but I was more afraid for Shy because I knew Jason was gonna kill him. If I had never believed how dangerous Jason was, I knew it at that very moment. I grabbed my head, closed my eyes, and cried. I had all kinds of thoughts running through my mind but I felt so helpless. I looked again to see what was happening.

Jason was standing there with a wooden baseball bat in his hands. He didn't have any type of remorse on his face or any type of sympathy. His veins in his hands and muscles in his arms were bulging out of his skin from holding the bat so tight. He looked so angry, so vicious, and I knew then there was no crossing this man and living if he found out.

He took the bat and smashed Shy in his back. Shy's body convulsed from the pressure of the blow, he screamed out a loud, eerie, screeching sound. Then he began to violently cough up blood.

I stood there barely watching, covering my ears and my eyes so I couldn't hear and see it all. I drew myself back a little in the shadows. I was terrified, standing there, shaking all over. I was overwhelmed with feelings for Shy. I wanted to run away but I couldn't move, and then I felt a little bit of the pee run down my leg, but I didn't move. I stood there, lifeless, against the wall.

I could feel my face getting wet from the tears that started flowing down my face. I thought about calling the police, but I'd left my cell in the car underneath my seat. I was stuck, and I gazed at the drop light that hung by the wire in the middle of the warehouse, swaying back and forth from the wind created by Jason from swinging the bat.

I finally mustered up some strength to say something. "Jason, what are you doing to him? No, Jason! Don't do this!" He didn't hear me; my voice was at a whisper. I thought I was screaming from the top of my lungs but I wasn't; fear only had let me whisper.

He leaned the bat against the chair and walked away. I watched him go over to his jacket and grab his stash of coke. He took it out, took his glove off, pulled a rag that was hanging from his " True Religious jeans" back pocket, and wiped the sweat off of his face. I thought, *how ironic.* He then put the rag back in his pocket. He poured some coke on his wrist and sniffed it in. He stood there a moment, closed his eyes with his head leaned way back, then shook his head from side to side, put the tube back in his jacket pocket, and walked back over toward Shy.

"Woo! That stuff is somethin' else, man!" He clapped his hands together and picked back up the bat. He started doing a li'l dance and hollerin' out at Shy, "You ready? You ready, baby? Round two, only one left!" He laughed, patted Shy on the top of his head, then said, "See, I love you too, man, I gave you a li'l break. All I'm askin' is, what did you tell 'em?"

I wanted Shy to tell him, then maybe Jason would stop. I wanted to scream out, "Tell him, Shy, please tell him!" But I didn't. I didn't open my mouth.

Nobody could have told me that I would see Shy on the floor and Jason standing over him. I covered my mouth and cried out. I knew Jason was going to kill him. I couldn't take my eyes off of Shy pleading with Jason to stop. Neither one of them had heard or seen me, yet.

"Jay, man, please. Don't kill me, man. Somebody feedin' you the wrong information." Shy's hands were together as if he was praying, but in actuality he was begging Jason not to kill him.

Jason didn't say anything; he just shook his head no as if what Shy said was making him even angrier. He took his foot and kicked Shy's body while blood, vomit, and urine drenched Shy. "Shy, you tryin' to tell me you ain't talk to the po-lice?" With each syllable of the word "police," Jason kicked Shy. The expression on his face was pure evil. "You must think I'm a fool if I believe that one." Jason bent down and put his hands on his knees, then hollered in Shy's face.

"Come on, man. It's almost over now, go 'head and tell the truth." Jason stopped and started walking away from Shy with his back toward him, as if he was thinking.

He took the bat he was holding on to and laid it over his shoulder, as if he was thinking; then he started talking to Shy again. "You been in here for what?" He continued to let the bat lie on his shoulder while he circled around Shy slowly. It was like watching a lion getting ready to devour its helpless prey. Shy lay there, seeming like he was passing out; there was less and less movement coming from him. Then Jason hollered, "Shy! How long you been here? Three days? Yeah, three days. No food, no water, no nothing; just tied up waitin' fo' me to get here." He bent down and looked at Shy. "Look at me, Shy, look, li'l bro. I'm here now."

He started circling him again. "I'm God to you right now, understand me? I'm the only thing between you and death." He bent down beside him again, "Look at me. I'm here fo' you, baby. My jeans getting dirty, my shirt covered wit' yo' blood. It's you and me, baby. Tell me what you told the police."

The coke had started in his system and he felt the power of the chemical. Jason was toying with him. "You tell 'em where Reese live? Huh?"

I hid myself again, and closed my eyes. I stood against the wall in the shadows and leaned back away from the light. What did I have to do with this, and what did Shy tell?

Shy cried out, "I didn't tell nobody nothin', Jay, I swear it to you." Shy's eyes were bloodshot red. I could tell he hadn't been sleeping. Now I understood the conversation Jason had back at the house while he was on the phone. Jason was ruthless. I thought back to the last three days and examined them; he wasn't doing anything that prohibited him from coming here to talk to Shy. He was just being vicious.

"Man, I don't wanna hear that. I want some answers, Shy." Jason walked away again. He shook his head in frustration and put his hand on his head. Then he turned around and went back to Shy. "Shy, the crew had you here for three days. You been gagged with duct tape, you a trooper, I give it to you, but I need some answers. Now!" He swung the bat, hitting Shy again, but this time in his stomach. Then he took it and swung a few more times. I couldn't watch. I bent down and covered my ears from hearing Shy's screams; however, I couldn't get away from them.

I thought about what Jason had just told him. And I thought how Shy thought he was among friends who loved him. Then Shy got my attention and I looked.

"Stop! My momma tried to tell me to quit running around with y'all!" he cried. He was beaten, scared, and alone, but he gathered courage to say that to Jason.

Jason laughed, then stood over him and spit on him. "Tell yo' momma that!"

Shy looked up to Jason like a big brother or a father he never had, so when Jason came at him with his accusations it hurt Shy's heart, and that right there was enough to kill him.

He was squirming on the ground and his face was swollen and disfigured from the beating he was taking. There was blood and saliva coming out of his mouth as he tried to answer.

Shy cried out, "Jay, you know me better than that, man. You my big bro. I would never do that to you."

Jason walked away from him as if he was thinking for a second, and that's when he noticed I was standing in the warehouse. I stood there with my eyes big and I was shaking all over. Jason walked over to me, trying to explain what was going on. I put my hands over my face for protection, thinking he was going to get me too.

"Shy been talkin' to the police. It had to happen like this." He grabbed his head and turned away from me then walked over to me. "I know you don't understand, but trust me, he's a snitch. This what we do to snitches."

He walked back over to Shy and hit him with it again. I jumped and covered my ears.

"Stop, Jason!" I screamed.

"Baby." Jason looked at me. He was holding the bat in his hand and coming toward me.

"You wit' me right?" He smiled. "Ride or die!" He smirked.

I couldn't even respond I was in such shock. He made his way back over to Shy. He dropped the bat and scooted Shy with his foot and hollered out, "Snitch!"

Shy was just lying there in pain, moving around, trying to find an ounce of comfort and peace. *Maybe even callin' on Jesus in his silences,* I thought.

"But, Jason, he loves you," I whispered. "He wouldn't have . . ." My words trailed off as I shook my head.

Jason looked at me. "Loves me? I been downtown answering questions 'cause of him, and you say he loves me?" He laughed. "That's love?"

Jason tried to reach out to me and touch my hand, but I pulled back and screamed out, "Don't touch me! You gonna kill him! Why did you do that? He's so young, he wouldn't hurt you; he loves you!"

"Reese! Calm down and shut up!" Jason was tryin'a get me to calm down but I couldn't. I was scared, hurt, and angry. "Reese, stop flippin' out!" He grabbed me by my arms again but I snatched away from him.

"You're a monster, Jason!" I screamed frantically. I was crying and shouting all kinds of things. "I'm telling! I don't care what you do to me, I'm telling! I'm going to tell his mother! You are going to jail, Jason! And anybody else who is a part of this!"

I yelled out all of it while I ran toward the exit. I wanted to get out of there and away from him. I figured if I could just reach the front door I could scream out before he caught me and someone outside could call the police. I was wrong. Jason ran up on me before I could escape and grabbed me by my neck. He slung my body into a concrete wall.

"Why you come in here? Huh? I told you to stay in the car, didn't I? Huh?" He pulled his hand back and slapped my face with the back of his hand. "Shut up, Reese! Shut up! You ain't gonna say a word or I'll kill you, you understand me? It'a be two murders!"

He glared into my eyes. I gazed back into his and thought, *This is the same man who looked into my same eyes and called them beautiful and hypnotizing. Now he is looking into them as a murderer, ready to kill whatever comes in between him and freedom.*

He grabbed me by my face, pushed my head into the wall, and hit me again. "Get all that crying and anger out before we leave this warehouse, 'cause I don't wanna hear it no more. This had to happen. I'ma ask you one more time . . . you wit' me?" He let my face go and walked toward the exit, then turned around and said, "You wit' me?"

I turned from looking at Jason. I couldn't answer that; now my eyes were fixed on Shy as he lay on the ground. I was numb. My heart felt like it was beating through my chest. I never even felt the second blow to my face when I failed to answer him. I couldn't even feel the blood running out of my nose but I saw it.

Jason walked back over to me and put his hand around my neck.

"I asked you were you wit' me?"

I looked at him, then looked away. I was scared but I couldn't answer him.

Jason loosened his grip around my neck, making me stumble a little. I stood there another second in an out-of-body experience, then started to follow Jason as he walked out the warehouse. Jason never looked back. I knew I only had a second, so I bent down by Shy.

He sat up slowly and reached out and touched my hand. “Reese,” he whispered. “Please don’t leave me like this, please.”

I couldn’t hold it together. My heart was overwhelmed. My very soul yearned to help him. I took my hand that was shaking and I cried out trying to wipe my face. It was filled with tears and snot coming from my nose. I couldn’t catch my breath; the anxiety, fear, and reality had closed in on me on so many different levels. Then Shy reached for my hand and squeezed it.

“Reese, look at me. It’s okay. But I need your help. Please, I need you to get it together.”

I nodded my head up and down: *yes, yes*. I closed my eyes, wiped my face with my shirt, and listened to him.

Shy’s eyes were full of tears but he was still strong. He was lying on this cold concrete floor alone, weak, beaten like an animal but still saw a light for himself; he never gave up. As he talked I watch blood come from his ears, and nose. I took my hand and rubbed his head to comfort him, and I watched the door for Jay.

He laid himself back down on the ground slowly and the face he made showed that the pain was unbearable. He was pleading for help.

“My mom, Reese. I need you to get my mom,” he pleaded with his mouth and his eyes.

I thought about if it were my boys scared, beaten, and begging for their lives. I became hysterical at just the thought. I almost hyperventilated. I couldn’t speak clearly, so Shy reached up and touched my face with his trembling hand.

"Reese, calm down. It's gonna be all right. Just get my moms."

I nodded my head so he could see I understood him. I took a deep breath before I tried to speak again. "I'll be back for you, okay, Shy?" I smiled at him then said, "I promise."

The ride back to the house was silent. Both of us had a lot on our minds. Jason was probably thinking that he solved a problem, but I was thinking about how I could get out of Jason's custody to go get Shy.

Oh my God! I spoke in my mind. *Oh my God! What kinda animal is this? Lord!* I shook my head back and forth and stared out the window, feeling like my heart was going to burst. I continued to pray. *This is horrible; what am I gonna do, God? Huh? Please help, Lord! Please don't let that boy die. Please save him, Jesus!* Tears fell down my face as I watched Jason speed up the freeway.

"Reese!" Jason smacked my leg, startling me. "Everything is gonna be all right. Look, I'm sorry for hitting you like I do but you be on some stupid stuff. Just stop getting in my way. I don't like to hit you. It always messes yo' face up for a minute! I don't wanna look at that, so stay out the way. Okay, baby?"

My flesh was clenching from the very touch of this monster. I never even responded.

"Aey, you hear me?" He waved his hand up and down in front of my face. I saw him but I wanted to kill him. I hated him. The Bible taught to hate evil and so I did.

"I didn't want it go down like that. I didn't. I cared fo' Shy, but, baby, when it came between me and him, I had to pick me." He kept driving. "Tell you what; tomorrow we'll go get you that ring you wanted. Huh? That sound good?"

I never moved, never responded, so while I looked the opposite way he startled me by smacking my thigh again. I jumped and looked down at my leg. It was red and hurting. I busted out in tears. Jason never acknowledged my response; he just continued to talk.

"It better, for five Gs!" He laughed. "I'll get it wit' the stack I got out of Shy's pocket. He ain't gonna need it!" He began to chuckle. "Okay, bad joke." He continued to laugh. "But fo' real, it'a be a miracle if somebody find him," he whispered.

I shook my head. *Jesus, please get me out of this!* I screamed within. *Please!*

We pulled up to the house and went inside.

"Go ta sleep, babe, you'll feel better in the morning," Jason said while grabbing a soda out the fridge and turning on the game. He was acting as if nothing had happened.

What a cold-blooded murderer, I thought.

I acted like I didn't hear him and went straight in the bathroom and locked the door. I ran some bath water and noticed that my hands were still trembling. I couldn't stop thinking about Shy. I had to do something. I grabbed my cell out of my purse and dialed 911, then hung up.

I sat on the toilet with the same familiar tears that constantly fell, and covered my mouth with my hands. I hurried and put the toilet lid up and started vomiting. I was so scared that I couldn't stop shaking and trembling and crying. I knew I had to do something about this, so I got on my knees and continued to cry and try to figure out a way to go back and rescue Shy.

"Jesus, I know I was wrong by walking away—both from you and Shy—but this is important. So please listen to me. Help Shy, God. He is in trouble, God." I looked up and continued talking. "I didn't even have a chance to see if he even knew You before I left that warehouse." I grabbed my hair, then fell out on the floor. "I'm sorry for that God, I am."

After a few moments of praying, I got a clean washrag out the cabinet and wet it to wash my face. I looked in the mirror at myself and I saw my swollen eye from Jason hitting me. *I don't recognize myself any longer. Who am I?*

Not just the black eye, swollen lip, and bruises changed my appearance, but I was speaking about the inside of me, too. How damaged I was, how abused I was, how lonely I was. It wasn't just seeing myself in the mirror, but also how scandalous I had become, how deceitful I had become, but most of all, how I looked at myself and couldn't see God, the Father, anymore. That worried me the most.

I let a loud, screeching cry out. It had escaped from out of nowhere. I hurried and covered my mouth from fear of Jason hearing, but reality had smacked me in the face; someone was dying! I went back to the mirror and stared until I felt the water from my bath touching my toes. I hurried and turned the water off, put the cold rag on my eye, and I watched my lip quiver from fear.

I soaked in the tub for about forty-five minutes and was interrupted by Jason banging on the door. "What you doin' in there? You all right?"

I closed my eyes then yelled, "Yes, I'm okay."

"I'm goin' to bed. The game is over," he said.

I could hear him walking to the bedroom. I got out the tub twenty minutes later, put on my nightclothes, and got in the bed with my back turned to Jason and his snoring.

I drifted in and out for a while, then finally fell asleep. I woke up in a cold sweat with visions of Shy lying there in the warehouse alone.

I rose right out of my sleep. I decided right then and there it was a perfect time to go get Shy and take him to the hospital. This life was over for the both of us! I watched Jason while he slept peacefully facing toward the wall. I thought how Shy could go to school and live a successful life if I could just get to him and save him. If I had to, I was willing to testify against Jason, anything to get away from Jason at this point.

I got out the bed quietly and put on my shoes, grabbed my keys, went down the stairs, and shut the door behind me. It was time to rescue Shy. I never even changed my clothes or cared that I had on pajamas.

I prayed as I drove toward the warehouse in downtown Columbus. "Lord, please, let him be okay."

I raced down the freeway doing eighty-five until I came to the exit. I turned left on to Front Street and noticed lots and lots of police cars, ambulances, and fire trucks in front of the warehouse. The media was also there with their cameras.

I jumped out the car and walked up to the warehouse where the other bystanders were; then I noticed the yellow caution tape. "Oh no," I whispered to myself. I knew what yellow tape meant. It meant someone was murdered.

My eyes got big as I watched them carry out Shy in a black body bag. I was too late. I wondered who had found him. My emotions were starting to pour out of me and people were noticing something was wrong. They began asking me if I knew the boy.

I didn't reply. I just hurried and walked back toward the car. I thought about telling the police everything, but the realness of what Jason was capable of doing just hit me in the face. I was too scared Jason was going to get me, maybe even my boys, so I unlocked the vehicle fast and slid in.

My heart was racing and my mind was running wild with thoughts of killing Jason in his sleep. That was the only way I could think to escape him. I was crying hysterically and screaming out, "What do I have to lose? He's a murderer!" I hit the steering wheel with my fist. I looked around at the crime scene one more time, then started my car.

I wasn't a fool. I understood if I opened my mouth it would be the last time I ever said a word. So I kept it all inside.

Chapter 13

Stabbed in the Back

I really wanted to go to the police after Shy was murdered. Go in, run to the front desk where the receptionist sits, and scream at the top of my lungs, "He's a killer! Jason Kinney is a murderer!"

But, I didn't. I thought about it; however, it wasn't the reality I lived in.

I had to handle this situation, this craziness, madness, evil, a whole other way. I had to be smarter than what terrified me, what slept with his arms around my waist at times and around my neck other times; I had to be smarter than Jason.

Looking back at things, when I got with Jason, I thought I just wanted to escape the pain of a bad divorce and have a little fun. I had to admit it to myself at least that getting with Jason was exciting and new. He was romantic and swept me off my feet when we first met. I was attracted to the chase to get Jason to myself, but unfortunately it never worked. He ended up having me, which included my mind. I couldn't live this way much longer. But what other choice did I have?

I was trying to get back to a normal in my life; unfortunately for me, I never knew what that was, seeing I never had it before. I had learned that things could change in your life in a blink of an eye and that sometimes, almost every time, how that change affects a person is all up to them.

***

After Shy's death my life had come to such a reality that the man who swept me off my feet was a murderer. He let it be known he had no problem killing again if he needed to. Jason wasn't different, he was the same ol' monster as before. He continued with the drugs and the women and it seemed like after he killed Shy, his money was even longer than before. The whole thing made Jason even more arrogant, if that was possible. He was buying up property, jewelry, and cars. And he made sure I didn't have an inch to breathe a breath if he didn't say so, it seemed. I thought part of him suspected I was gonna get him. He just didn't know when and neither did I until the day came when he gave me some air to breathe on my own.

I decided that life was short and I needed to work on getting myself together, so I quit smoking weed and going to the clubs. I spent as much time with my boys as I possibly could. I also started looking for another job in my field as an electrical engineer. I didn't know what I was getting myself and my boys prepared for, but I knew I was making some moves for our future.

Jason had to suddenly go out of town, he said, to make sure things were set up in Detroit. He had been gone for three days, and while he was gone I spent every day and hour with my boys. I took them to the movies, read to them, took them to the park to play, and prayed with them.

I had one more day left before Jason was to return and decided to get me some me time. I took the boys to Cleveland to spend a few days with their father and when I came back I called Eva to see if she wanted to go hang out, but she never answered her cell. So I got myself dolled all up to go to dinner and a movie alone. I had to admit it felt good to get out of the house and off Jason's chain for a while.

Once inside the theatre I went straight to the concession stand for some popcorn and a large soda. I paid for my stuff and entered the movie. I went to my favorite seat, so I could put my feet up. I snuggled into the large oversized seat, and put the soda in the cup holder, but I held on to that good-smellin' buttery popcorn I was about to demolish. I leaned back, put my feet across the rail, and took a handful of popcorn to my mouth.

I glanced over at the entrance and watched a few people walk into the dark place, when I had to do a double take. I thought I saw Jason walking in with some chick. But, in his defense, he was out of town. *I must be trippin',* I thought. But he did walk like Jason and he did have the same swag just like him. *But Jason is in Detroit, isn't he?*

They went to the front of the theatre and sat down. I turned my attention back to the screen to watch the previews, but this lookalike got up, I'm assuming to go to the concession stand or bathroom. When he turned around toward my seat, it was Jason. He was in the same theatre I was in, with another woman!

I sat there like a fool, but I really wanted to go down there and smack the taste out of his lying mouth. *Here I am putting up with all of his shenanigans and he continues to make me look like a fool,* I thought. I kept my eyes on him and started talking to myself under my breath. "I'm so tired of this idiot! Ugh!"

He walked out the theatre, then snapped his fingers and turned around and headed back toward his seat like he had forgotten something. I leaned up in my seat to make sure I didn't miss anything. He motioned his hand for the chick to come with him, so she got up to follow.

The theatre was pretty crowded and the previews were still rolling so when the light from the screen shined, it lit the theatre up for a second, long enough for me to see the chick. She got up and turned her head around toward my seat; my mouth went wide open. Imagine my surprise to see my best friend, Eva, taking my man's hand as he led her out the theatre. First off, I thought he was out of town, and second, there's the Eva factor; now I knew why she never answered my call. I was so embarrassed, like everybody in the theater knew he was my man and she was my best friend. My emotions were raging within me. One minute I wanted to hurt them as bad as I was hurt, the next minute I wanted to storm down there and confront them, give 'em a piece of my mind.

I sat there dumbfounded and staring at the movie screen with no idea of what I was watching. My happy little getaway was out the window.

A few minutes later they came back in, hand in hand with treats. They were seated a couple of rows down from me and hugged and kissed the entire time. They had me in my seat mumbling under my breath, "This chick is dirty! Look at them. Oh my God I'ma get her. I'ma snatch her weave out as soon as we leave. Better yet, I'ma call her husband, Adam, and tell him to come up here. Then let's see what's gonna happen. If I called him that would sure enough kill both those birds down there!"

Even though my anticipation to question them was off the chart, I decided to wait. I knew I needed to calm down and figure out how to confront them without Jason going bananas on me. I knew if I showed out in the middle of this flick he would beat the crap out of me right then, so I waited.

As soon as the movie was out and the credits rolled I got out of my seat and made sure I was standing in the lobby when they came out.

"Jason!" I hollered while I watched them hold hands and look into each other's eyes, talking and giggling.

Jason turned and Eva turned around too. Eva's whole expression changed when she realized it was me who called Jason's name. She wasn't all giggles then. She couldn't even look my way and she immediately let Jason's hand go.

He, on the other hand, looked like he couldn't care less. He looked at Eva when she let his hand go and laughed, then turned to me and hollered back, "Yeah, what's up, boo?" He was so arrogant and obviously didn't care that he was busted at all. "What up, Reese?" He smiled, and held up his finger as if to say "wait a minute," then he whispered something in Eva's ear, and walked away from her and over to me. He grabbed me around my waist and kissed me on the cheek.

"Wha' you doin' here? You smell good, girl." He kissed my neck, then held on to me a little longer before he finally let me go. There were all kinds of thoughts racing through my mind. I couldn't believe him, I was outraged. *No, this man isn't gonna play me like this. After all he has done to me, and to top it all off, the woman he has been cheatin' with is my best friend.* I never saw this one coming at all. They both had pulled the rug from underneath me.

I was tensed up and pushed him back. "Jason!" I said; then I punched his chest as hard as I could. I didn't care if he hit me back; this was the last straw.

He quickly grabbed me around my waist again and whispered in my ear, "Listen." He tugged me, making my body jerk. "You better not make a scene in here you understand me?"

I never replied. The whole time he spoke in my ear I watched Eva looking at us. We met eye to eye and I gave her a nasty look, letting her know there was no me and her ever again. She stood there twirling her weave through her fingers and then she looked away.

Jason continued, "I'm not playin', Reese." Then he whispered, "I'll be home in a few. We can deal wit' this then." He kissed me again on my cheek, long this time, backed away, and went back over where Eva was standing.

I was confused. Here he was standing there with my best friend, the woman who knew everything there was to know about me. The woman who cried with me when I was going through it and laughed with me at better times, the woman who Jason sent with me on trips. She was my best friend, and now here they were, standing in front of me, together? I never imagined this one in a billion years. I missed that bulletin.

The only thing that could possibly come out of my mouth as I stood there looking like a helpless puppy was, "Wow! Really, Eva?" I held my hand out and pointed to her. She turned her head and looked away as if she was sorry. "Eva, forget about what you're doing to me. If you think about nothing else remember that you are married!" I screamed.

They both laughed, Jason showing his white teeth and his cute dimples. I stood there furious, holding my cup of soda. I watched Eva and waited for what I thought would be an apology. She gave me an apology, all right, one she could have kept! She swung that weave around, then said, "I'm sorry, Reese, but he was too much of a temptation for me to pass up. I didn't want you to tell me how he was; I wanted to know for myself." She laid her grimy hands across then down Jason's chest. She confessed with a smug look on her face. Jason stood there smiling like the whole thing was hilarious to him. I was gonna get her.

Jason answered his cell and walked away. I knew that was my chance to get her so I walked toward her. While I watched him, Eva interrupted my thought.

"This doesn't have to get ugly, Reese, please let's just—" she said, backing away from me before I cut her off.

"Let's just what, Eva? Huh? You're supposed to be my friend! I guess now I get what Julius was saying all those years ago when he tried to tell me you tried to get at him too, huh!" I yelled. My eyes shifted to Jason over to the side, laughing on his cell with someone, probably a whole other chick while we stood there looking absolutely stupid.

"My husband doesn't have to know. Please, Reese." Eva ran her hand across her face nervously while she whispered.

I watched her move her hand, making her wedding rings bling. I walked up to her, looked around the crowded theater, and whispered. "Oh, he gonna know this, guarantee ya that one!" If her husband found this out, it would get even messier seeing he's the one who kept Jason out of jail. Eva knew this just as much as I did.

I couldn't take it anymore, her pleading and Jason standing there, laughing on his cell like this was some kinda joke. I was so tired of being disrespected and somebody was gonna pay for it tonight. My emotions were through the roof, felt like killing her.

I took my cup of soda and threw it all on Eva. It felt good, too, and messing up her designer clothing felt even better 'cause I knew how much she loved them. I laughed and thought, *she probably loves the clothes more than she loves her husband, to tell the truth.*

"Oh my God! Why you do that?" she cried.

I was breathing hard and mad as fire at her. "'Cause you are a scandalous skank, Eva, that's why!" I screamed out in tears. Even though I didn't think before I threw it, it was on. "You wanna stand here with that crappy apology? You're supposed to be my best friend!"

A crowd of people had gathered around, laughing and pointing. Eva was drenched in soda. She was shaking all over and her yellow sundress was turning red from my red pop.

I watched her standing there, crying; then I turned and looked at Jason putting his cell up and running over to me.

"Didn't I tell you to go home?" He smacked me as hard as he could in the middle of the theater. I stumbled backward, falling into a movie display. Jason came right after me. He bent down next to where I fell.

"I told you don't make a scene, didn't I? Go home now! Before somebody call the police, stupid!" I was humiliated and once again all he was worried about was himself!

He walked out the theatre, never looking behind, leaving Eva and me in the theater.

I never told Eva's husband anything because I knew Jason would kill him and I would feel terrible and responsible if Jason did something to that man.

The police came before I could leave, and arrested me for assault. Heck, they never got arrested for throwing drinks on reality shows. *Guess this is real life.*

At the police station I called Jason's cell but he wouldn't answer. I was stuck down there without bail and without anyone but Jason and Eva knowing where I was. Go figure, a few hours ago both of them would have been the first two I would've called to come to my rescue if I were in trouble; now they were the last.

I heard the guard come in again. "You can make another call since you never reached anyone."

I cried I was so happy. I knew they didn't give you two calls, or I didn't think they did. I walked down the hall in an orange oversized jumpsuit and some brown plastic sandals they had given me in place of my heels. I watched my pretty pedicured toes as I walked because they didn't give out socks, no matter how cold it was.

All I wanted to do was enjoy one night out to myself before Jason came back and continued to make my life a living nightmare. Not only did it get spoiled, I lost a so-called friend.

I wondered who I should call. It couldn't be Julius 'cause he was already wanting to take the boys from me. That was all the ammo he would need. I picked up the phone.

"Five minutes, ma'am." I turned and saw the guard behind the desk.

He must have seen me hesitating. "Okay." I wanted to bust out in tears right then, but instead I just dialed.

"Toya, hey, I'm in jail." I didn't know how else to say it.

"What? Oh, my God. What happened?" She sighed.

"It's a long story, but I need you to come get me out of here, please." I sniffled.

"I don't have any money, Reese, I'm sorry," she cried. "I feel so horrible, but I just paid rent," she explained.

I had a bad taste in my mouth from all of what happened. Not only were my friend and man messin' around, but I was sittin' in a jail without the bail! *What sense does this make?* I couldn't think straight. *Who can help me?* I wondered. I closed my eyes and laid my head against the wall beside the phone.

I knew there was only one more person who could help: Kev. I opened my eyes.

"It's okay, but can you call Kev and tell him I need his help?" I knew in my heart that he would help. "Let him know I can give it right back to him when I get released." I gave her his number and hoped. "Okay, I gotta go," I cried and hung up the phone.

I prayed that Kev would help because we hadn't spoken since we had words a few months back. They took me back to the lockup and I sat watching the news for what seemed like years. I didn't talk to anyone else, just sat there in front of the television.

I dosed off a few times but within a few hours I heard the guard calling my name.

"You made bail," she said. Those were the best words I had heard all night! I was so relieved to be out of there. The guard gave me my clothes, my ID, and all my other belongings and pointed to a place to go change.

"Thank you." I smiled at the woman.

Once in the bathroom I put my things on the sink and I looked in the mirror at myself, held my face in my hands, and broke down. I couldn't imagine going back to that house where Jason was. I was furious at him. He never came and got me; he really let me sit in there. And after he cheated and hurt me with my best friend. What an ultimate betrayal. I could still feel the knife twisting deep in my back.

I grabbed a paper towel and wet it in the sink, and put it over my face to refresh myself.

After I got dressed I was escorted to the lobby where Kev and Toya had shown up to get me. I saw Kev first, standing there, putting his wallet back in his jacket. What a beautiful sight for sore eyes.

He was on his cell and shaking his head like he was angry. He saw me and gave me a half smile, then put his finger up as if to say "wait a minute." I nodded okay.

"Jay, we got her. I'ma take her to get her car, then she can do what she wants." Kev looked frustrated.

I frowned my face up. "He called you?" I asked Kev. "He wouldn't even answer me when I called him to come get me out of here." I couldn't control my feelings anymore. Kev looked at me. Then put his finger up again as if to say "wait a minute" again.

"Jay, I'll call you right back." He hung up, walked up to me, and gave me a hug. He smelled so good. I closed my eyes, feeling so connected to him. I started crying and he took his hand and wiped my tears.

"Don't worry 'bout Jay, you know how he is," Kev proclaimed.

I did know how he was but it didn't change the fact that I was on fire. "Kev, he's messin' wit' Eva and he left me here like it was my fault!" I screamed out, then cried.

"You all right, you know I wasn't gonna let you sit in here." He looked at me with sincerity in his eyes. "I got you." And I believed him.

I went over to Toya and hugged her. "Thanks so much."

"You know who to thank, he paid your bail." Toya smiled and looked over at Kev who was now sitting down.

I turned around and looked at him. He nodded, and I smiled. "Thank you. I got the money to pay you back. We just have to go to the ATM," I told him.

He frowned and put his hands out as if to say no. "Naw, you good. Don't worry 'bout it." He smiled.

I gave Toya another hug. "Thank you, thank you, thank you for being there for me."

"You my girl! But, you need to leave Jason alone! Fo' real! Kev is his boy and he even agrees," Toya fussed.

We both looked over at Kev, I could tell he was tired even though he was in and out of our conversation.

He was sittin' on the bench with his elbow on his knee and his hand on his head, leaned over, half asleep. He looked up. "Come on, ladies, let's get out of here." He said, gettin' up, then yawned.

I looked over at the clock in the police station it was five in the morning. I thought, *no wonder he's yawning*.

Toya interrupted my thoughts about Kev when she blurted out the reality of the night. "Jason wouldn't even come get you. He runnin' you in the ground, Reese. You too good for this!"

Toya was right and I had a plan. When I sat in that cell I came up with a plan for Jason all right! I had no love for that scum. I wanted revenge! Jason was going to pay for his action. I wanted to get Jason for all that he had done, including what he did to Shy.

Jason was going down!

He made a mistake when he showed me his whole operation. Part of my plan was to convince him to let me help him out with the little things so he had more free time. I needed to prove I was really ride or die by getting my hands dirty. But I was smarter than him 100 percent, and that's where my revenge would come in. I would make him look foolish and get him where it would hurt: his pockets!

Chapter 14

Come Get Me

I fell asleep in the truck, thinking about how to convince Jay to let me have a role in his affairs. When I woke up I looked over at Kev driving. He was such a beautiful man. He turned and looked over at me.

"You all right?" he asked.

I shook my head.

"You had a long night." His eyes pierced through my soul when he looked at me. It was like sunlight does in the A.M.

I replied with a slight smile. "Yeah." I looked back out the window. When I looked over at him again he was deep in thought, so I looked in the back seat to talk to Toya, but she wasn't there.

"Where's Toya?" I asked.

I'd pulled his mind from his thoughts. He ran his hand across his eyes. "Oh, yeah, I dropped her off. You was over there, asleep. She said she has to work in a few hours. We had been sitting in the police station for over five hours." He yawned.

"Wow, I didn't know that. You guys are such good friends."

He nodded and kept driving. There was some tension in the air between us. We hadn't really talked since the gun incident.

"So, what's wrong? Why aren't you talking to me, Kev?"

"What you mean? I do talk to you."

"Yeah, but it's different now. I knew sooner or later we would have to have this conversation."

"Reese, you actually stopped talkin' to me when you found out about the business we were in. I couldn't make that man tell you what or who he really was. It wasn't my place." He kept driving, looking over at me every few minutes. "So? If I might ask, how did you think I was supposed to handle that fact?"

He laughed. "Why do you care, Reese? Huh? Why do you care what I think? That's been almost a year ago. You haven't left Jason and he dogs you. You don't talk to me, you got yo' sons here and there, and we pickin' you up from a police station for assaulting yo' best friend! Anything in this picture make sense to you? Huh?"

"But, Kev, we supposed to be better than that. You could have said somethin' instead of smiling in my face like everything was everything!" My voice cracked as I spoke.

Kev stopped the car and pulled it over. "Okay, you wanna know, really know, how and what that man think about you?" He looked over at me. He was yelling at the top of his lungs. "Huh? You think you ready for this wakeup call?" He lowered his voice and calmed down a little. He waited for me to reply.

"Yeah, I'm ready," I said softly.

Kev pulled out his cell and dialed a number. "Shh, don't say nothing, Reese." He looked me in my eyes.

"I'm not, I promise."

He dialed. "What's up, Kev?" It was Jason. He blew smoke out when he answered the phone.

"Man, why you ain't go get Reese? That's foul." Kev looked over at me.

"I wasn't goin' to get her! She clowned at the movies, Kev!"

"Jay, you wrong. You was supposed to be in Detroit for one, and two you sittin' in her house right now! That's grimy, Jay, real grimy."

Jason laughed. "Yup, I am sittin' right in her crib wit' my feet up. She better be glad I didn't bring skanky girl back here instead of takin' her to the motel," he yelled.

"Jay, you a dog. You know that's shady!"

Jason laughed. "Whatever, man. Reese needed to sit in there for embarrassing me and herself! Maybe she will think next time."

Kev looked over at me. I was moving around in my seat, and as much of an embarrassment the call was, it was still very painful. Kev could see I was irritated by the call. Jason was still talking when Kev interrupted him. "All right, Jay, I'm headed home so I can get some sleep."

"Aey!" Jason yelled.

"Yeah?" Kev answered.

"Where she at?"

Kev looked at me before answering. I shrugged my shoulder, raised my eyebrow, and told him with my eyes the answer to that.

"I don't know."

"Oh, all right. She must be on her way here. I'll talk to you later, one," Jay said.

Kev watched me; then he nodded his head and poked out his lips as if he was disappointed. "One," Kev replied. Kev hung up.

I sat there feeling so stupid. I was a fool to believe Jason cared, when in actuality all he cared about was himself. Kev looked over at me. He started his truck.

"I only shared that wit' you 'cause I want you to make some changes, Reese. Listen, that's my boy but . . ."

I couldn't believe Kev was talkin to me like this. Who gave him the right to tell me, even if it was the truth? And it was. I couldn't even respond to him 'cause I knew he was right. So I just sat there and listened.

"Look, Reese, I'm sorry, but you need to get it together. You are special and beautiful, inside and out. You don't deserve to be treated like this!" Kev's voice was starting to rise. I could tell he was passionate about this situation. "I love, Jay, I do, but he ain't worth what he taking you through, baby. You need to cut yo' losses and move on."

I didn't have anything to say. I stared out the window the whole time he spoke.

"I'm not tryin'a tell you what to do, sweetheart, but I'm out. I'm leaving Ohio real soon and getting myself out of this life. It's not worth it. I know better than this." He looked out the window. "My moms tried to tell me."

He pulled into the parking lot of the movie theatre where my car was and drove up to it slowly. "I look at what happened to Shy while I was out of town. He had just turned eighteen, on his way to college wit' a full ride, and they still ain't found out who killed him."

He had tears in his eyes. He wiped his eye before the moisture could spill over. "Reese, I can't be responsible for no more of these young boys' lives. I don't have the heart for this anymore."

I looked at him and my eyes got big. I realized he didn't know that Jason killed Shy. And just like he'd told me, it wasn't my place to tell him.

I reached over and gave him another hug; then we looked at each other and I closed my eyes and kissed him on the lips. I smiled. He smiled back.

"We okay?" I asked, getting out.

He seemed a little dazed. "Um, yeah, we okay."

Chapter 15

The Thief

When I kissed Kev I knew it was the end of Jason and me. Never had I ever crossed the line before in either of my relationships. I was always loyal to Jason in spite of his blatant disrespect for me. Regardless of what feelings I had for Kev, I never let it go past friendship . . . until now.

I held back from my feelings for Kev that were now spilling over and were displayed by a forbidden kiss.

I often wondered what Kev thought about the kiss. Did he think about my lips touching his as often as I did, or did he think I was just saying good-bye?

I got fed up with what could have been. I, of course, was fed up with Jason. It wasn't only Jason who I was fed up with, but my whole attitude had been infected by the things I had experienced in life. I no longer called home for advice from my grandparents, and more often than not I dodged their calls and ignored their concern for me. I had become some of what I had seen in Jason. Really, I was no better than him because, regardless of what I had seen him do or what he did to me, I knew right from wrong. Ultimately I knew that I could call on God and He would come to my rescue. However, my anger had the best of me and I decided I would deal with my situations on my own. First things first, I had to convince Jason that I could be useful for him in his business.

"Jay, I'm just saying, I can help. You keep saying it's you and me. Well, let me prove it."

I watched to see what he would say. He didn't respond so I added, "It will give you time to relax a little with me helping out. After all, Kev is leaving soon and you need somebody you can trust."

He sat there smoking a cigar and watching the news. "That might work." He looked up and smiled, then went back to watching the news.

I knew that reasoning would do it because all he wanted to do was chill, spend money, and give orders. I had him!

It started off simple, with me collecting all the money from their crew from drug sales. After that I made sure he trusted me enough to pick up the big money; not just the $2,000 and $3,000, but also the $200,000 and $300,000 that was ready for pickup. Eventually I was taking a little of it at a time, picking off a couple thousand here and there. No one noticed.

Kev wasn't feeling the fact that I was involved, but he stayed out of it. I looked at it like he had to still care. He even came to me and tried talking to me about what I was getting myself wrapped up in.

We all met up one day before I was scheduled to make a pickup. Jason wasn't there yet; it was just Kev and I.

"Reese, what you thinkin' 'bout?" Kev asked. He put his hand on his head and leaned back in his chair. "I mean, why are you doin' this? You got so much to lose. You don't need to be wrapped up in this life. What you tryin'a prove?"

I sat there listening to him. I wanted to tell him what my plan was and how much I hated his best friend, but I knew I couldn't. I played stupid. "What? I'm just trying to help my man." I couldn't keep a straight face telling him that, so I walked over to the window and watched Jason get out his truck and walk toward the door.

Kev blew out a loud breath. “Oh okay, thought you was smarter than that.” He rolled his eyes and got up, looked out the window at Jay walking to the door, then sat back down and continued. “That’s why I’m out of here soon. No time for this, and you know he’s usin’ you,” he huffed.

I didn’t say anything. I continued to look at Jason walking; then I walked past Kev and sat on the couch. “Yeah, what do you care? You out of here, right?”

Jason opened the door. “Hey, what’s good?” I could feel the cold air when Jason walked in. “It’s cold out there! Sorry I’m late. I had to handle some business.”

He came over to me, bent down, and kissed me. I didn’t even care where he had been. My mind was on one thing and one thing only: taking his money.

Kev watched Jason kiss me, and then he looked away.

“All right y’all, let’s get this done so I can go. I got other things to do.”

Jason and Kev talked and agreed that with me hiring and picking up the women, there would be less attention. Kev and Jason had been to the airport so many times, they knew they were hot and the police could possibly notice their activity. It made more sense if someone they both trusted would do it; only thing was, the person they both trusted wasn’t the one to trust.

They let me hire females to travel back and forth from New York to Columbus. I would pay the females $1,000 each but get $5,000 from Jason for their trips. That right there was a $4,000 come up every thirty days. Not to mention before they reached Jason, I would have the females get undressed and take dope off of one, then take the other girl and split her dope between them. Then I'd give the chicks another $1,000 apiece.

One time he noticed that one bag was a little short. "No big deal," he said.

I thought I was slick. I'd laugh behind his back knowing I got over on him.

I would then sell the dope I took in Dayton, Ohio to some high school friends who'd turned into drug dealers. In my mind everything I did was justified by what he had done to me and Shy. I knew that the one thing men loved was their money, and I promised myself to take it away from Jason little by little.

It was crazy, since our relationship had started off grand, with Jason buying everything I could have imagined: furs, cars, brand new furniture, and all the trips around the country I wanted. Jason had spoiled me, but now we were at the end of this relationship and Jason's true colors had shown. Not only was he a womanizer and drug lord, he was a woman beater and more than all of that a murderer.

But I had underestimated Jason. I had never thought about how he and Kev stayed in business for so long and never got caught or why they kept their crew so tight. I only saw Jason for what he did to me and how reckless he was; and that was my downfall. I forgot that Jason knew the drug business well and I hadn't counted on that, but still I had to do what I had to do.

Jason had been in the game for years, so when money came up missing, he knew something wasn't right. He just didn't know who was taking it, but he knew it was missing.

I was at home one day chillin', watching some movies and relaxing, when I got a call from him.

"Reese, get dressed. I'll be there in a minute to get you," he demanded, then hung up.

I worried and wanted to know what was going on. I could tell by his tone he was angry.

By the time I got myself dressed he was outside the house blowing the horn. I hurried out, shut the door, and got in his truck. "What's up, Jay? What's goin' on?"

He didn't answer, just pulled off fast. He got halfway down the street before he started talking. "We need to meet up wit' Kev before I go out of town." Jason had a look in his eye I had seen before. It was the same look he had when he murdered Shy. I was nervous.

"Somebody been taking money," he blurted out. He turned the music up in his car and kept driving until he stopped at a restaurant.

Man, what did I do? I knew it was me. I knew for sure they were going to kill me. I thought about running when the car stopped. *But where to?* I reasoned with myself.

Jason had set up a meeting with Kev at a restaurant downtown after he noticed. We got there before Kev showed up. I hadn't seen him in a while but through all of what they suspected I wanted to see Kev.

Kev came in looking at his watch. He knew he was running late. He walked up and started talking to one of the waitress and using his hands to describe what Jason looked like. I watched his every move while Jason sat there at the table on his cell, fussing at someone. It sounded as if he was speaking to one of the fellows in the crew, asking them about some business. The waitress knew exactly who Kev was talking about and pointed to Jason and me. All the females in the place had their eyes fixed on Kev. They watched him like he was a piece of meat as he walked toward us.

"What's good?" Kev said and put out his hand to shake Jason's. Then he looked at me. "I didn't know you would be here. What's up, Reese?" He smiled, bent down, and kissed my cheek.

Jason interrupted. He stood up. "I can't call it." Jason's expression told it all. He was frustrated and wanted to know who the thief was.

"What's up, Jay? Why you lookin' like that? What's goin' on?"

Jason sat back down, then took in a deep breath. "Man, somebody stealin' from us." Jason looked over at me. I saw him but I was trying to act as if I wasn't really paying attention to them. I was very nervous sitting there and praying they didn't figure me out.

"Reese, I'ma need you to go over there and sit for a minute." He nodded his head over to another table nearby. My eyes and Kev's followed his. I got up and went over there and sat down. No questions asked, but I did wanna hear what he knew. So I positioned my seat to hear it all.

Kev was surprised and responded to Jason, "Naw, man! Jay, you sure you didn't spend some on one of yo' li'l honeys? You know how you splurge, man," Kev whispered. They both looked over in my direction but I never allowed my emotions to show. I sat there acting like I couldn't hear a thing. I didn't care what Jason did, not even a little bit at this point. Kev shook his head back and forth and watched Jason's face. He was serious.

"Naw, man, that money comes out my stash at home. I don't get it confused wit' this," Jason claimed.

"You can't be serious," Kev said.

"Yeah, they stealin'. I'm tellin' you when I find out who it is . . ."

I started talking to myself in my head. *Oh my God! They gonna kill me!* I knew I had another pickup scheduled in the next few days while Jason was out of town so I figured that would be my last. My revenge had to end; it was time for me to stop. Jason stood back up, then put his hand on his gun underneath his suit jacket.

"Lower your voice, man," Kev stood up and demanded of Jason.

Jason was loud and others in the restaurant were watching.

Kev looked around the crowded restaurant, then took off his jacket and sat back down. He was getting angry too. They shared this business, starting it off with a hundred bucks apiece back in the day, and now they were bringing in well over a couple of hundred thousand dollars a week.

"Who is it, Jay? Do you know?" Kev asked. I sat there and looked over at Jason's mouth to see what he was going to say.

"Naw, I don't know." I was so relieved. Jason leaned in across the table real close to Kev. "I'm tellin' you, when I find out I'm gonna kill 'em." He was serious.

"Aww, I feel responsible since I'm the one in Columbus the most. You travel to and from New York, Miami, Jamaica, Detroit, and L.A. getting our business set up nationwide." That left Kev doing the business in Columbus and he couldn't believe he had let someone sit up underneath him and steal. It angered Kev and frustrated his brain trying to figure out who would do it. He kept saying, "We treat everybody good. We share the money. Who's greedy, Jay?" He shook his head in confusion. He couldn't understand it.

"Man, don't worry 'bout it. It will come to the light. It always does," Jason stated, showing Kev his pearly white teeth and the dimples in his face.

"Yeah, I guess you're right. It will come to the light," he responded, not sounding so sure of himself.

"I tell you what, though," Jason said, "I'ma get 'em whenever we find out who it is."

From that point Kev was suspicious of everyone. They decided not to share what they had found out with anyone, not even their closest workers. It was between him and Jason until somebody slipped up. I didn't know why I was worried because by the conversation, they never even suspected me.

They figured they could lose a few more dollars and a little more dope to find out who it was.

Jason and Kev shut their mouths and opened their eyes and continued to do business as usual until the thief was brought to the light.

Chapter 16

Love Is Blind

After Jason told Kev and me what he suspected I was feeling paranoid and nervous. I wrote it off, thinkin' my nerves were shot. I promised myself this was it.

It was a couple of days after Jason was in Miami on business when I got the call from Jason that it was time for a pickup. "Sweetie, I need you to go to the airport and pick up my sisters for me," Jason said to me on the phone. That was the code to get to the airport and pick up the women.

"Okay, are they here yet?" The inside of my palms were sweaty and my stomach was flipping somersaults.

"Yeah, babe, they there. Hurry up! I don't want my sisters waiting, you understand?"

"Yeah, I'm on my way." I hung up the phone and hurried and put a pair of jeans, a T-shirt, and my coat on. I ran down the stairs and out the house.

It had to be all of twenty degrees outside that night when I left. My cell rang constantly as I drove toward the airport. I looked over at it but never answered. I knew it was Jason and I knew he would be yelling and calling me every name in the book because I wasn't there yet.

I zoomed down the freeway, not even really paying attention to the other cars on the road. I was just trying to get to the airport as quickly as I could.

I reached for my phone to make the arrangements to get some of the dope off the ladies before meeting Kev and the crew. I dialed one of the ladies who was waiting for me at the airport.

"Hey, you out there?" she asked.

"Not yet, pullin' up in a few minutes. Where y'all at? Is everything okay?" I was concerned.

"Oh, girl, yeah." She laughed. "I had to use the restroom so Money walked wit' me that's all."

I shook my head. I was in disbelief how naïve these girls were. Here they were in the airport with all this dope and money attached to their bodies and they were joking and laughing. *Wow,* I thought, *how silly*. "Well, be out front, we need to hurry and get this taken care of fast." I hung up then speed dialed another number.

"Hyatt hotel, how may I help you?" the nice, pleasurable voice stated.

"Hello, I have reservations for today and wanted to confirm," I said. I would take the ladies to different hotels around the city to get some of the dope and money off them. I read the clerk the confirmation number, hung up, and continued to drive toward the airport. I figured I needed to call Kev. I dialed him and waited for him to answer; then I explained.

"Hey, Kev, what's up?" I said.

"Nothin'," he said dryly. "Jason just called, I'm letting you know." His tone was laced with attitude.

I knew Kev was upset with me from our last time together. I figured his attitude was from that.

"You ready to meet up? I'm ready," he said.

"Well don't meet me there yet," I stuttered. "I think they took a later flight," I lied.

Kev paused. It was a weird, long pause. So I added, "So I'll see you in a few," and hung up. I would make up stories to buy extra time to get the dope off the women and back on them before we reached Kev or Jason, depending on who was there.

While I drove I started feeling bad. I hated that my scheme was going to affect Kev. He would definitely be hurt and betrayed by my actions.

"He picks my sons up and takes them to the park. We eat out all the time and hang out and now I'm playing him for a fool." I shook my head back and forth as I approached passenger pickup. I slowed down and looked for the girls. I pulled over and stopped. I waited a few minutes anxiously. I patted the steering wheel fast and surveilled the exit until I saw the two of them walk out. Chantell was holding her cigarette in one hand and on her cell phone letting someone know she made it okay. Money, the Caucasian girl, grabbed her tote and got in the car.

"What's up, Reese? How you doing?" Money asked.

"What's goin' on, Money? Just trying to get this done fast," I said while I watched Chantell get in the car.

"Hey, Reese?" Chantell opened the car door and got in. "You call Kev, Reese?" Chantell asked.

"I was supposed to call him as soon as I picked y'all up." We were all driving in silence. Seemed like we all were questioning what we were doing this time. I decided it was time for me to call Kev. I looked at my cell to see if he had called me; he hadn't but Jason had been blowing me up. I knew Jason was furious that I hadn't called him yet. And I knew he wouldn't think twice before killing me.

I whipped into the Hyatt and we got out the car. I thought I was smooth; I handed the keys to the valet attendant and walked into the hotel. It was well after nine in the evening. I knew we had to hurry.

"Come on, girls, we need to hurry up."

I went to the front and got the keys; then we rushed to our room, they put their bags down, and then it was time to get down to business.

"Okay, Money, how much you got on you?"

"I'm not sure, maybe one." Which meant one kilo.

"Okay, let me have it." I put out my hand and waited for her to give it to me. I poured a fourth into some Saran Wrap and then we put it back on her body. After I finished sorting out Kev and Jason's cut, then mine, I walked over to my cell and dialed Kev.

"Hey, Kev, sorry I'm late but we got caught up. They were at another terminal than I was. You know they remodeling the airport, too." I was trying to give a reason for the loss of time.

"Yeah, I hear ya, caught up. Everything everything? The girls get here okay?" he asked. The two of them didn't play when it came to business. They wanted to know every move that was made when it came down to their business.

"Yeah, yeah, they fine. We had a misunderstanding and I was at the wrong terminal," I said again so convincingly.

"All right, Reese. Let's do this. Things have been changed. Meet me on Miller," Kev said calmly.

"Why, everything everything?" I asked because we were originally meeting up on the north in some condos on Morse Road. "Thought we were meetin' north on Morse—" He cut me off.

"It changed. I'll be there in a few." He hung up.

I held the phone a few minutes longer, wondering why the drop was changed. I picked my cell back up and started calling Jason, but I thought about it and figured that was a bad idea because he wouldn't understand or care why I was running behind. After we wrapped everything up we left the hotel.

I pulled up to the apartment on Miller about fifteen minutes later. I knew Kev was there already because his car was out front. I was relaxed by now. I had my money and the dope, and had paid the females their little bit.

As we walked toward the door I noticed there weren't any other cars there besides Kev's. I wondered where the rest of the crew was but didn't think too much about it. I opened the screen and knocked on the door. As we all three waited for Kev to open the door, we all shivered from the cold air blowing on us. I looked up in the sky and watched the snowflakes fall on my face. I smiled at that moment, and then Kev opened the door.

"Ladies, come on in." He reached his arm out, directing us into the house. Then Kev turned and looked at me. He was smiling. "What's up, Reese?" Kev said real smug, closing the door behind us.

"What's up, Kev. What's wrong?" I knew him well and could tell something was wrong with him.

"Nothin'," he said and rubbed his hands together. "Let's do this, ladies. Did Reese take care of y'all?" He looked at the females, meaning did I pay them. Kev's voice was smug and real slick, like he was making a point. And on top of that, when he took off his suit jacket, he had a gun tucked in his back. I never knew him to carry guns, or he didn't carry them out where I could see it.

"Yeah, Kev, she took care of us," Money stated.

"All right then, Reese gonna give y'all her car so y'all can get back to New York."

"What?" I was surprised. *Why do I have to give them my car?* I wondered. "What you mean?" I asked. The girls were happy. They smiled at the thought of getting my whip.

"You gonna give them your car to drive back, it's paid for, right?" he asked, smiling.

He knew I loved that car. *What the heck is going on?* But I didn't want to stir up drama, so I never said a word. I just tooted my lips up and stood there looking at Kev as if he was crazy.

"We'll get you another one." Kev eyed me with intensity.

I knew right then he suspected I was thief.

I was scared; I didn't know what he was up to. I was busted. I lost my car, lost respect from someone I deeply cared about, and most likely was about to lose my life. I felt that Kev knew based on his sarcasm and his actions. My gut feeling was telling me I was caught red-handed with my hand in the cookie jar, and I had eaten so many cookies that I was starting to feel sick!

"Kev, is Jason here?" That's all I wanted to know. I was looking around the room and thinking Jason was gonna jump out and beat me down.

"No, didn't you talk to him earlier, Reese? He won't be back for a few days. You should know that. That's yo' man, right?" Kev asked. There was that smug look and acting tone again.

"Yeah," I said softly. "Okay, girls, let's get this stuff off of you so y'all can get on the road," I ordered, clapping my hands together and then rubbing them. I didn't want them to be involved because they were young girls and didn't really know what was going on. They were just trying to get some money and if he knew we were gaming them, all of us could get hurt. I didn't want that to happen to Chantell and Money so I hurried to get them out of there as fast as I could.

Kev stayed downstairs. He sat on the couch and started playing the PlayStation 3 while he waited. He lit himself a blunt and turned up the stereo in the house and started puffing on his weed.

I watched him in silence for a second then I went upstairs where girls the were. I was trembling, my knees were knocking together, and my hands were shaking. I prayed we would all get out of this safe and I promised God I would never do anything like this again.

I couldn't believe I could ever find myself afraid of Kev. I never thought he would hurt me, but for the first time ever, I felt like he could and definitely would! I had the girls go in the bedroom and I was headed back down the steps for my cell that I had left in my jacket pocket. I heard Kev on the phone with someone, but when I heard him say Jason's name, I stopped at the top of the steps and listened. Kev had turned the music down so he could hear Jason.

"Jay, man, what's up?" I heard Kev say. "Yeah, she here. They upstairs. I'll call you when they leave," Kev said as he continued to smoke. Jason must have said something else because Kev asked, "Huh?" Next I heard him say, "Ah, man, it was too hot at the other spot, so I made a decision to do this one alone."

Kev sat there and listened. He leaned forward and put the ashes in the cup on the table. "Naw, I never did find out who was stealing." *He knows something. I know he does.* I nervously walked back in the room with the girls. I was in a daze and thinking twice about keeping the money I had just stolen. However, it was too late. In spite of what Kev knew there wasn't any proof. Just as long as I didn't open my mouth I would be okay.

When I returned downstairs I threw the duffle bag of dope on Kev's lap. Kev got up. "Look, man, I'll call you in a minute, I got to go." He hung up the phone.

I just stood there waiting for Kev to say something. He stood up, walked right past me, and went over to the females. Kev reached in his pocket and pulled out a stack of money.

"Here, ladies." He looked down and started counting the money; he gave both the girls $200 extra a piece. "This is for gas. I'll get that title to you in a couple of days. I'm sure somebody in the crew will be up that way before the week is out." He cut his eyes at me. "I'll make sure they bring it to y'all."

I was angry that Kev gave my car away but, I sucked it up, took the loss, and thought, *better a car than my life*.

Kev walked the ladies to the door, said good-bye, and shut the door. I sat down on the couch all smiles, but I trembled on the inside.

"Reese, I followed you! First to the airport, then to the hotel! What was you thinkin'?" Kev hollered, walking toward me in complete rage.

I was caught and I couldn't lie my way out of it. "I don't know," I said, trying to keep my eyes from filling with tears. I was busted. It was official. I covered my face and tried to escape what I knew was bound to happen: my own death.

Kev walked toward me and reached behind him as if he was going to pull the gun out. "I should . . . Reese! Why you do this? Huh? Do you know what happens to people who steal from us? Huh? You think Jason a joke?"

He was standing over me, breathing hard, and huffin' and puffin'. I just sat on the couch lifeless, like he was talking to the wall.

He bent down real close to me and yelled, "You hear me talking to you, woman?" He grabbed me by my T-shirt and pulled me off the couch. He looked into my brown, oval eyes and watched the tears form in the corners and said real soft, "You think I'm a joke?"

I stared back at him, then turned my head away from him and answered very low. "No." I couldn't even look him in the face.

Kev released my shirt from his grip and walked away from me. I guessed he was furious and needed a moment to cool down. He put his hands on his head and rubbed his head. He walked over to the dining room and sat in a chair, looking at me. I just stood there in the living room crying my eyes out, not because I was busted, but because I had hurt Kev. In the beginning I never once thought about Kev in my revenge, and I never wanted to hurt him.

"Reese, if you tell me what I did to you to deserve this, I promise, I'll let you go."

I stood there. I had no answer for him. I didn't know what to say.

"Reese, you hear me?" he snapped. "I know you hear me. Tell me why you did this?" He pointed toward the bag of dope. Kev got out of his chair and walked back toward me again.

I could feel the heat from his body and so I knew he could feel the vibrations from my trembling. As angry as he was, I could tell he was distracted by my beauty. He hesitated, then said with a firm voice, "Reese, you need to tell me somethin'. Come on now, tell me somethin'. You bad enough to steal and now you wanna stand here and act scared?" He walked away from me and grabbed at the gun in his back. It was as if he was ready to pull it out and shoot, but he didn't for the second time.

He turned toward me. "Say somethin'." He stood there in the front room and waited for me to reply. I finally found my voice. I owed Kev that much.

"Kev, I didn't mean to steal from you." I sniffled and used my hands to explain. "I didn't even think about you when I did it. All I thought about was what Jason was doing to me and what he did to . . ." I caught myself from letting what I knew about Shy's death slip out.

He stared at me a few more seconds, then sucked his teeth. He shook his head and walked back into the other room and sat down. "Reese, tell me this; you put me in a real spot here." He came back in the front room where I was and stood in my face. "What you want me to tell Jay? Huh?" He was so mad he was talking through his teeth, and so close that spit was hitting my face as he talked.

I covered my eyes and screamed, "I don't know!" I fell to my knees and covered myself up with my arms. I feared he was going to hit me.

Kev walked away from me, then walked up to me and pulled the gun out, cocked it, and aimed it at my head. His hand was trembling and his eyes were welling up with tears.

He watched me cry and hold on to myself like I was a little girl. I was terrified. I knew he was going to shoot.

He stood over me aiming the gun and thinking about what he was getting ready to do. Maybe he was thinking about my sons. Maybe he was thinking about how much he cared. He sighed aloud and put the gun away. He couldn't do it. I knew I was supposed to be dead.

I was so thankful it was Kev who figured it out instead of Jason. Jason would have killed me but Kev didn't do it.

"Get up! Get up, Reese!" he demanded.

I didn't move. I stayed on the floor in a fetal position, crying and trembling with fear.

His voice became softer as if he was beginning to feel sorry for me. "Reese, come on, girl, get up. You know I ain't gonna hurt you. We gonna figure somethin' out, okay?" He gently touched my face. "Hey, you okay."

Kev reached for me, then balled his fist up and turned away. I could tell he had so many emotions going through him. He finally bent down beside me and put his arm around me. "Everything gonna be all right. Okay, Reese? I promise you."

He closed his eyes and held me right on the floor, for hours it seemed, only being interrupted by our cells ringing constantly. Neither one of us answered our missed calls.

I knew at that very moment I loved him . . . and he loved me.

Chapter 17

The Bathroom Floor

"Jesus, how did I end up here?" I asked, thinking about my upbringing in the church and my relationship with Christ. But now, years later, here I was on the floor of my own bathroom with blood streaming down my face from Jason hitting me in the mouth with the handle of his gun.

I shook myself, pulled myself out of what used to be in my life, realizing that I was now in a whole different place. "I can't call on Jesus." I felt I had let Him down. I covered my mouth with the horrible thought and cried a little longer, then felt the corner of my mouth with my tongue. It was still burning and I wondered if it was going to swell.

For a moment I thought I was dreaming. *Is this indeed a nightmare?* I asked myself. *Or did my life really turn out to be this bad?*

Watching my hand move toward my face, involuntarily shaking dramatically as I reached for my lip, I closed my eyes tight. I feared I was going to die in my own house by the hands of the man I had shared the last few years of my life with. I was confused; I was perplexed as to how I'd gotten here. With my failed marriage and two babies later, I didn't get it.

I took a deep breath and put my head back down. Deep down I knew I was seeing the consequence of

Jason thinking I was the one stealing. He had finally figured it all out: me hiring women, me collecting money, and money missing. It was me all along.

The only problem was he couldn't find the money and so that left a doubt that it could possibly be someone else. That probably saved my life for now.

I was scared to death in my place, trapped like a caged animal, but I was still reckless. All I could remember was Kev telling me to stop . . . stop stealing or else. I did I stop for the next couple of times. This last time was going to be just that, the last time. This was going to be the time that embarrassed Jason and left him standing alone, looking stupid!

Kev reminded me that it was out of his hands. I thought about him holding me that night on Miller Avenue and what he said then.

"Reese, before we leave let me make something clear."

I looked Kev in the eyes, still scared from all the drama and still a little frightened of Kev.

"You can't beat Jason, baby, you gotta let it go." He touched my shoulders with his hands as he talked to me. "Jason ain't to be played wit'. Listen, that's my boy, I wouldn't tell you nothin' wrong. You need to just walk away."

I honestly was ready to stop and I knew in my heart it was only a matter of time before Jason figured it out that I was stealing.

"Okay, Kev, I promise you." I smiled.

I knew Kev was telling me the truth but I couldn't walk away. I wanted to get Jason back, and that was what led to me now being on the bathroom floor hurt and scared. I lifted my head up and looked around the tiny bathroom. "Sorry, Kev, but I just couldn't stop there . . . Not until I had it all," I whispered.

I kept having flashbacks of what happened before Kev got him to leave.

"Where is it, Reese? I know you took it! Tell me where the money is." He huffed while he, Kev, and I smoked weed.

I smiled, puffed on the blunt, and looked at him. "Jay, I don't know what you talkin' 'bout." I smirked.

Jason stood there laughing. "Girl, you gonna make me hurt you! Who do you think you talkin' to?" Then he turned to Kev. "Man, who do she think she talkin' to? Man, you better get her." But I couldn't help it. I knew I had made him look foolish even if he hadn't figured it out yet. I was high and sick and tired of all his mess and I didn't care at that moment what he was going to do to me. I laughed.

Jason got up from the couch and stood over me while I continued to laugh. Kev stood up too realizing our fun moment of smokin' some weed was gonna turn real bad. And it had. But it had been worth it.

"Reese! Where's my money?" he shouted while walking up to me and hitting me in the mouth with the gun."I ain't got time fo' this! Give me my money! You the only one who could have it. Before we included you in the game, we never had this problem." He kicked me in my side.

"Stop, Jason!" I screamed. I was tired of his abuse. "I hate you, Jason, I hate you!" I continued to scream from the floor. I tried covering myself the best I could but he did it so fast that even Kev couldn't stop him from hitting me.

"Jay! Man, what you doin'?" Kev tried to get him to stop but he wouldn't. They scuffled a little; then Jason walked away.

I watched to see what he was going to do next. He went in my kitchen. I could hear him pulling out my draws 'cause I heard silverware moving around. He came back in the living room and he began to tear open my leather sectional with a knife from my kitchen.

"Jay! Come on now, it ain't that serious," Kev tried reasoning with him.

I got off the floor slowly and followed Jason going up the stairs. He went straight to my bedroom and cut open my mattress. He turned around and looked at me.

"So you wanna play this game?" His eyes were piercing through me. He walked up to me and grabbed me."Reese, now you gonna make me hurt you!"

"Stop, Jason! I don't have yo' money! I swear I don't!" I lied. It was too late to turn back now and if I had admitted to having it I was surely dead.

I heard Kev coming up the stairs.

"Hey! Y'all chill out before somebody get hurt."

"Kev, stay out of this," Jason ordered; then he went in my sons' room and flipped their mattresses up, lookin' for any missing money and /or drugs. My heart started beating fast, then faster. I knew that Jason was completely out of control.

I was scared; if it hadn't been for Kev I knew I would've been dead.

"I know I need to get it together. I need to get out of here now, huh, God?" I questioned. I'd even asked God a time or two what to do, but not even He had given me the answer. But then again, my life was so full of mess, how could I have even heard God's voice through all the noise, although He was giving me plenty of signs?

I scrambled myself together, first grabbing my head with one hand, then grasping for the toilet to get off the floor with the other one. I trembled from head to toe, hoping that I reached the front door in time to lock it before Jason decided to come back and finish the job.

I tiptoed to the bathroom door and opened it slowly, just in case Jason was still there. I thought I'd heard them pull off, but wasn't positive. I watched the front door while I walked down the stairs and prayed it wouldn't open. I reached the door and locked it, then went over to the picture window and looked out the blinds.

"He's gone," I said with a heavy sigh of relief.

I lay back on the couch and closed my eyes a second, trying to catch my breath. I opened my eyes, then smirked and grinned. Regardless of what I'd gone through, what I'd been through with Jason, I'd gotten over on him in the end.

I got up of the couch and I ran to the kitchen. I opened the door to the washer and dryer room and pushed the dryer forward. I lifted up a loose floorboard and there it was: all the money I had taken.

I put the Saran-Wrapped money to my nose, closed my eyes, sniffed it, and started laughing. "Now, it's over." I cracked up thinking back to how Jason looked for it earlier and never even came in this room.

I started talking out loud. "He wasn't gonna find this!" I began to mock him by sticking out my chest and putting my shoulders back. "Where is it, Reese? I know you took it! Tell me where the money is."

The final part would be me and the boys leaving Columbus, Ohio and leaving my broken past behind.

I looked around at how Jason had torn up the place looking for this money I was now holding in my hand. "Ha, you wasn't gonna find this, stupid! It's over!" I walked back into the living room while I talked aloud. I screamed and fell back on my soft sofa with the money.

I ran back up the stairs, two at a time, and went into my bedroom. I looked around at the new bedroom set that Jason had just purchased for me. It was a cherry wood canopy bed with the dressers and nightstands to match. "I don't care about what that fool has done for me or given me. He deserves this!"

I opened up my closet and reached past the furs and all the designer clothes that were hanging there. I went straight to my little pink .22 revolver that Jason had given me for my last birthday.

I did exactly what Jason had taught me; I put the gun in the back part of my jeans between my skin and pants, securely tucked away. I grabbed my luggage, threw it on the bed, and packed my bags.

"What am I forgetting?" I said, standing in the middle of my bedroom, looking around the room. After seeing I hadn't left anything, I headed to the kids' room to pack them up some things.

I knew I was going to have to either go online and get a plane ticket or run out to the airport. I figured when I went passed Toya's with some clothes for the boys I could stop at the bank, run in, and put the money in my safety deposit box, then head to the airport for my ticket.

I then rolled my eyes, then shouted aloud, "I can't stand Jason. I wish I could have gotten to my gun while he was in here clownin'. I would have . . ." Thoughts of Jason angered me as I gathered all the luggage and took it to the front door.

I grabbed my gun and pointed as if I was gonna shoot somebody, never finishing my sentence because I knew down in my heart I wouldn't have done such a thing. Moreover, I knew I wasn't a killer, I just wanted Jason to pay for every awful thing he had ever done, and I believed that vengeance was mine and not the

Lord's to give! I hated fighting with Jason and despised the beatings he gave me. It often made me remember my painful past and how I had seen my momma die when I was eleven years old.

I cried out, "Lord, I will not end up like Momma!" Then I whispered, "If I can help it. Every time I think I'm gonna have peace in my life something always comes and steals it."

The expression on my face told it all. I was tired. I stood there for a moment in between my room and the boys' thinking and debating within whether I should continue my plans. It was scary now with Jason suspecting me of stealing the money that was missing. I remembered what happened to my mother when a man thought she had stolen from him.

"Well it's too late to turn back now!"

I had to admit I was a piece of work, in my own right. I was really a good girl turned bad, and through all the fiascos I could still hear the voice of God telling me to turn from my wicked ways. As scared as I was of Jason, the pain and betrayal, the hurt and ambition rang over the voice I could clearly hear telling me to just stop, but I wouldn't. I had gone way past the red light and now I was out of control.

"I know I shouldn't be doing this, I hear you, Lord, but I'm tired. I just wanna start over with my boys. You always said you would be here for me, God, but you let Jason beat me for years! You let my son's father cheat on me and embarrass me! That was so painful. I wanted to ball up in a corner and just die after Julius cheated. He was my high school sweetheart, my together forever, and I believed it." I had to sit on my bed for a second because thinking about Julius brought me to some unresolved issues. I cried thinking about all the promises and dreams we shared together and how it never went that way. I jumped back up and continued talking to God.

"You let my momma get killed! I'm doing it my way, Jesus. It works for me!"

Chapter 18

Eighty Grand

"Hey, Toya." I looked down at my watch while I waited for a response on the other end of the phone.

"Hey," Toya answered.

"The flight leaves at nine tonight; it's noon now."

Toya was listening, but I knew she was concerned about the boys and me. She knew about all the drama and had witnessed the damages too many times. She had seen Jason knock holes in my walls and remembered bruises on my legs and arms, and even black eyes on occasion.

"Okay, you comin' by here to say bye to the boys before you leave? They keep askin' for you." Toya was the only person who knew we were leaving for Atlanta. The plan was for Toya to take the boys to their father until I was settled in. It was the summer so Michael was out of school.

"Yes, of course. I will be by there in a bit. I need to take care of few more things; then I'm headed there."

I shared where I was going with my friend and I even told her wc wouldn't be back, but I never told her about the stolen money and drugs. I knew Toya would tell me to return it. She wasn't for all of that. She was saved and wouldn't agree with getting even. Toya would have said something like, "Let God deal with him. You shouldn't be living with him and y'all ain't married anyway." Toya had standards and always reminded me of them.

"Don't worry about it, we'll be fine. I know you're worrying." I tried to lighten up the conversation. "You are too young to be worrying about me. I'll be fine," I assured her.

"Reese, I don't know what's going on, but I got a bad feeling that something is wrong. You keep saying Jason isn't dangerous but every time I turn on the news one of his friends is dead. Man, you better hurry up and get away from him. Sis, all the diamonds and furs in the world ain't worth you losing your life over. Please get out of that!" Toya cried.

"I am. I will be out of it today, promise."

"I'm praying for you and I asked the Lord to cover you and the boys with the blood of Jesus. The blood of Jesus is the answer."

I closed my eyes. I could feel the emptiness in my heart. I almost felt like there was a black hole where my heart should be. The hurt of my life had given me an excuse to walk away from Jesus, but still I replied to Toya, "I hear you, sis," then hung up.

I didn't wanna think about Jesus, not with the things I had gotten mixed up with.

I knew I was messing up real bad, but I kept it moving in the house after I hung up with Toya. I made sure I had everything I was going to need. I ran back in my room with the cash, sat on the edge of my bed, and unraveled the money. I laid it all out on the bed, and when I was finished counting, I had taken over $80,000 from Jason. I jumped up off the bed, went to the window, looked out, then turned around and glanced at the money on the bed.

"Oh my God, what have I done? I gotta get this out of here!" I yelled while packing it all up.

I did one last once-over of my room and saw my Victoria's Secret tote. I grabbed a shirt on my bed, bent down, and wrapped the money in the shirt and put it in the tote. I knew I had to get the money out of there, so I decided it was time to take it to the bank and put it in a safety deposit box.

I heard a ringing. I looked around the room until I found my cell in my purse. "Hello," I answered.

"Hey, you all right over there?" It was Kev calling to check on me.

"Yeah, I'm fine." I went over to my bedroom window to see if Kev was pulling up. "Where you at?"

"Out and about."

"Where's Jason?" I said as I peeked through the blinds, looking up and down the street for his Hummer.

There was a brief silence.

"Man, this dude left! He went out of town! The thing that's messed up is he had a business trip to take and now I gotta go."

I felt guilty. "Oh, Kev, I'm sorry."

"It's all right. It's not yo' fault. Just wanted to make sure you was all right. You sure you all right? Reese?" Kev asked with concern.

I was in a daze thinking about getting out of there. "Huh? What?" I looked down at the tote. "I don't know," I replied. "So, he went on a trip? Wow." I cracked up laughing. Jason was a hot mess. Nothing stopped Jason from doing what Jason wanted to do. "You sure?"

"Yeah, I'm sure, Reese," Kev replied.

I sighed nervously. "Anyway I'm good, Kev, but I gotta go."

He didn't know I was headed to Atlanta. I didn't want to get Kev any more involved than he already was.

"I know you busy and got more stuff to worry about than me," I proclaimed. I was scared. I wanted to make sure Jason was gone and the only way I felt I could do that was if Kev found out for me, so what could it hurt? "But can you make sure he's out of town? You know Jay can be lying. Please check."

"I will make sure. I'll call you right back," Kev stated then hung up.

I sat on the bed and waited for Kev to call me back. A couple of minutes later my phone rang and it was Kev. "Reese, I can't get through to him. He must have turned his phone off," Kev explained.

I could tell by his voice he was frustrated. My heart started beating faster when Kev said he couldn't find Jason. I wondered where he could have been and if he was really on a cruise or headed back to my house.

"Hold on, Reese. I got another call comin' in."

I anxiously waited for Kev to come back to the phone but in the meantime I could kill two birds with one stone and work on getting the money out of here. I grabbed the tote with the money in it, threw on a pair of shades and a baseball cap, and headed for the door. I knew I needed to get that money out the house.

I looked up and down the street, still fearing Jason. I ran to my car, started it, and zoomed down the street. Kev finally came back to the phone.

"Reese, Jason is gone. Trust me on that. You don't have nothin' to worry about. He's gone."

"Are you sure, Kev?"

"Positive," he assured me.

I gasped a breath of relief. It made me feel better knowing Jason wasn't in town.

"You hear me, girl?" Kev asked.

"Yeah, I hear you." I kept driving to the bank, not telling him anything. "Okay, Kev, I will talk to you a little later. I need to check on the boys. Thank you so much for checking for me."

"All right, Reese, I'll see you later."

I hung up. Dang, I felt so bad! I hated lying to Kev. He didn't deserve that from me. He'd always been a good friend to me.

I pulled into the bank and went inside.

"Hello, I need to get into my safety deposit box please." I smiled at the banker.

"Yes, ma'am, right this way." The tall, blond-headed lady smiled. She led the way to the safety deposit boxes. I followed her. I wanted to get in and out of the bank fast.

"Here we are. I'll leave you alone." She shut the door where the deposit box was and left me there alone.

"Okay, thanks." I smiled back and waited for the blonde to disappear from the room. I opened the box, counted the money again, then wrapped it back in the silk shirt and locked the box with the key.

"I'll be back." I sighed, took a deep breath, and then walked out, headed to my new destiny.

Chapter 19

Vegas

When I walked into Toya's house, the boys ran up to me. They jumped up and down and screamed at the top of their little lungs with excitement. I had already prepared myself before I got there that seeing them would be bittersweet. I had cried and wished I didn't have to leave my boys any longer. I felt bad because I had left them so many times just to do me and now, I was plottin' so we all could have better lives. When I thought about it, I only had myself to be mad at 'cause it didn't never have to get as bad as it did if I had just walked away a long time ago.

I hadn't seen my boys in a few days so for me the time I shared over at Toya's with them was priceless. The boys seemed to have grown so fast. My youngest was talking more and both of them needed their curly hair to be trimmed. I found myself sitting there, stuck, and staring into space thinking about my poor choices and wishing I had just stayed connected with Jesus. I felt Michael tapping me on the arm, trying to get my attention.

"Mommy, what happened to your face?" Michael rubbed my cheek with concern. "Did Jason do that, Mommy?" he asked.

Oh my goodness. It tore my heart apart with the realization that I had been letting my sons see me like this. But there was no way I would leave without saying good-bye.

I looked over at Toya before I answered my son. “No, son, Jason wouldn’t do that to Mommy. Men don’t hit women.” I had to lie. Yes, they’d heard a couple of the fights between Jason and me, but they’d never seen him put his hands on me.

“Okay. Mommy, I’m so glad you here. Are you coming to take us home?” Michael’s eyes were so bright and so full of hope.

I rubbed his curly brown hair and closed my eyes before I answered. Staying away from my boys was the hardest thing I ever had to do and to think it was the best thing for them made wanna kick myself.

“No, Michael. You guys are going on an adventure with Toya. She’s taking you to Daddy’s house! I will be there to pick you and your brother up in a week.” With the disappointment I saw on their faces, I tried to add, “We are going to a new place.”

Gabriel, my baby boy, came and wiped my tears away. “Don’t cry, Mommy.”

I talked with Toya for a bit about the boys’ trip to their dad’s, making sure she had everything she needed to get them there safe. I stayed with them and held on to each of them, drowning them with my kisses before I had to hurry off and get back home to complete the plan.

I sat in the car and cried before heading back home. “God please help me,” I asked. “I don’t want this life! What happened to me? Jesus, please.”

I picked up my cell to call my grandma, but I didn’t want them to worry about me. And I knew I wasn’t good at pretending everything was good. So I opted out of calling them now.

I got back home and sat in the living room for a minute with the TV on. I couldn't help but think how Jason had put a gun to my head. I got up and walked over to the kitchen to get something to drink out the fridge, then laughed out loud and thought how stupid Jason would feel when he realized he would never find his money or me.

I sat down at the kitchen table. I thought about how right I was to take Jason's money and I reasoned within that he definitely deserved this. I got up walked to the fridge and took the lemonade out. I poured myself a glass, took a drink, then set it down on the kitchen table.

"I wish I could be a fly on the wall when he comes back here and realizes I'm gone." I finished my drink and got up from the table, went to the patio, and looked out. "But I'll be long gone," I whispered.

Today proved that it was time to get out of Columbus.

"All I said was he was wrong for leaving Kev here all the time to take care of the business while he was always out of town kickin' it. Then he changes the subject and says last night he counted his money after he picked it up and it was short; it had to be me that took it!" I smirked. "He gonna spit on me!"

I was hype; my arms were moving up and down and I was pacing the floor back and forth as I recalled all his abuse. "He reached over and smacked me, saying I talk too much. My mouth too slick and gets me in trouble," I hollered. "He pulled that gun on me because I fought back this time. Well I'm tired of him hitting on me!" I screamed.

I stared out the patio doors with my leg crossed over the other one, shaking my leg in anger. "I hate Jason. I took him in and let him stay with me and my sons and this is what I get. He cheats on me with my friend, he beats on me, and I hate him! Who does he think he playing with?"

Deep down I wanted to be loved right, loved the way my grandpa loved Grandma. I wanted to be loved unconditionally, without any boundaries or betrayal. However, I knew I wasn't doing what it took to find that kind of love. I knew I was outside the will of God for my life and I knew that in the will of God was where I would find true love.

"I'll get it right, Jesus, just give me some time to get all of my struggles out the way, and then I'll do your will. Please, Jesus, give me some more time to get it right."

I knew the love I was looking for and searched for only came from Jesus Christ. I sat there and thought, *what more could a man want?* But I knew in my heart it wasn't about the love of a man. I was being stubborn and fighting against the will of God for my life. I walked away from the patio door and went back upstairs.

As I headed up the steps I thought about how Jason had killed Shy and how earlier he could have very well pulled the trigger and killed me too. I screamed out, "You saved my life, Jesus. You did. Why, Jesus?" All of a sudden I just dropped to my knees. "All the hell I have caused You over and over again and you are always here. I gotta get it together, Jesus," I whispered.

I looked up at the ceiling as if I were looking at heaven, knowing I wasn't pleasing God. "I've done so much and seen so much. I know people say 'fake it until you make it,' but that ain't me, Jesus. I gotta keep it one hundred with You. I'm all messed up. I need to give it to You. Everything? This stuff is too much . . . It's so hard."

I looked to the ground, then back toward the ceiling after a moment's thought. "You have my heart no matter what I go through. I will always know that, Jesus. I'ma get it together."

In the midst of my heart-to-heart with Jesus, I heard a knock at the door. My first thought was that Jason had come back. But then I realized Jason would not have knocked. I quietly went and looked out the peephole. It was Kev. I exhaled. I debated within if I should answer but decided to open the door.

"Hold on a second," I hollered. I grabbed my luggage and hid it in the closet from Kev. I didn't want him to see what I was really up to.

I opened the door. "Hey, what you doin' here?" I questioned him.

Kev was standing there, grinning from ear to ear. "Reese, I got a solution to yo' problem!" He held up two airplane tickets and smiled. "Come go to Vegas wit' me for a few days. I gotta go handle some business." Before I could answer he continued, "I just thought you could use the trip after everything that happened earlier. You wanna go?"

I didn't know what to think. *Where is this coming from?* I walked from the door to the couch and sat down, pondering his offer.

"I mean you will have your own room. I was just thinking it would be a good break for you; some time for you to think."

What is Kev up to? Does Jay have anything to do with this? Maybe they are setting me up. Maybe they know I'm leaving. I gotta think. What should I do? I better go; at least Toya can get my boys out the city.

Kev was waiting for me to make a decision. He had been talking the whole time about the trip but I couldn't hear him.

"Okay. I will." Then I remembered and touched my lip. "When?" I asked.

"That's the thing, we leaving in a few hours. It's one of those last minute things that has to be taken care of now." He sat down beside me on the couch. He rubbed his head and tried to explain, "Jay was supposed to do this but he up and left, leaving me to do it."

He was upset; his nose was flaring out and his face was turning red.

"My face is swollen." I held my head down.

He lifted my head up. "You're still gorgeous." He grinned, trying to make me feel better.

"I don't know, Kev; what about Jay? He will—"

Kev interrupted me. "Trust me, I won't tell Jay nothin'. He don't have to know you comin'. After today I figured you could use it."

"Well, let me call Toya and let her know. How long we gonna be there?"

"Just a few days, that's it."

I daydreamed for a second and saw myself in the warm Vegas weather, and at the point it didn't matter to me if I was in Atlanta or Alaska; I just didn't wanna be in Columbus, Ohio! And since I was already packed, I figured I would go. I told myself it would be the last time I could spend with Kev before I disappeared.

After we landed in Vegas, I rode with Kev while he went to meet some men. He wanted to grab a bite to eat and get me to relax a bit from all the drama.

I was waiting while Kev was taking care of the business they had there. I was on my phone with my credit card company. I'd found out Jason was charging everything he did to my card. Guessed that was his way of getting even with me for taking some money.

“Yes, ma’am, please cancel that card immediately!” I instructed the rep and then ended the call.

Kev came jogging back to the car. I was so angry with Jason, but I wasn’t gonna let him spoil my time in Vegas. ”Okay, okay! I’m hungry; let’s go!”

“Girl, what you been out here doin’? You done put on some lip gloss and eye shadow, and let yo’ hair down! You did all that in the car? I’ma have to fight these goons off of ya!”

We both laughed. I hit him in the arm when he got in the car and we were off to dinner. I put on my shades and enjoyed the wind coming through the window while he drove. I wondered if I could trust him enough to tell him I was running off with Jason’s money. After all, he forgave me when he found out I took the money back in the day. However, that was pennies compared to what I knew I was taking now.

When we got to the restaurant and sat down, Kev watched me. He smiled when I caught him looking.

“What? Why you keep lookin’ at me like that? What’s wrong? Is my lip still swollen?” I reached for my face but Kev grabbed my hand.

“No, nothing’s wrong. I’m just admiring your beauty.” He leaned in across the table. “Reese, you really brighten up a room.” He shook his head, then continued watching me. “You’re one of a kind. Jason doesn’t know what he has.”

I blushed, wanting to believe every word Kev was saying. *He’s just being nice,* I told myself. For the first time I was at a loss for words, sitting there stuck for a few seconds; then I blurted out, “I was thinking about you.” *Oh, my God! Did I just say that aloud?* My heart was beating fast because my words were now out there and I couldn’t take them back.

"So? What were you thinkin'?" Kev grinned.

"Um, um," I replied, too slow to tell him.

Kev stood up. "I'll give you a second or two to answer that. I gotta use the bathroom, excuse me." He stood, and walked toward the bathroom.

I watched Kev walk away. I felt like I was on a roller coaster going down the hills and sharp turns and twists. Man, I wished so much that Kev and I could have been, but under all these circumstances I knew it was impossible. I thought, *maybe a different day and different time*. I daydreamed and imagined being loved back, but realized I couldn't continue to look for love; it had to find me.

"He who finds a wife finds a good thing. Humph. How far away am I from that, Jesus?" I laughed to myself. I was thinking about that scripture; then I heard my cell ring. I didn't recognize the number. Maybe it was the credit card company calling me or something.

"Hello," I answered.

"Reese, what's goin' on? You at home?" Jason asked.

I sat in my seat and tapped my nails against the table. "What do you want, Jason? I can't believe you calling me after all the hell you have caused. What do you want?"

"Who you think you talkin' to? You better remember who you talkin' to!" Jason yelled through the phone.

"Jason! You in Aruba wit' my so-called girl and you want me to sit here and pretend I don't know?" I looked around the restaurant, then remembered I was in public and quieted down.

"Woo, wait a minute. Who told you that? Huh? Kev said that to you? Sweetie, I'm not I'm in New York takin' care of business that's all. I been here since we got into it. I was hurt after all that stuff at the house wit' you," he convincingly said.

I laughed, got up from the dinner table, and walked into the hall so I wouldn't disturb the other guests. "Jason, the credit card company called me because of all the transactions in the last day in Aruba! And on top of all of that, tell Eva her husband is probably lookin' for her!" I took a wild guess that was who he was with.

Jason sighed, exasperated. "Now, I let the money go and wanna believe you don't have it! But don't make me mad by disrespectin' me!" he fumed and hollered.

But I wasn't trying to hear him anymore. I was out of the city. My boys were out the city and there was nothing he could do about it, or the money missing. I hung up on Jason, walked back to the table, and noticed Kev sitting there. I tried to hold back the tears before I reached the table, but they continued to flow. It was painful, to be betrayed and disrespected by Jason and Eva, and what they were dishing out still hurt. No, I didn't want Jason in my life anymore, that was clear, but to think I had done all I could to be a good woman to him and he did me dirty like this. And Eva, my girl, was icing on the cake!

Kev noticed me crying and came over and hugged me. "What's wrong? You okay?"

"Yes, I will be. It's Jason. He and Eva—"

Kev cut me off and started talking. "Listen, we ain't gonna worry 'bout that mess. Leave it in Ohio. You in Vegas. We gonna enjoy ourselves, okay?" He kissed my forehead. "I didn't wanna tell you. I just thought you didn't need to hear what Jay was doin' or who he was with. I'm sorry, okay? I thought I was protecting you."

I believed him and nodded. "Thanks, Kev, for everything. You're a good friend."

Kev released me from his embrace, looked at me, and kissed me on my cheek, then my nose. We both laughed, then we looked into each other's eyes and he kissed me on the lips.

We stood in the restaurant and kissed for what seemed like eternity.

I couldn't help but wonder where this was headed.

Chapter 20

360

Kev sat back down at the dinner table after releasing our embrace. He leaned in and grabbed my hand. "We have been kiddin' ourselves. You feelin' me as much as I'm feelin you. It's been that way since we met, but now I need to know where you are goin' from here with Jason. With me."

My heart was fluttering. I squeezed his hand tight.

He continued to hold on to my hand while he talked. "I know Jay, but what you gonna do, Reese? You stayin' in it?" He motioned circles on my hand as he held it, and he waited to ask me the next question. He rubbed the side of his face where his shaded facial hair was. "Are you movin' on?"

I paused for a moment, and tilted my head while I squinted my eyes at him. I wanted to make sure I meant the words I was about to say. "I'm movin on."

Kev waited for those words to roll off my tongue. He grinned. "Watch that, Reese, 'cause if you mean that, then that opens the door for me to enter in."

I smiled, and took a deep breath. "Enter then."

Kev's grinned widened. "Okay, so you didn't hear me knocking? I've been standing out here knocking for months; it's about time you let me come in."

My very dream was coming to pass. The man I wanted to spend forever with was standing at my door.

"Reese, I wanna turn it around. I want us to do this together. I mean no more drug life!" he demanded. Then he got serious. "You know we can't stay in Ohio, don't you?"

I listened then replied, "I know." I felt so warm all over; I was so in love with Kev and now I knew what I suspected was true, he felt the same about me; no more hiding it.

Then reality crept in and hit me. My eyes got big and I panicked with thoughts. *Oh no! How can I tell him I'm leaving Ohio and headed to Atlanta? How can I tell him I took that money?* I wanted to tell him the truth but how could I?

I decided to just play it by how our conversation would go from here on. I knew he would never trust me after I told him what I had done. What I wanted was now in front of me and ready to start a life with me, but because of my determination to get revenge on Jason it would never happen.

Kev told me how relieved he was to finally know that I felt the same way he was feeling all along. I listened to him go on and on but the money issue was all that was on my mind. I wished I had never taken that money. Dang, what was I thinking about? I wished I could have returned it without him ever finding out, but it was too late. Then I started wondering if this all was a setup. If Kev was just trying to get me to tell him the truth. After all he and Jay had been best friends since they were kids. *What would make me think they aren't playin' me? They might be planning to kill me or something!*

I was getting paranoid, tapping my nails on the table again; then I started biting them. I crossed my legs and shook them, then uncrossed them and repositioned myself in the chair. I kept looking at the entrance, thinking Jason was going to come in any minute. "Kev, what's goin' on? You talk to Jason? Did he put you up to this? Please tell me the truth," I pleaded.

Kev frowned. He looked confused. "Oh, wow, you believe I would do something like that to you, Reese? Huh? All I have ever shown you was love, girl. Even before I fell in love with you I looked out for you."

He got up from the table and went over beside me and bent down. "You think I'm setting you up with Jay? Yeah, right. I ain't got time for games, Reese. Look, I love you. I don't know why I feel like this but I'm willing to betray my best friend for you, so please don't think this is a game. I don't play games!" Kev was upset as he walked back over to his seat.

"I'm sorry, Kev, but I'm scared that's all. Please forgive me. I didn't want you to get upset, I just wanted you to be honest," I explained.

"I do, I forgive you, and I can understand a level of fear being there because I know all the stuff you been through with Jay. But I need you to believe me when I say this: I love you and I want nothing else but for you to be by my side until the day I die," he proclaimed.

That took my breath away. *This is what love is really about right here: a man willing to do whatever for me. God, give me a sign if this is real.*

Once dinner was over we walked the strip, laughed, and talked about the possibilities of starting a new life together, away from Ohio and away from our old lives.

Kev grabbed me and we stood face to face. He bent his head down and softly bumped his forehead against mine. He hugged me. I closed my eyes and thought, *I wonder if he thinks I have the money.* I would have loved to enjoy this moment but that continued to haunt me.

He kissed me again. I had dreamt of being in his arms for so long, and now he was mine and the kiss was everything I could have ever imagined. It took my mind off the money for a moment, that's for sure.

"Reese, marry me," I thought I heard Kev say.

I looked up at Kev as if to say, "are you for real?" *Am I hearing things? Did he just propose?* Truly I was speechless. I knew we had spent a lot of time together over the years and I knew we both had deep feelings for each other, but I never expected him to say this, never.

Marry me. Those words rang in my ears. I wanted him to be my husband but at the same time I was torn. I had begun to believe I wasn't worth anything and would never be married again or happy. Besides that, I knew Kev was in the game deep. Was he really getting out the game like he said? All of this was something to think about. Love would not be enough any longer to make me stay with someone. Logic had to be there, and when I looked at this picture in full, Kev was a drug dealer, plain and simple.

"Kev, what about the dope?"

He took my hand and led me over to a bench outside the hotel near a beautiful water fountain. I sat on his lap and put my arms around his neck. I laid my head on his chest and relaxed.

"I'm out the game," he stated. "I'm serious, Reese. I came to Vegas to help Jay. That's all."

I lifted my head and tilted it and watched him explain.

"I'm serious. That money that came up missing was for some people here. I told Jay I would pay it for him."

Oh my God. I felt so bad. "Kev, about the money . . . I'm sorry." I was about to spill the truth and just give the money to Kev when he cut me off.

"Look, Reese, I don't wanna know." It's like he knew what I was about to say. "It's covered, that's all you need to know. Don't bring up that money again."

I wanted him to know I had it and I wanted to give it back to him. *I have to tell him I have the money. No if, ands, or buts about it,* my mind ordered.

"I told you a while ago I wanted out of this and this"—he pointed to me—"you . . . you are my reason." He grabbed my hands. "Marry me? I promise I'll take care of you." He waited for a response by never taking his eyes off of me.

I sat on the bench and looked him in the eyes for a moment longer, asking myself if I could trust him. I loved him. I knew I did. I believed him. It made sense with him. Love and logic.

"Yes, Kev, I will marry you," I blurted.

He picked me up and swung me around, then we kissed.

"Let's talk for a minute," I said. I was concerned with my salvation for the first time in a long time and I wanted Kev to understand that getting it right with Jesus was my focus.

I led him back to the bench to sit. I grabbed Kev by the hands and said, "I have to get it together, Kev, because I know God is looking at my life and seeing a big mess. I can't be a part of drugs anymore. Please let's just get the boys and leave. Please, Kev, promise me you will get on the plane with us? Jason isn't going to do anything. God will protect us."

He paused a moment before saying, "I'll seriously think about it. I may have to stay in Ohio for a few months to play it off. I don't want nobody to suspect anything. I want you and the boys to be safe, Reese, that's all. I don't care about the business, just you."

Chapter 21

Fairytales

We got rid of our rooms and decided since we were engaged we could share a suite for the night. We promised each other no funny business. We wanted to be close to each other. I knew I didn't want to spend another day away from this man. We left the lobby and went upstairs to the new room together.

The first thing I noticed in the suite was the peanut butter–colored leather couch with Moroccan pillows all over it. Then I turned and looked across from the couch and saw the fireplace. I went toward the window that was as wide and long as the whole wall and looked out on to the balcony. *The view is amazing!* I opened the balcony doors and walked out and could see all of Vegas in the far distance.

Kev stood back and smiled as I took everything in. He then sat on the soft, plush couch and watched me. He was so happy that I was going to be his wife and even happier that he was making my dreams come true.

I inhaled the Las Vegas wind that was blowing through my body, not even once thinking about any mess; I was in my moment.

I was interrupted by Kev's cell ringing. I turned and saw him looking down at it. He picked it up and looked.

"Reese, don't worry, okay? I'ma take this. It's Jay. I'm going to put it on speaker so you can hear everything." I knew Kev was only doing that to show me that I could trust him.

"Hello," Kev said.

"What's up, Kev. You make it? Nobody in Ohio can get a hold of you," Jason said.

"Aw, man, I'm good and, yeah, I made it here. I'll be back there in a couple of days," Kev said.

"Okay, you take care of that. Um, you seen Reese?" Jason wanted to know.

Kev looked at me for a minute to think about what he was going to say. "Naw, I ain't seen her since the fight you two had. I talked to her but I ain't seen her and as far as that thing, you in the clear."

"Good lookin' out, man. I did speak to Reese a couple hours ago. She was upset I spent money on her credit card and she found out I was here wit' Eva in Aruba. Crazy huh?"

"Jay—" Before Kev could finish Jason interrupted.

"When I get back to Columbus I'ma stop treatin' her like this. I don't really have proof that she took that money, you know?"

I stood there listening. I knew Jason was lying. He was trying to get sympathy from Kev. He probably figured if Kev felt bad he would tell him where I was.

Kev held his head down and started walking with the phone. "Yeah, I hear ya."

I shook my head and mouthed, "He's lying!" Kev put his finger to his lips to tell me to be quiet; even my whole expression changed. I was paranoid and started looking around like Jason was going to come around a corner any minute. I walked up to Kev and watched his motions as he talked.

He took his phone off speaker and put it to his ear. He listened to Jason talk but pulled me close to him to let me know I was protected. We stood there holding each other while Jason was on the other end of the phone, not knowing a thing.

"All right then, I'll speak to you a little later, Jay." Kev hurried to get off the phone and stood there holding me.

He looked down to the top of my forehead all squinched up and kissed me on it. He took his finger and rubbed the wrinkles I was making on my forehead. He then patted me on the back and said, "Loosen up. You don't have a thing to worry about." Kev held me and let me know I was fine.

"Kev, what do you think?" I was nervous; I thought Jason must have known something. "I mean, he callin' you, actin like everything's okay and stuff." I pulled myself from Kev's arms and started walking around the suite, closing up curtains and the balcony door.

Kev followed me, watching me and shaking his head. "Reese, sit down. He don't know nothin'. I will protect you. I'm not afraid of Jason, not at all." He went and sat down on the couch. "Come on, sit down, babe." He patted the empty spot next to him.

I sat down beside him, and then leaned under his arm until I almost fell asleep.

Kev stayed there with me until he knew I was okay. He covered me with a blanket from the hotel room's bed.

"Reese, I think I'm goin' to get my own room, baby. You need your space. I'll see you in the mornin' okay?"

I sat up and pulled on his shirt to stay, but Kev stopped me. "Baby, I'ma go get me a room. I know we are engaged, but I will be your desire unto God and wait 'til I'm your husband. If we are going to start a new life together, then we are going to start it off right with a threesome: you, me, and God."

I smiled and went back to sleep, after thanking God.

Chapter 22

The Ceremony

The next morning Kev surprised me. He knocked on the bathroom door while I was finishing putting on my makeup.

"Hey, beautiful," he said when I opened the door.

"Hey, you," I replied. "Give me a sec, Kev." I walked back to the bathroom and finished with my face by adding some lip gloss.

"Take your time, beautiful. I'm not goin' anywhere," I heard him say. "You feeling better than you did last night? You all right?" He was concerned.

"Yes, I'm okay. I was just a little worried when he called," I called out from the bathroom. "Everything is good, babe," I added.

Kev came over to the bathroom door and stood. "I have a surprise for you this morning. How would you like to go down to the spa for a nice, long, intense massage?"

I listened while I touched up my makeup. I looked at myself in the mirror and smiled. "Yes! Let's go!" I opened the door and I gave him a big hug.

Downstairs, as we lay side by side on the deluxe massage tables, I fought with remembering so much. I wanted to think about the future and forget the past but for some reason every time I closed my eyes my past appeared. I heard Kev calling me, so I opened my eyes.

"Baby, come on, we're finished."

I woke up, got off the table, and Kev handed me a glass of water while I put on my robe.

"Why don't you go to the salon in the hotel and get yo' hair done for this evening. I need to go handle some business while you do that, okay?" Kev offered.

"Where you goin', Kev? I thought we were staying together." I was scared to be left alone.

"Trust me." He gave me a kiss, put his robe on, and walked out the massage room.

I went in the salon to get dolled up. I was actually excited about being there. They had everything there: a nail salon, hair salon, body waxing, and a makeup artist. I told the stylists and nail technicians about my knight in shining armor and it melted their hearts. All of them wanted to come to the ceremony and bring something since we were away from home.

I was sitting there getting my nails finished when Kev called and wanted to know what was taking so long, seeing hours had went by.

"Baby, you told me to get it together and that's what I'm doing. Beauty takes time," I answered.

"Well, you're already beautiful. Come back upstairs. I miss you."

"Aw, I miss you too. I'll be there in a minute, okay?"

"Hurry up; I have a surprise for you."

"What?" I hesitated, then put on a big grin. "What do you have for me?" I raised one of my eyebrows, displaying my interest and curiosity.

"Come and see," Kev teased.

I hurried and finished up. I wanted to see what the surprise was, and moreover, I wanted to see Kev, so I hurried back upstairs.

Kev was waiting and watching football. He was screaming at the TV as if it could talk back to him. "Oh, come on, man! Where's the defense?"

I laughed and opened the door. He was wearing a pair of jeans and a plain T-shirt. It was the first time in a long time I had seen Kev dressed so casual. Usually Kev stayed tailor made up. I looked down at his feet and even his shoes were off.

I stood in the front room of the hotel. "Hi," I greeted him.

"Wow, Reese you are breathtaking," said Kev. When Kev looked at me he made me feel down in my soul what he felt about me. I could see how he felt about me in his eyes. When he looked at me he made me feel like I was beautiful.

As soon as he saw me standing there, he instantly turned the television off. My heart was racing. I felt like I had a middle-school crush, all warm and fuzzy on the inside. I felt like the hair on my arms was standing straight up as he got closer and closer to me. It almost was as if we had an electric, magnetic connection. *Whoo! I love that man!*

He grabbed my hands gently then closed his eyes and kissed them. "Hey, you have a nice time down there? Did they take good care of you?" he asked, putting my hands to his chest. "You look beautiful."

I nodded and blushed.

"I love you, Reese. I hope you know this. I'm not playin' games. All my cards are on the table, baby, and I want a fresh start, with you and your sons by my side. You understand?"

I couldn't help my eyes from getting moist. The gentleness of this man was so unreal to me. I had never experienced such a love in my life, except the love of God.

"Yes, I understand, Kev."

Kev got down on one knee, then reached in his pocket and pulled out a four-carat heart-shaped diamond ring. I wasn't expecting him to have a beautiful ring. We had just decided to get married, so it made me lose my balance and Kev had to lead me to the couch. He sat me down then got back on his knees.

"Reese Taylor Bradford, will you marry me?" He paused then said, "Right now?"

"Yes," I said without hesitating.

Kev took my hand and put the ring on my manicured finger.

I was in the bathroom soaking in the bubble bath whirlpool tub. The minister's wife was waiting for me to finish so she could lead me to the chapel. She was an older, gray-haired woman, jazzy though. Her hair was cut in short spikes and her clothes were saucy.

"Honey, you almost finished in there? We need to get to the chapel," she yelled from the front room.

"Yes, ma'am, I'm ready," I said. I got out the tub and put on some sweats to go downstairs and get prepared. I grabbed all my belongings and walked with the lady. We went down the elevator to the main floor where the sanctuary was.

"Here we are, baby." She motioned her hand for me to go in the room. She looked down at her watch. "You still have a little bit of time to get ready. Do you need any help?" She smiled.

"Actually, I do need some help. Thank you," I replied. "Can you help me with my dress?"

She was such a sweet lady. She had so much joy. "Of course I will." She got my dress off the hanger. "Is your mother and family here?"

I got quiet then said, "My mom passed. She's in heaven. I don't have any other family besides my two sons and they're in Ohio right now."

She grabbed me by the hand and said, "Oh, I'm so sorry to hear that."

I thought about the question the lady asked. *Wow, Momma. I so wish she were here with me.* It made me so sad but I was determined to enjoy and remember this day for the rest of my life. *I am going to make him an excellent wife,* I said within myself.

I stood up proudly.

"All right, beautiful, you ready to do this?" The woman turned me around to a mirror that stood in the hallway.

I looked at my reflection. "Beautiful," I said, touching my face. "I can't believe this is me. I can't believe this is me in this wedding dress about to get married." The gown was extraordinary. I selected a soft gold gown that was beaded from top to bottom. It was fitted to my body, showing off my curves in good taste. The back of the gown dropped real low, showing the small of my back.

Once again I had to fight the tears away. "Don't cry, Reese; wait until the ceremony. You don't wanna mess up your makeup, baby." The woman smiled, crying herself as she looked on.

I took the woman by the hands and rubbed one of them. "Can I have a minute before I go out there?"

"Yes, of course. If you need me, I'll be right inside my office here." She left and I watched her go into her office.

I continued to look at myself in the mirror. "I look so beautiful." I then backed away and said, "God, if I haven't said this in a long time, I love you. Thank you so much for my new life. Thank you, Jesus, for my husband. Please bless us and allow us to spend the rest of our lives together as one."

I hesitated for a moment, then said, "In you, Father." I looked up at heaven and cried inside with joy.

I was sure Kev was inside the chapel, losing his mind waiting for me. He was so nervous and excited all at the same time. I went and peeked inside the sanctuary and watched Kev for a minute. He walked back and forth looking toward the door every few seconds to see if I was there yet. He looked suave standing there ever so debonair, with a black tux with a white vest, and his shoes were black-and-white snakeskin. He had gone out and got him a fresh cut and the shadow on his face was edged up real tight. He looked so good.

I shut the door back, closed my eyes and I was ready to walk in the sanctuary and heard my cell ringing. I thought maybe it was Jason and he was there, so I went and looked at it. It was Kev calling. I picked it up and answered it. "What are you doing calling?"

"I'm out here on the other side of your door." He told me. I was curious to why of course. I was a little nervous, thinking maybe he changed his mind. I went up to the door and leaned my head against it to hear what he had to say.

"Hello, Reese?" he asked as if it weren't me. I believed he was just a little nervous. "You ready?"

"Yes, I'm ready," I said nervously.

Both of us were nervous. We were stepping into a new life, and all we had was each other.

"Reese, there's something I need to tell you before we do this." He paused and my heart beat a mile a minute. "I love you."

I closed my eyes, locking in my tears so that my makeup wouldn't get ruined. "I love you too."

We held the phone in silence for a few seconds, then said a couple of "You hang up first. No, you hang up's." Then we both hung up.

I couldn't take it any longer as I opened the door wide and entered the sanctuary, ready to become his wife.

Kev looked toward the door and that's when he saw me coming in the room. You would have thought time stopped when he first saw me.

He said out loud, "You are a picture of art in motion."

My hair was pulled back off my face with a couple of spiral curls that fell ever so gently across my forehead and the makeup was done just right. I remembered the makeup artist telling me I didn't need a lot because I was already beautiful.

"You are everything I ever wanted," he said.

At that moment, as I walked toward him, I could tell he was thinking about us. *No more drugs, no more, good-bye to it all.* Kev walked to get me. I noticed the tears coming out his beautiful eyes and I smiled at him, knowing that his tears were that of joy. I was sure Kev didn't count on breaking down like this; he usually knew how to keep it together. He was cool and laidback but today was the day that Kev let his emotions show.

He reached for me and stood in front of me, gazing in my eyes. He took my hand and led me to the minister. I trusted him, and never felt like I was going to stumble or fall.

I looked around the chapel and that's when I saw my sons and Toya. I covered my mouth with my hands. I looked at Kev and put my arms around his neck and held on to him. I whispered, "Thank you, baby, thank you."

It was spectacular to think he pulled all of this off in next to no time at all. It was amazing. I was overwhelmed.

The ceremony was by candlelight. We continued to hold hands when we approached the minister. He was a tall and distinguished man and I noticed how together he was. He had on a black robe with a little white design down the front of it. His hair was gray and cut short to his head. He was a dark, older gentleman with the sternest look upon his face, letting me know that he was there strictly for business, which I knew was the Lord's work. He held the Bible in his hands, opened to a page, and began to speak.

"Reese Taylor Bradford, do you take Kevon' Joseph Valan' to be your husband?"

I thought for a moment and stared down to the ground, looking at the beautiful marble floor; then I looked at Kev and squeezed his hand real tight and said, "Yes, I do, I take you to be my husband." Before I could finish my sentence I was crying like a baby.

Kev was posed the same question. "Yes," he answered. Kev held me real tight, showing in his actions that he would always protect and love me until death do us part. We heard the minister's instructions; he sealed our union with a kiss. *Death do us part.*

We smiled and listened as the guests cheered us on. I looked around and saw my new friends from the hair salon and the workers at the resort. My boys ran up screaming, "Mommy!" I smiled, bent down, and embraced them both with a long hug and kisses. I was so thankful that they were there with us. We were all there to start our new life together.

Kev had arranged for a lovely dinner after the ceremony. Then as we listened to the live band we danced cheek to cheek. We didn't separate after the wedding; we stayed side by side.

Me and Toya talked and I danced with my sons, hugged on 'em, and took as many kisses as I could. "Toya! How did y'all pull this off? I know Kev had you in on this."

"You know he did," Toya said. "Girl, when he called me and told me y'all was getting married I cried like a little baby! I knew y'all was for each other. I told you. I dropped the phone for a second and started shoutin'!"

We laughed and hugged again before Toya took the boys back to my room. After we said good-bye to the boys it was time for us to leave as well.

I stood there for a few more seconds watching the boys disappear on the elevator. Then Kev slipped his arm around my waist and whispered, "Let's go."

In the elevator to the room Kev let out a big sigh. "Baby, can you believe this?" He smiled, staring, waiting for my reply. He reached down and touched my hand then looked at the ring on my finger.

"I know, huh, this is crazy. I never would have thought that we could be together, Kev." My eyes were lit up like a Christmas tree. "Kev, thank you for bringing the boys. When and how did you pull all this off?"

Kev put his arms around me. "I love you, Reese. I'd do anything for you, baby." He kissed me on the cheek.

The elevator stopped at the top floor. "Kev, this is the wrong floor. We're on the wrong floor." Puzzled, I wondered, *why is Kev getting off like he don't remember where his room is?*

He shot me this smirk and nodded for me to follow him.

I finally got off the elevator and followed him. "When did you do this?" I said, following him and still puzzled.

"Earlier, Reese, come on, babe," Kev said while carrying my shoes. He was excited. He wanted to show me how much he loved me.

Kev opened the door then said, "Wait." He put my shoes inside the door, and then ran back over where I was standing and picked me up. I put my long arms around his neck and my head into his chest while he carried me inside the room and over the threshold.

I couldn't see the room well because he was holding me, but when we finally reached the bedroom and he laid me on the bed I jumped up and went to look around. I couldn't help it; I was so excited.

There were three rooms in all, all of which were lit up with candles. The bathroom was off the hook with a Jacuzzi, tub and shower also. I ran to the front room and looked around at the place. I noticed there was a chandelier hanging and the whole front room floor was marble, and that's when I saw all the roses on the floor.

Kev sat down and watched me move around in the dress and said, "Um um um, how beautiful your light brown skin looks in this dress."

He came over to me and took my hand and spun me around. He stretched our arms out and we looked into each other's eyes. He then pulled me close for a dance with him. His chin lay on my head and he rubbed my back as we moved together. I thought to myself, *now this is true love.*

He spun me around again, but this time my back was facing him. He put his arms around me and noticed my skin glistening when the light hit my back, he confessed. He turned me face to face to him, shook his head back and forth, embraced me, and started to kiss me on the neck.

I felt the chill bumps rise on my skin.

"There's bathwater for you," he said.

I turned to him and kissed his lips. Kev softly slipped his arms around my waist, closed his eyes, and kissed my neck until he reached my lips. Then he whispered in my ear, "I wanna bathc my wife, will that be okay?"

My heart raced as he carried me into the bathroom and shut the door.

Chapter 23

Kev's Story

The next morning I opened my eyes and smiled thinking about the wedding. I was still in the bed but Kev wasn't there and I wondered where he went. I turned my head toward the balcony that was just off the bedroom and saw him sitting out there. He was looking at me, I smiled as soon as we locked eyes.

"Good morning sweetheart," he said. "Good morning," I replied. His shirt was off and he had on his pajama bottoms, smoking a stogy and reading the paper.

I was still sleepy so I closed my eyes and tried to sleep a little longer, but within a few minutes I heard Kev say aloud,

"Look at my beautiful wife, she's flawless, God. You gave me her." I peeked over at him. He was still sitting in his chair looking over at me. He couldn't tell I was awake because my eyes were peeking through at him.

He got out of the chair and looked over the balcony at the Vegas strip. He put the cigar out and looked down at his cell vibrating then at the number but never answered it, pushing the call to voice mail. "Twenty missed calls." He glanced again seeming to be contemplating calling the number back then he said, " I don't care I'm on my honeymoon and nothing is more important than that." He walked over to the bed and sat down beside me.

“I want you to get some rest, we been up all night long.” He whispered in my car. Then I felt him get up and he walked back out to the balcony. ”I keep havin’ flashbacks of our wedding night.” He laughed then sat back down in the chair on the balcony. He continued to stare over at me, all while I pretended to be asleep. He smiled and flicked his ashes in the ashtray.

I realized I wasn’t gonna get anymore sleep so I sat up in the bed.

“Baby?” I yawned. “What you thinkin’ ’bout?” I got out the bed and walked toward Kev on the balcony.

“You surprised me, I didn’t know you were awake.” He got up and started toward me and met me with a kiss. “How did you sleep? You okay?” He was so concerned . . .

I was so happy that my checks were hurting from smiling so much. “I slept great. Never felt better,” I proclaimed and kissed him again. “The best part of the whole ceremony was seeing my boys. Oh, Kev!” I placed my hand over my mouth and stood there, looking at him. “That was priceless; thank you, babe, really.”

I appreciated him so much and the love and care he gave me. I knew it was a priceless kind of love. Kev had done so much for me. He had shown me nothing but love and respect from the time we met, but now I was thinking how I hadn’t given him the same thing.

I lied to him and had that money and on top of that he didn’t know about Shy. I wasn’t feeling very good about myself.

“Kev, I have to tell you something. Please, I need to tell you something, babe,” I confessed. Kev started shaking his head no as if to say not now.

"Babe, let's enjoy today. We can talk when we get back, okay?" Kev pleaded.

I smiled, gave him a big hug, and agreed. I wanted to get it off my chest, but realized it wasn't the right time so I changed the subject with a question.

"So, what we gonna do today, Kev? What you wanna do? I want to go everywhere!" I smiled and looked over the balcony on to the strip.

Kev couldn't get a word in edgewise because of my excitement. He walked up behind me and rubbed my back, looking over the balcony with me. "We can go wherever you want," he said.

"I wanna go shopping! Let's go get the boys some things, then we can go get us a little somethin' somethin'." I laughed.

"All right, that sounds good to me," Kev said, looking at his cell. He looked at me, and then answered the phone. "What's up, Jay?" He pulled me close to him. I could hear their conversation. "Kev, where you at? You leave yet?" Jason said, sounding concerned.

"No, not yet, man. I needed to take care of somethin'. I'll be back there in a couple of days." By Kev's actions he seemed relaxed and confident that Jason didn't have an idea of what was really going on.

"Handle yo' business then. I called Reese but she isn't answerin' me. I figure she isn't ready to talk, you know. I went a little too far this time. I shouldn't have hit her with that gun; that was messed up. I don't know if she will forgive me, man. It's messin' wit' my head, Kev." Jason sighed. I couldn't believe he was saying all that! He was lying through his teeth! I couldn't hear anymore, I walked away from Kev and went into the living area of our room and sat on the couch. I was disgusted.

Kev walked over to me, bent down, and kissed my lips and held my hand trying to make me feel secure. Then he continued talking to Jason.

"Jay, I don't know what to tell you. It was pretty bad between y'all. Reese may have moved on, so if I were you, I wouldn't expect her to understand. I told you to stop treatin' her like that, man. You wouldn't listen, Jay."

Kev was getting upset. "Look, Jay, I still have flashbacks of you beating on Reese and me having to get in the middle and stop you. Just leave her alone." Kev was angry. His voice had gotten louder while he continued to explained to Jason.

"Jay, man, I gotta go. I'll call you when I get to the CO," Kev said, ready to end the call before his anger got the best of him.

"All right, man," Jason responded dryly. Kev was about to hang up when Jason said, "Kev, I can't eat. I can't sleep. I can't get that woman off my mind."

Kev looked at me as if he was going to say something, but he didn't. I sat there watching him and it was apparent he didn't know Jason, his best friend from the time they were eight, would break down like this; Kev was showing mixed emotions. One minute he was feeling guilty, the other he was mad, because all in all he loved Jason. They were friends.

"Kev? You hear me?" Jason sighed. "I did this, I went too far, man." His voice was low.

Silence fell between them on the phone, then Kev said, "Man, I don't know what to tell you. You may have to chalk this one up."

"All right, man, I got to go. If you hear from Reese tell her to pick up the phone. Okay, Kev?" Jason asked.

"Yeah, man. I'll tell her," Kev agreed, then ended the call.

Kev continued to walk around the room, not expecting the call to have been like this.. He rubbed the top of his head and sat on the couch, looking serious.

I knew something wasn't right. I could see it in his eyes.

He gazed into space for a few more minutes without even hearing me ask, "What's wrong?" I was getting nervous now because he wasn't responding. I had never seen Kev like this. "Baby, what's the matter? Do he know about us?" I jumped up off the couch and walked around the front room of the suite franticly.

Kev watched me panic, holding my hands together and pacing the floor. He watched the roses be trampled as I walked back and forth across them with my bare feet, not even remembering how beautiful I thought they were the night before.

Kev watched his wife lose control of her happy new life.

"Stop!" Kev said. "Reese, calm down, everything's okay. I was just thinkin' 'bout Jay. He sounds so sad because of what he did to you. That's all, baby. No big deal."

He watched me sit in the middle of the floor where the roses were. He came over and sat on the ground with me in the middle of the roses and held me. He bent his head down and kissed me softly on the forehead.

"Everything is fine. You have to remember that's my best friend. I'm gonna feel a little down at times. I just can't talk to him right now." He looked at his cell and turned it off. He got up and threw it on the couch and walked away. Even though Kev fell in love with me, he and Jason were friends and the fact that everything went down the way it did was hurting him I'm sure. Seemed as if he was realizing that his relationship with Jason was no more; he had to close that door for good.

"Come on, let's get ready to go." He smiled and led me to the bedroom.

I followed him, deep in thought.

Kev must have known I was very worried. Because he continued with his reassuring words. "Don't worry, baby, everything is fine, you understand. Don't you worry about a thing. I'm with you, you're my wife. You hear me?" He touched my chin and pulled my head up. "You hear me?"

I knew he was for real. "Yes, I hear you. Everything is everything." I smiled halfheartedly.

While I sat waiting for Kev to come out the bathroom I got angry thinking about Jason's call to Kev. I didn't feel sorry for Jason. I knew it was some kind of act or trick to get me back.

"Manipulation!" I shouted and shook my head. I knew Jason knew that Kev could get in contact with me and possibly talk me into going back to him like he had done so many times before.

"He got a lot of nerve!" I chuckled. "He sitting in Aruba with Eva and claiming to be worried about me. Wow, he's crazy, a dang-on psychopath!" Then I whispered, "I was crazy too for putting up with him. No more!"

"Reese! Reese! You okay, babe? Why you sitting there like that?" Kev asked, exiting the bathroom.

He was touching my shoulder and trying to get me to respond. I finally looked at him and said. "Oh, hey, you scared me." I grabbed my heart as if I was frightened. "What did you say?" I asked.

"I asked you if you were all right, baby. You were sittin' here in deep thought. What were you thinkin' about?"

I looked at him for a long time and meditated on my response. "Babe, I'm fine," I lied, not wanting to ruin the day any more than Jason's phone call had. "I was just sitting here thinking about you."

I got up off the couch and put my arms around Kev and gave him a hug and a kiss on the cheek. "I love you," I said as I was holding him tight. I glared into the wall as I held on to his muscular frame and wished that I could tell him everything.

"Where we goin' first, honey?"

"To eat, I am so hungry." I held my stomach to show him.

"Let's go," he replied.

I showered and got dressed. I grabbed my purse and walked out of the suite behind Kev.

"Let's walk," I said. "It will be fun." I smiled.

"All right, let's walk." He pointed down the street toward McDonald's and laughed. "You wanna go there?"

I smiled and said, "No. Stop playin'. I can eat McDonald's in Columbus. I didn't come all the way here for that."

"Babe," Kev said, "I think we both got far more than we came here for."

Chapter 24

Confessions

By the time we got back to our suite, we were exhausted and had all kinds of shopping bags. I went through the shopping bags looking at all the things we had bought for the boys while Kev sat and watched me.

"You just gonna sit there and watch me? No help?" I teased.

"Babe, I'm exhausted, to tell ya the truth." Kev sat on the edge of the bed, taking his tennis shoes off.

I was ranting on and on about everything I had seen on the strip that day, the crazy people, and the hustle and bustle of Vegas. "I absolutely love this place!" I screamed, then ran over to where he sat and jumped on him. "I wonder what the boys are doing."

Kev laughed because he knew I wanted to call them or have them come up for a little while. "Baby, go 'head and call 'em. Maybe they can come up and eat with us or something."

"Okay, I would love that." I went over to my purse, grabbed my cell and dialed Toya. "Hey, what y'all doing?"

"Hey, Reese, we at the pool. The boys are havin' a blast! We met a nice guy who has his sons here too, and they are about the same age as the boys," Toya added.

"Okay, sounds like you met a friend," I joked.

"I don't know. He's pretty cool though. I didn't think I'd hear from you for a few days!" Toya laughed.

"Yeah, I just missed the boys."

"I can bring them up if you like."

"Oh, no, they sound like they are having fun. I'll call them later. Tell 'em I love them." I smiled and hung up, walked back over to Kev, and sat on his lap. "Well, back to you then."

I gently touched his face, then I took my finger and outlined his eyes and nose with it. "You are so beautiful, Kev," I whispered in his ear.

"Reese, baby, men aren't beautiful."

"You are."

He took off my sandals and massaged my feet. "Let me take care of you tonight."

He called room service and ordered us a romantic dinner in our suite before going to bed. He ordered two lobsters, baked potatoes, salad, and chocolate cake for dessert. It all sounded so good to me.

"Let's just relax," Kev suggested as he yawned. I could tell he was worn out. To be honest I was tired too. I loved the fact that he was so attentive to me. The way he kissed me, touched me, and loved me made me feel beautiful.

"I want you to enjoy the time we have together here and not meditate on anything else or anyone else, but I did want to tell you that I think I have everything planned out so we can get out of the situation with Jason and move away without a trace behind us."

Room service knocked on the door shortly after and Kev got up, went to the door, and got the food. I got off the bed and went on the balcony and Kev followed me with the food. As we ate we continued to talk about the plan.

"Okay, Kev, what's the plan?" I was excited. I wanted to know everything that our future held. And to get another shot of happiness was a blessing that I knew came from heaven.

"Not now, Reese. Trust me, I got this, but now is the time to focus on making you happy while we are here."

"Well, baby, I wanna hear. I wanna know what our next move is."

"We will discuss it later. You have been through hell and all I want to do now is create a little bit of heaven on earth for my wife."

I knew Kev well. We had become friends and gotten close over the years so I knew that Kev learned from his father how to treat women with respect and to protect his wife at all cost.

"Baby, what you thinkin' 'bout?" I asked him.

He smiled and looked down at his watch. He got up. "It's after ten. Time is going fast."

"I didn't realize it was that late. I'm getting sleepy," I said while I stretched my arms over my head.

"I know you're tired. A lot has happened in the past few days." He looked over the balcony with me, then massaged my shoulders.

"Umm, that feels so good." I turned to him, "Thank you for the massage. You know exactly what I need. I love you."

Kev had his hands on my shoulders. I was standing face to face with my husband. He took his hand and moved my hair out of my face with his finger. "I love you too. I want you to know that I am so proud that you are my wife."

Knowing there was still so much I needed to share with Kev, I didn't feel so proud of myself. "Kev, I need to tell you something." I took a deep breath. "I was so angry and have been so angry at Jason for some of the things he has done to me." Kev tried to interrupt and tell me I didn't have to explain any of my actions. "No, Kev, I have to tell you this. You're my husband," I said with a stern look. "Jason did a lot of things to me. He has raped me, he has beat me, he has spit on me, he has taken away a lot from me and I do not like him for that."

I didn't know what was going to happen after I came clean. *Will he divorce me? What will he do?* I wondered. I hoped he knew how much I needed him. "Kev, out of all that he has done and as much as I hate him, nothing compares to when I saw him kill Shy." Kev sat down in the chair on the balcony.

Kev put his hands on top of his head, then his eyebrows slanted in, his eyes turned red, and his face turned redder. He began to cry. "What are you talkin' about Reese? Jay wouldn't do that. Tell me you lyin'. Tell me!" He yelled and got up from his chair, pushed it out the way and walked out the hotel room, running into the server from our room service.

I laid on the bed, put my hands over my face, and cried. I thought it was over that fast. He didn't even believe me.

I waited in our suite for hours and he never showed up. I cried myself to sleep and when I woke up and looked at the alarm clock it was four-thirty in the morning. I didn't know where Kev went or if he was coming back. However, I knew he needed to know the truth about everything.

I got up, put my Nike sandals on, and decided to go find my husband. We were going to get through this together.

I looked for him in the casino but he wasn't there so I went outside. That's where I found him sitting on the bench with his head down and his elbows on his knee. A hand was on his head and he was deep in thought.

"Kev," I called out.

He looked up and saw me coming. He then put his head down.

"Where you been, babe?" I asked.

"I've been outside the hotel pacing back and forth." He lifted his head up and looked at me. "Baby, I know you wasn't lying. I could feel it. Besides I always felt Jason was hiding the truth about the situation with Shy. Jason's story never added up. I'm sorry, babe, it's just blowin' my mind. I could have . . ."

I bent down and put my head down where his was. "Kev, don't do that. Jason did this. It's not your fault."

"But, babe, I could've . . ." His words trailed off as he shook his head and stood up. He helped me up and walked away from the bench. He had his back turned toward me.

"Jason is out of control, Reese. I didn't know he was gettin' down like that and I thought I knew everything about him." He turned around and looked at me. "Babe, I gotta get you and the boys out of here."

I looked over at the bench and thought how a couple days ago we sat at this same bench and he had proposed. I went over to him and stood there in front of him. He looked into my eyes.

"Baby, your eyes are bloodshot red from crying. Babe, don't cry anymore. I got you. I promise Jason will not hurt us." Kev held his arms out and I slowly walked over to him, and leaned against him.

"What really hurt me more is knowing you had to see him do that to Shy."

I pulled his face up with my hand and made him look at me. "I love you," I confessed.

He turned his head away again; then he looked back and grabbed me closer to him. “I love you too.” He went and sat back down on the bench.

“Kev, I have something else to tell you.” I sat down beside him on the bench.

“So, what else is there?” I could hear the frustration in his voice.

I closed my eyes for a moment longer, then opened them and said, “Kev, I took the money.”

Kev didn’t move. He didn’t change his expression or body language. He just sat there.

“I’m sorry, Kev. I am. I just—”

“Where is it, Reese?”

“It’s in a safety deposit box.”

“Where?” Kev asked anxiously.

“It’s in Ohio,” I explained.

Kev grabbed his head and swiftly put his head down, then jumped up off the bench. “Ohio? So you tellin’ me I gotta send you back to Ohio?” Kev turned away.

I remembered that I had forgotten the key at my place back in Columbus. I didn’t say anything to Kev though; I knew he was upset and he had thought we could leave from Vegas and never return to the city. Now, because of me, we would have to make a pit stop back to Ohio.

I watched Kev and could tell he was flaming mad at me, but I also worried he would do something to Jason because of Shy. I wanted him to walk away from it all. I was even willing to leave the money if need be.

Kev didn’t say anything else. He walked back toward the hotel.

I stayed on the bench and cried. I thought I had lost him because of my lies. I held my head down and stared at the concrete, wondering what to do.

"Hey, you comin', baby?"

When I looked up Kev was standing there. He reached out and grabbed my hand. He kissed my hand, then he said, "Babe, we in this together."

I loved that man. I realized I had never felt this way before nor had I ever felt someone love me with the type of intensity that Kev did.

I whispered, "Thank you, Jesus, I love you. You are a great big loving God."

"What you say? I heard you talkin'. Were you talking to me?"

I smiled, then responded, "No, I was talking about you." Kev and I headed back to the hotel. We now had to come up with a plan B.

Chapter 25

Movin' Backward

"Reese, Reese." Kev shook me, trying to wake me. "You're havin' a bad dream, honey, wake up!"

I opened my eyes. I was still breathing fast, panting, and holding my heart with my hand. I sat up in bed and took a deep breath and turned to Kev. I stared at him a few more seconds before I spoke.

"I had a nightmare!" I proclaimed. "Jason is crazy!" I said while I held on to Kev's cheeks softly with both of my hands.

"Babe, I got him under control."

"The dream was so real, besides, God don't like ugly and I'm tired of living like this. If we walk away from it all and dedicate our lives back to Christ, He will fix it. I know it's true, Kev. I've seen Him do it before."

"Look, Reese, I hear you. I don't even care if we take the money and give it away. I just know Jason isn't going to stop looking for us if I just disappear. He will suspect something; he's tricky, baby. I just want you and the boys to be safe. Let me handle Jason, okay?"

He hugged me and held on real tight. "Reese, we been here for almost a week and tomorrow we're goin' back to Ohio. That wasn't the plan for you to go back to Ohio, but now that you came clean about the cash . . ." He looked at me. "When we get back you go clean out the safety deposit box and I'll go to Toya's and get the boys.

So when you go in, hurry and grab what you need. I'll get you and the boys on the first plane out of Ohio." Kev was serious. I listened as he orchestrated the plan.

"Well at least you get your money back you gave Jason." I laughed.

"Reese, now is not the time for jokes, baby, this is serious. Jay is dangerous," Kev explained.

I knew better than anyone how dangerous Jason was. I watched him murder Shy. I experienced him beating me and leaving bruises, black eyes, busted lips, broken fingers, and so on and so on. "I'm sorry, baby, really I am. Okay, where we going?" I asked.

"I'm not telling you that until you're on the way to the airport. The less you know the better this plan will work, besides, I know you, woman. You'll tell the women you met here, call Toya and God knows who else." Kev was so tense. "Plus, Jason been blowing my cell up. He says he needs me to find you, so I'll play into his wishes until you and the boys are safe."

"I wish he would stop looking for me and just leave me alone."

Kev held my hands together and used one to softly rub the other; I was nervous.

"What time we leaving in the morning?" I asked.

"Nine-thirty."

"Okay," I agreed. However, I was afraid. I had seen Jason in action when he felt betrayed.

"Good night, honey, we need to try to go back to sleep. See you in the morning." Kev yawned.

"Night," I said and then, immediately, I started praying. "Lord, we need you. We are ready to end this life and serve you, just one more day, Jesus, I promise." I closed my eyes and fell back to sleep.

***

Kev had gotten back up out of the bed. My eyes were closed but I wasn't asleep. I guessed he couldn't sleep either. I could feel him look at me; then he kissed me on the lips softly. He took me out of his arms and laid me on my pillows. I never moved as he thought I was sound asleep.

I definitely couldn't sleep with him out the bed 'cause I knew he was worrying. I started to think and wonder if all of this was worth the chance we were taking to get away. One thing I knew was the crew would definitely side with Jay because they would feel we, me and Kev, had betrayed him. That was a whole other can of worms we opened. My stomach was sick. I was so scared and I was feeling that this was gonna end real bad; for us, that was.

Kev had been up 'til four-thirty in the morning trying to work through his plan. I heard him talking to himself. He sounded frustrated. He had it together but we both knew he couldn't trust anyone to help him. We couldn't take that chance.

I must have dosed off waiting for Kev to get in the bed. I woke up and turned to the clock that hung in the bedroom of our suite. *It's six in the morning*. I sat up in the bed and swung my legs around to the side, put on my house shoes, and got out of bed.

"Kev," I called out. "Where are you?" I reached the front room and saw him sitting on the couch, drinking orange juice and reading the Vegas newspaper.

"Hey, honey, how you feelin' this morning?" Kev got up and escorted me over to the balcony where my breakfast awaited.

"Oh, babe, thanks," I smiled.

He pulled the chair out for me, and I gave him a kiss. "Don't tell me you been in here all night? It's not that serious, Kev. Jason isn't coming after us. We are being paranoid because we feel we did something wrong, but, babe, I thought about it and thought about it all night. I know we didn't do anything wrong. We're in love, that's all," I said so convincingly.

"Yeah, babe, I hear you, but wit' Jason, you have to be careful." He sat across from me and we ate. "Enough talk about him." He jumped up and clapped his hands. "It's time to go! I'm excited about goin' home and you should be too. We picking up the boys after all. Huh?"

I nodded my head in agreement and smiled. "I am excited. I get to see and hold my boys again." I swung around and held myself as if I were dancing. "I know they're here, but it seems like forever since I've seen them, touched them, held them." My voice grew softer and softer as I spoke about them. "I love them. I can't wait to get settled somewhere and just live. You know what I mean?" I stared at Kev, waiting for his reply.

"Yeah, I do," he answered.

Kev decided not to say anything else about Jason; not even in spite of Jason calling and texting him with concern about me. He thought it would be best to let me relax on the way home.

Kev looked around the suite at all the bags packed and chuckled. "We had nothing when we got here and now it looks like we have everything but the kitchen sink packed up."

I joined in laughing.

"I'm gonna call downstairs for help so we won't be late to the airport." He reached for the hotel phone.

My eyes glanced around the room to see if we were forgetting anything. The couple of things I spotted I hurried and added to our things. Shortly after he called downstairs someone was knocking on the door to assist us. We left our suite, and called Toya to make sure she and the boys were on their way to the airport. Once in the lobby Kev turned in the hotel keys. We loaded the rental car, then headed to the airport. While Kev drove I questioned him about leaving Columbus for good.

"Kev, when do you think we are leaving Columbus?"

"Oh, you and the boys will be in Ohio just long enough for you to get the key to the safety deposit box and only the things you need out the house." He looked at me, making sure I understood. I nodded my understanding.

"I will pick up the boys while you do that. After I pick them up I'll swing back by your house to get you. Be ready. Okay?" Kev said firmly.

"Okay, okay, I'll be ready." I was being sarcastic. I wasn't interested in camping out in Columbus any longer than I had to.

Once we arrived at the airport, Kev unloaded the rental in the front. Me and Toya got the boys out and we waited for Kev to return the rental and come back so we could get situated and then board the plane.

Kev took the car down to the end of the airport strip; we could still see him. Toya chased after the boys running wild and I stood and watched Kev. He went to the front of the little desk at the rental car place and handed them the keys. He signed off on the paperwork, put the paper in his back pocket, then jogged back down to where we were standing.

"You ready?" Kev asked and gave me a big hug.

"Yes." I admired him.

"Let's go." He looked over to the boys who were running all around the outside of the airport. Kev shook his head then said, "Boys, come on. It's time to go." He grabbed an airport cart and began putting the luggage on it.

We went through the airport and security, then boarded our plane. Shortly after we sat down I'd fallen asleep and the boys were right beside me. Before waking us I'd heard Kev and Toya talking.

"I'm excited about sharing a life with Reese and the boys," he told her.

"I'm so happy for y'all, Kev. You both deserve it," Toya replied.

"I'm so ready to turn it all the way around. I'm tired of the so-called gangster life and all the drama that comes along with it."

"Praise God!"

"I remember being in church as a boy and believing Jesus, Toya. I want my family to experience that."

"Wow, Kev, I didn't know that about you. Now Reese, she knows Jesus real well, so I am happy she has someone like you to lead her back into His arms."

"Toya, Reese been tellin' me about Jesus since I've known her and how we both needed to get it together. I'm ready now." He smiled then said aloud, "I remember you, Lord. It's over for me, Jesus. You got me. I hated some of the choices and decisions I've had made in the past. I know I had to change. I even hate some of the things I witnessed or ordered to happen to people." He paused. "Oh God, I'm sorry, Jesus. I'm so sorry, Lord; please forgive me."

I was so blessed, so grateful, and realized I didn't deserve anything that God had done for me. All the hell I had caused but yet God! I thought.

Although I'd been half awake listening to Toya minister to Kev, when he woke me I flinched from been fully asleep. I stretched my arms and sighed and said, "Okay, okay, I'm up."

Kev was standing and getting the luggage that was in the overhead. He got the boys up and Toya helped.

"You ready? We need to get the tickets to Arizona and go to baggage claim and get the luggage."

My eyes got big and sparkled. "Arizona? It's beautiful there." I smiled. I could have gone anywhere as long as my boys and Kev were going.

"Yeah, but did you hear me? I'm going with you, now. We need to stay together. Forget Jason; let's just bounce. That sound good to you, baby?" he asked.

"Yes!" I jumped up, threw my arms around his neck, and wouldn't let go. I kissed his cheeks for what felt like the thousandth time. After I stopped, Kev picked up Gabe, and put his arm around me as we walked slow through the airport hallways. "We will never be in Ohio again."

I had stopped at the baggage claim and watched Kev continue to walk. I looked at him and allowed him to take a few more steps then yelled, "Hello, here's the luggage! What are you thinkin' about?" I asked.

"Nothin', just excited 'bout where we are goin', you know what I mean. Fun in the sun, baby!" He grinned, showing his pretty white teeth.

"All we need to do now is check this luggage in so we don't have to bring it back in. I'm gonna walk over and take care of that while you and Toya say good-bye. Come on, boys, you guys can help me!" The boys ran over to Kev, excited. Kev came over to me and kissed me. "We'll be right back."

Toya was walking up after going to the bathroom. "Oh, Lord, now what?" she joked.

"We are going to Arizona."

"I'm gonna miss y'all. Kev taking my babies away, but I understand and I'm glad, 'cause Jason is unpredictable and he's gonna be upset when he finds out you two are married. And that's an understatement! But, Reese, I am so happy for you; you deserve a good man like Kev and he absolutely adores you and has for years." We hugged.

"I remember a few years back we were all at your house. Jason had got mad and tried to fight you. But I watched Kev; he watched you and he talked to Jason so he wouldn't hurt you. I knew then he was in love with you. It was the way he looked at you that made me know."

Toya said, "Me and him were outside talkin' that night and I asked him." She giggled. "I wanted to know." Toya held her hands up like, "I'm caught." "He denied it at first but then he watched you from the outside, in the window, and his eyes never left you and I knew then his heart wouldn't either."

"Aw, Toya. Why didn't you ever tell me that story?" I hugged her again.

"Reese, you wasn't ready. And besides Kev was cool but he was in too deep back then."

I whispered, "But look at how things change."

"Look at God." Toya pointed upward and smiled.

"Hi, Mommy!" Michael was excited. He and Gabe ran from where Kev was over to me and Toya. "Did you get us somethin', Mommy?"

"Of course I did. I got you a bunch of stuff I think you'll like." I grabbed him and kissed his cheeks all over.

"Mommy, Kev said we getting on another airplane today. Are we?"

"Yes, baby, remember I told you we were going to a new place?"

"Yes."

"Well, Kev is going with us too. Will you like that?"

"Yes, Mommy, yay!" The boys jumped up and down.

I kissed the boys good-bye. I sniffed in and smelled their little-boy scents. I then let them go with Toya for the last time. I would soon be the mother they deserved.

Chapter 26

Letting Go

I knew I couldn't have any ties with Toya once we left Ohio. I knew Jason would do something stupid and I didn't want him to do anything to her. He knew how close we were.

"I will call you when I get settled okay?" I told Toya.

"Okay," Toya replied.

"Thank you, little sis, I love you."

"Love you too."

"Okay, talk to you soon. Be good and let me know if you need anything."

"I will."

I was going to miss her. I watched them walk out of the airport until I couldn't see them anymore.

"You okay? Baby? You okay?" Kev sounded very concerned.

I looked up; I didn't realize Kev was standing there talking to me. I wiped my eyes and said, "Yeah, I'm fine. Just saying my good-byes to Toya. I realize I'm gonna miss her so much." I stood up and lay against Kev's chest for comfort.

He put his arms around me. "Don't worry, babe, it's all going to work out," he assured me for the millionth time, yet I still needed more convincing.

We loaded up in Kev's truck that we had parked at the airport. I watched Kev dip in and out of the traffic as he drove. I knew that I was getting closer and closer to walking right out of my miserable life. I was excited. I could feel somersaults in my belly flipping.

"I'm so nervous," I said aloud.

"Why?" Kev responded.

"I don't know. I guess it's from everything that has happened over the last week. It's been a crazy ride, huh?" I said, then looked up at Kev with my head still lying on his shoulder.

"Yeah, I guess it has." He smirked.

"But you know what?" I touched his hand softly.

"What?" He glanced over at me.

"I am so glad it happened." I sunk my head deeper into his arm.

"I knew I loved you from the first time we had a conversation. There was something special about you, Reese." He kissed my forehead.

I just shook my head, still in disbelief I was about to live a fairytale life. "I love you so much. I am so excited." I put the visor down and looked at myself in the mirror. Kev watched as I fiddled with my hair and gave a few model looks. He laughed to himself while watching me.

All of a sudden his phone started vibrating.

"Hello," he answered.

"What's good? You in Ohio?" a deep voice asked. His volume was turned up so high, I could pretty much hear everything the male caller was saying. I just hadn't made out the voice yet.

"Who is this?" Kev questioned.

"It's me, Jason."

"This don't sound like Jay, who is this?" Kev demanded.

"It's me, Kev. I got a new cell. Maybe it's because you don't recognize the number or somethin'. I don't know but it's me, man. Where you at? You in the CO or what?" Jason asked.

"Oh, what's up, man? Na, I'll be back there in a few. What's good?" Kev lied.

"Nothin', man, just wanted to see where you are."

"You in Columbus?" Kev asked.

"Not yet, I'll be back in a few," Jason answered.

"What is a few? Days? Weeks? Hours? What, man?" Kev replied.

"Hours. We just got to Florida." Jason chuckled. "I'll be there in a few hours. All right, man, I guess I'll see you then," Jason said.

"Yeah, I'll see you then. One," Kev said and waited for Jason to reply.

Silence fell between them, and then Jason answered, "Yeah, one," and the line clicked dead.

Kev hung up the phone. I never said a word about the conversation, I just said softly, "Let's hurry and get out of here."

"Okay, babe, we will." Kev reached over and touched my shoulder for comfort. After the call I was nervous again. I looked over at Kev and stared at him.

"Jason wants to ring my neck! Not to mention I'm married to the man of my dreams and can't even share it with the ones I love. This is crazy!" I stared out the window as we got closer to my house.

"Baby, we have to be smarter than Jason. He has the whole crew behind him. It would be nice to ride off into the sunset, but in order for us to live normal lives, we need to bounce. Plain and simple, babe, bounce."

Kev was getting anxious. And I didn't blame him. I didn't know whether we could trust Jason's whereabouts.

Kev took me by the arm and pulled me over to him and hugged me. "We will be out this city within a few hours, babe."

I nodded, trying to stay positive.

"You know, Reese, I gotta tell you, I've been really thinkin' bout what you said about Jesus, and I think we need to get it right with Him too for real."

"Kev, we have to. We have to change our lives around because if we don't, nothin' will work out for us. I don't know about you, but I've done a lot of dirt that I ain't proud of and I know better than doin." I put my head down 'cause I felt horrible about leaving my walk with Jesus.

"I know what you mean, but we gonna get it right, okay? Don't sweat it. My grandma always told me that God would forgive."

"I can remember walking in the will of God and trusting Him no matter what," I whispered as though I knew God was listening. I looked over at Kev as he drove, slowly turning into my driveway.

"I just don't know what happened, or where I went wrong. I just don't know," I softly said.

"Don't worry 'bout it, Reese. One day we'll both be sharing testimonies to someone who needs to hear them."

We both laughed.

"I just look back at my life and think how much my grandparents instilled in me about Christ, living right, and making the right choices, and here I am jacked up," I cried.

"The good thing about Jesus is He forgives. That's something you never need to forget," he said.

"I don't, but I understand that sometimes we wait too long. Sometimes we need to repent to Him a little sooner and cry out to Him a little more frequently before He decides enough is enough and He sends His judgment on us," I said, then turned and stared out the window.

"Reese, don't be so deep," he said. "We'll be in Arizona in a few."

I watched his bottom lip curl up as he smiled and that made me feel a little better. "Yeah, you are right. God will forgive us. He has given us a new day! I'm gonna stop all this drama and go in the house and get everything together. I'll probably be standing on the curb when you get back, 'cause that's how bad I want to get out of here!" I laughed.

"That's what I want to hear!" Kev replied. "Reese, before you go I want you to take this." He reached under his seat and pulled out a gun and laid it on my lap.

I started trembling and shaking my head no. "No, Kev, I don't want this. Please, get it off of me," I screamed.

"But, Reese, just in case he shows up here actin' silly."

I stopped him. "Kev, I'm okay. Look around. Jason isn't out here. By the time he gets here we will be gone."

"Look it's already ready. All you have to do is aim and shoot. Please, baby. Take it, please," he begged.

I looked at the gun on my lap for a few more seconds then said, "No, I trust God has this under control. We are getting it together, Kev. Jason isn't here. God is." My eyes started to water because I truly felt the presence of God. I smiled and touched Kev's hand. I picked up the gun and laid it on Kev's lap softly, touched his chin, and guided his face to look in my eyes.

"Get rid of it. We don't need this. You don't need this anymore. God is our protector now!" And I meant that with all of my heart. Hopefully it was true.

Chapter 27

Leavin' Ohio

I touched the handle of the car to exit when Kev stopped me. "Babe, you not gonna give me some suga' before you go in the house?"

I turned around and looked at him. He had his eyes closed and lips poked out for me to kiss him. I leaned in to him, closed my eyes, and kissed him.

"That's better. Love you." He smiled.

"I love you too. Let me get in here and get this stuff so we can leave. I'll have everything ready when you get back."

"All right."

I turned and looked at him as I was getting out the car. "Kev, what made you give me that gun?"

"I don't know, just in case, you know? I really don't believe Jason is here but for a moment . . ." His words trailed off. He didn't finish his statement.

I got out the car and walked toward the front door. Kev rolled down his window and hollered, "You want me to come in with you? I can wait for you, then we both can get the boys and leave."

I didn't think he needed to come in. I figured I was good. "Don't be silly, I'm fine. I'll lock the door soon as I get in the house. Kev?" I frowned up my face and stated, "Jason ain't thinkin' about me." I then smirked. "He's moved on to the next hottest thing around, you know how he do it."

Without ever saying another word to him I opened the door, turned, and blew Kev a kiss with my hand. He sat there for a minute watching me and slowing down the last few minutes we were sharing in silence before I went in the house. His eyes were stuck on me while I puckered my lips and closed my eyes and aimed that kiss at him.

I walked inside my house. I thought how odd it was that the television was on. *I don't remember leaving it on,* I thought. I walked from the foyer into the living room. I took my shoes off and went to walk through the living room to the kitchen for a soda. As I stood there fiddling with my shoe strap, someone grabbed me around my waist. I turned around and looked; it was Jason. I tried to run. I reached the front door and turned the knob, when I saw Jason's hand on the lock. He stood behind me and whispered in my ear. He never moved his hand off the front door.

"I'm not playin' wit' you. If you go out the door everything you love will die today!"

I cried out hysterically, knowing that this was my end. I turned around and let the doorknob go slowly. I walked toward him then stopped, deciding to take the punishment. Better me than everything I loved.

"Well, I see you been busy the last week in Vegas. Oh yeah, congratulations. You did get married didn't you?"

My eyes got big. Jason knew everything. I dropped my purse right there on the floor. I was afraid but the way I saw it, the only way for survival was to hear exactly what he knew. It was a surprise, but I let him continue.

"Reese, what you think? I wasn't gonna find out about this? Come on now, baby girl, you been around me for too long. You should know I find out everything."

He dropped pictures on the table of me and Kev while we were in Vegas. I glanced down a t them. We were holding hands, walking the strip, and he even had some from the wedding ceremony.

"I can't wait to get Kev, he's dead! Supposed to be ma'boy!" He started tearing the pictures up.

My eyes were gazing around the house, looking for a way to escape, but I couldn't think of anything. *If only I had taken the gun Kev was trying to give me.* I noticed the gloves he was wearing, then the black clothing he had on along with plastic Baggies that covered his shoes. I was scared.

"So, Reese, let's get this party started." He put the blunt he was smoking in the ashtray on the table in front of him, turned the television off with the remote, leaned back in his seat, and folded his hands.

"You don't have nothin' to say? Huh, Reese, you don't think you owe me anything? You was just gonna leave me and not say a word? Huh? That's not right. I told you, baby, the only way out of this is a body bag. You didn't believe me? You must have thought I was kidding, huh?"

I started to cry harder, and that's when I noticed the gun lying on the table. I thought about trying to grab it quickly. *What do I have to lose?*

His eyes traveled to where mine were looking. "I wish you would reach for that gun." He laughed, and then his face went grim as he got off the couch. He picked up the gun and walked over to me.

"You really gonna stand there and not beg me? Beg for yo' life, Reese. Beg me, like Shy did that day in the warehouse. Remember that?"

I couldn't control my body from shaking.

"Beg me, Reese!" he demanded. "Beg for your worthless life!" He touched my face with his hand, then put the gun to my temple.

I closed my eyes. I knew he was going to shoot me. "No, Jay, please! Don't do this!" I stooped down and covered myself.

"Get up!" he commanded and stood me up. He was hurting my arm 'cause he snatched me off the floor fast and hard.

"Let me look at you one more time." His voice softened. He took the gun and began to stroke my face with it softly. "You are so beautiful, Reese. Too bad your husband isn't here to protect you this time, huh? You thought he would always protect you. Is that what you thought?" He was now eye to eye with me.

"I'm gonna do him, Reese. This is real personal. I don't care what happened between us. Kev was never to touch you! And he went off and married you? I'ma kill him!" He shook his head back and forth real slow. "I just wish he would have come in here with you. I would have killed you right in front of him before I tortured him. What kinda friend steals their best friend's woman?"

I never responded. I just watched him and knew he was insane. He pushed my head with the tip of the gun and I stumbled back. "Jason, please, I'm beggin' you not to do this. What about my boys?" I pleaded.

"Oh, da boys will be fine. They got a daddy, matter of fact, they got two now!" He laughed. "Besides, they too young to remember this. They won't even remember you when they get older. Oh yeah, their daddy got a new wife, she'll raise 'em," he explained like it was nothing.

"You don't get it, I don't care. You tried to make me look like a fool, Reese. You out there in Vegas wit' my boy!" He hit his chest in anger. "And on top of all of that you marry him? Seriously, I started to come kill you there!" He continued in my face, one minute laughing, the next enraged. "But I waited. I wasn't about to spend no money to come out there for y'all. You ain't even worth it. Besides, I was havin' too much fun wit' Eva in Aruba." He laughed. "Yep, you were right. I was wit' Eva." He cocked the gun and kept it at my right temple.

I dared not open my mouth about him and Eva. But I dared not keep my mouth closed either. At that very moment I did the only thing I knew I could do. I began to pray aloud, "Jesus, I need you!" I screamed. I knew He was all I had. If there was to be a miracle, Jesus would have to be behind it. This man was standing in my face, in my house, with a gun to my head, and I knew without a doubt that he was going to shoot it!

Jason laughed. "Oh, now you wanna call on Jesus. You should have thought about that awhile ago don't you think? I don't think He's comin', Reese. You've done too much. It's over!"

The next thing I knew I heard a loud boom that deafened me. There was a ringing in my ears and I could feel the side of my head open. It was as if my head was exploding. I was dazed as I placed my hands over my ears. I staggered, trying to grab hold of anything I could so I wouldn't fall. That's when I saw it: my bloody trail of fingerprints.

I could see Jason standing silent, watching to see what I was going to do and looking on like a child that started a fire that was out of control.

Everything happened so fast after he pulled that trigger. I locked eyes with him while I was falling as if I wanted to ask him why. *Why would you do this to me? Was it really that serious to take my life from me*?

I hit the ground hard and Jason walked up to me, put his hands on his knees, and bent down. He kissed me on the forehead and stared at me for a few more seconds. He shook his head, sucked his teeth, and prepared to get out of there before anyone came.

He calmly walked over to my blinds and looked outside, I guessed to see if anyone was out there who might have heard the shot. Jason hurried and wiped off the gun and laid it beside my body. He wiped down everything he had touched as I lay there helpless, dying. Then he looked at me and started walking in my direction. My heart was pumping fast and my eyes screamed out, *stop* . . . I thought he was going to shoot me again. I closed my eyes and waited. . . .

"I love you, girl; sorry I had to do this to you," he whispered in my ear, then kissed me on the cheek. "Oh yeah, and Jesus ain't comin' for you."

I lay there and watched him put on his coat, and head toward the kitchen. My heart was racing and I even thought I could hear it beating. I heard a loud noise come from the kitchen; then I realized it was the back door shutting and that's when I knew he was gone. I remembered taking in one last breath before everything went black, and I was gone too. . . .

Chapter 28

The View From the Living Room Floor

My eyes shot open as if I'd been lying on the floor taking a nap and had awoken with a second wind. I couldn't move or reach for my cell but could feel it vibrating in my pocket as I lay there in a pool of my own blood. I knew it was Kev calling, telling me he was on his way, but there was nothing I could do. I felt paralyzed.

I thought, *I don't want my sons to see me die like this. Please, Jesus, don't allow them to see me like this.* I felt the blood running down the side of my face. *Jesus!* I screamed in my head. *Help me, Lord! Please!*

All I could do was lay there and cry out. My body was motionless. By now Jason was long gone I was sure, with a plan not to ever be caught or step foot in Ohio again.

However, I wasn't worried about him; I was worried about Kev and my sons, hoping they would make it safely out of Ohio without any problem. I knew Kev would know to get as far away from there as possible. He couldn't think about me; he had to think about the boys and himself now.

I waited in the midst of death and listened to my heartbeat slow down minute by minute. As I lay there I could see the portrait that me and my sons had taken for Christmas hanging on the wall. I smiled in my heart and made that my reason to hold on to life.

I love them, Jesus, please don't let me die.

Michael, my son, his brown eyes seemed to gaze in my eyes through the portrait. I wondered why I waited so late to realize how much they needed me, and beat myself up thinking how much I had let them down. I knew the choices that I had made got this outcome of what had taken place. I regretted every choice now and realized that what should have been important were the boys all along.

I stared at the portrait a few more minutes, blinking in between the stare and trying to force my eyes to stay open and focus on my boys. I tried to turn my head away from them for a moment because of the guilt I was feeling, but it was hopeless. I couldn't move. It was as if God held my head and forced me to see them.

So instead of looking at them I closed my eyes for a second; then I thought about the love I had for them and them for me, and I opened them back up and continued loving on my boys through the portrait, using them as strength to hold on. While I lay there in a pool forming of my own blood, I had to face the truth; I had put my own selfish needs over my sons.

When the truth hit me in my heart, oh how I ached. My God what a horrible feeling it was to learn something you can never do over again because its too late. What a horrible thing it was to be faced with death because I was a hurt, bitter, and a betrayed woman trying to get even with everybody who ever hurt me. What a price my babies would have to pay for my ignorance.

If I could do this all over again, I would do it different. But it was too late for that. I was in this and now realized that while I partied from state to state, sold drugs, used drugs, shopped, used and outsmarted men, I was the one being tricked all along. The devil had set me up, for my own life.

My eyes kept opening and closing as I became weaker and weaker and tried to hold on to life, but was so weak I knew I had to let go. My body fluids released out of me and my body started to convulse. There was nothing I could do. The situation was out of my control, and death was coming for me soon.

I felt myself stop shaking and then I drifted off.

Jesus, Jesus! I screamed out in my mind. *Please don't turn away from me! Please don't turn your face away from me.* I felt alone. I was breathing fast and loud, panting. *God, please! Please!*

I knew He was listening because I knew He loved me. I was just remembering, then realized my current situation. I could still feel my cell vibrating periodically but I couldn't do anything about it. I thought, *if only I could reach it and tell Kev what's goin' on.*

I opened my eyes and tried to focus on the portrait. It kept me hoping. I prayed someone would find me before it was too late. *Maybe somebody did hear the shot?* I wasn't sure; maybe they called the police and they were on their way to help me.

I cried while looking at the portrait. My boys were so happy and loved me more than anything and I knew it. The same way I'd loved Momma. I had watched Momma die like this. I couldn't share Momma's fate. I just couldn't. I begged.

As much of a fighter I was by nature, I felt I was in a hopeless situation. I knew Jason aimed the shot at my head, and even though I moved and it hit closer to my ear and neck, I understood that everyone I ever knew who was shot at point-blank range in the head died. I knew the odds were against me. I knew I was going to die.

My body was shivering and I could feel coldness and an eerie feeling running through my bones. I tried to sniff in some of the mucus that was coming out of my mouth and nose, but it didn't work. I tried to focus on the portrait until someone came for me. I stared at it for a few more minutes and began to dose off once again.

This time I couldn't open my eyes back up. This time there was nothing I could do but fall into what felt like a deep, permanent sleep.

Chapter 29

Heaven or Hell?

"Lord? Am I dreaming?" I felt a peace that I could not explain. "Lord?" When I opened my eyes I was in another place. I looked around the grand room and realized I was in someone's mansion. As I walked I thought that it seemed to be like a palace; something from a fairytale.

I began to walk around this extraordinary place with elegant pictures, drapes, and flooring unlike I had ever seen before in my whole life. I smiled and turned around in circles, amazed at the extremely high ceilings and the beautiful pillars and floors.

"Hello," I called out. I could hear an echo of my own voice. "Hello, where am I?" Then I continued to walk from one beautiful room to the next into this brilliant, warm light that seemed to create a warming sensation in my skin and bones.

I touched my arms and hands in awe of the tingling feelings I felt within. It felt as if I was glowing. A radiant light beamed on my face and neck. While I tiptoed across the golden floors I wondered where I was. I stopped for a moment and turned around to where I heard singing far off. It was beautiful music with awesome voices. I closed my eyes and imagined the beautiful and angelic faces of those who were singing what sounded like praises unto the Lord.

It dawned on me; I knew who I was looking for. I was looking for Jesus.

"Jesus?" I whispered. "Where are you?"

I grinned. I felt so good, like a little child looking for the one person in the world they loved the most!

I looked down at my feet and noticed I was barefoot; then I looked at the gown I was wearing. It was all white with gold and white lace woven down the front of it. I put my arm to my nose and smelled the most awesome fragrance coming from my body and wondered who cleaned me up, gave me this gown, and brought me to this beautiful place.

As I continued to walk the scene changed. I was now outdoors in a valley of green grass. I'd never seen grass this green before. And in the grass were all kind of flowers. Some flowers I'd seen before but others I had never seen. There was an aroma that was so overwhelming with the smell of the flowers. I went over to one of the flowers and closed my eyes and sniffed in. *How delightful,* I thought.

I came across a stream full of blue water and I bent down and cupped some of it in my hands. It was warm and smelled sweet. Just when I was about to drink the water I looked over to the right of the stream and saw a waterfall of water falling out of the sky. It amazed me; my eyes were lit up and I exhaled aloud.

I wondered how water could fall from the sky, and where was I to see such a thing? Then I saw little children running and playing in the water, jumping in and out with no fear. I laughed while I watched them play.

While all of this was happening I could still hear the singing and praising unto the Lord. I had a yearning to follow the voices. I turned to walk near the voices when some of the little children ran up to me and started singing, "Hosanna, Hosanna!" They were dressed in the same type of garment I was, but some wore gold and others wore white. On the little girls' heads were flowers made into wreaths. They continued singing and twirling around me and I laughed and sung with them. Then suddenly the children disappeared and I found myself all alone somewhere else, somewhere dark.

I turned around looking for the children. I was confused and wondered where they and the singing had gone. This scenery wasn't as pleasant as before. It was cynical and dark now. "Hello? Where did everybody go?" I was scared and felt alone. I wondered around slowly, looking at what seemed to be dead and burnt grass in the ground.

The brilliant light I once felt was gone and was replaced with gloom and despair in the air. I could hear growling and snarling and in the distance what seemed to be screams and pleas for help. I covered my nose with my hand from the unbearable smell that was there.

I walked around the place slow and cautious, wondering where I was. I looked down and noticed I was still wearing the beautiful gown and then I heard a voice saying, "Look at it again." The voice was strong and powerful.

"Who said that?" I turned around in a circle to find the voice that was speaking to me.

"Look at your beautiful gown again!" This time the voice seemed to be getting angry and closer, so I grabbed my head and covered myself. I was afraid of the voice. I was afraid period.

"My daughter, it's all right. I won't harm you. Look at it again. Please," the voice begged.

I stood up and looked at my hands first, then at the beautiful gown I wore. I began to scream hysterically and my hands shook uncontrollably.

"A-ha-ha! You killed Him! His blood is on your hands, Reese!" the voice proclaimed.

My hands and gown were covered with blood and I heard laughter that drowned out my screaming. I couldn't even hear myself scream it was so loud.

"We welcome today Reese Taylor Valan'." I could hear cheering and shouting all around. "See, Reese, you're special to us here because you are one of those humans who know God, served Him, then because of your own selfish desires decided to live and do what you want to on the earth, and that right there gets you attention when you come here," said the voice.

"I . . . I don't belong here. It's been a mistake, you're making a mistake. Please, stop, take this blood off of me!" I cried.

"No, no, we thank you because as I was saying you knew Him, like I did," the voice said quietly. "But, yet, you did it, exactly what I did. You crucified Him again. See look, look at His blood! Didn't you read your Bible, Reese? Peter 2:21 says, 'For it had been better for them not to have known the way of righteousness, than, after they have known it, to turn from the holy commandment delivered unto them.' Did you think He was joking when He said that? It wasn't a joke. You, my dear, have made a thousand promises to Him but never kept one of them!"

I shook my head back and forth, hoping to wake out of this nightmare. I was in hell!

"Jesus!" I screamed and went to the ground and lay as if dead, but there was no reply to my cry.

"Reese! Reese! Baby, talk to me! Wake up, Reese. Oh my God what happened? Did Jason do this to you, huh, baby?"

I opened my eyes to find myself at my house and Kev there with me. But I couldn't reply.

Kev was frantic, walking and pacing back and forth. He grabbed his cell and dialed 911. "Hello, my wife has been shot! Please send someone quickly. I'm not getting a response from her, please hurry!"

He grabbed his gun and bent down to me and whispered, "Hold on, baby, I'll be right back. Reese, is Jason still here?" Kev asked me but I couldn't answer.

I heard him go up the stairs quietly and slowly to see if Jason was still in the house. I heard him going to every room upstairs, looking everywhere; then he ran down the stairs to the kitchen.

"He went out the back door; the glass is busted back here!" I heard him hollering. He put the gun away and sat down beside me and gently picked my head and chest up and laid me across his lap. Kev began to cry. His tears dropped down on my cheek.

I was motionless, lying there with blood coming out the side of my mouth and head.

"Reese, hold on, babe," Kev demanded while he sat on the floor, rocking me back in forth for comfort. "I knew I shouldn't have left you. I'm sorry, baby. I should have stayed here; I know Jason is a snake!"

I could feel the tears falling on my cheek and into my eye. I looked up at Kev and tried to tell him with my eyes that everything was going to be okay. I formed my lips to talk but it was hard for me to get it out.

"What, babe? Take your time. What you trying to say?" Kev so desperately wanted to know. "Reese, I'm so sorry I left you here. Please forgive me. I didn't think he was gonna do anything."

I talked to him with my eyes, trying to let him know that it wasn't his fault and God was still in control of this. I continued to struggle to speak.

"Talk to me, baby," Kev said. "The boys are in the truck waiting for you. They can't wait to see you. Hold on, babe. The ambulance is comin'. You hear 'em? I promise they comin', Reese."

He looked down at me. I could tell by his face it was bad. My head was opened on the side, there was blood everywhere, and I had blood coming from my mouth.

I wanted Kev to know that God could do it, He could still give us a miracle. *He is able,* I wanted to scream. Tears ran down my face when I looked at Kev, not knowing if it was for the last time. I closed my eyes real tight and drifted back off.

"Reese! Reese!" a voice cried out in a singsong, teasing manner.

I lifted myself off the ground and looked around for the voice that was taunting me. I opened my mouth again and screamed out, "Jesus!" With everything I had I screamed and yelled for Him to come and save me. I had something to live for and I knew He was the only one who could save me from the pit of hell.

"Stop screaming that name! He's not coming for you! Don't you understand? You made an open shame of Him."

I grabbed my head and began to shake my head, then screamed out, "No," as loud as I could. "Jesus! Jesus!" I continued to say, looking around the pit for Him to come any minute. I knew my God and I knew if I called Him, whether it be heaven or hell, He would come.

The voice laughed along with what seemed to be millions of others; then the voice said, "Hebrews 6:6 says, 'If they shall fall away, to renew them again unto repentances; seeing they crucify to themselves the Son of God afresh, they put Him to an open shame'!"

I continued screaming and ignored the voice. "Jesus!" If there was one thing I remembered Momma telling me, it was if I were to call on Jesus, He would come.

Silence fell in the pit, and then I felt the brilliant light on my face and neck again. I lifted my head and reached my hand out to touch the light.

"Jesus, I knew you would come," I whispered.

I looked forward and could see His shadow in the distance but approaching fast. When He got closer the more my heart felt like it was melting and the warmer I got. I continued to look at His shadow when I started hearing laughter again.

"Look at what you did to Him!" the voice said.

I was eye to eye with Jesus. He was silent and standing before me. He was radiant and beautiful, and all I could do was cry.

I examined Him and saw Him with the nails in His hands and feet. He was hanging there right in front of me on the cross being crucified again for me. I felt horrible; this became as personal as personal could get. I knew He hung on the cross, naked, ashamed, and beaten just for me and my sins and my foolishness.

I bent my head down as close to the ground as I could, ashamed to even look at what my life did to Jesus. I could feel the pain in His heart for just me. And I knew at this moment there were only two words I could offer my Lord and Savior.

Chapter 30

Say It

After a few moments I had a deep desire to look at Him. It was as if He was silently calling my name. His eyes pierced my heart and soul as He displayed His love for only me on the cross.

I could no longer hear the voices of the mockers but only the voice of the King.

"I love you, Reese."

I couldn't hold my head up any longer but reverenced the Lord, and dropped not only my head but my whole body to the ground in a lifeless manner, and covered my face with my trembling hands in silence.

"See, I told you, He died for you ruthless, terrible creatures," the voice stated.

I grabbed some of the burnt grass that was in front of me on the ground in anguish. There was nothing I could do, no take backs, no starting over. I knew I couldn't take back the way I had lived life on the earth and the mistakes I had made.

My heart ached knowing that I caused Jesus to come to hell. It was my torment. I thought I had a little more time to clean up my life and get it together, to say "I'm sorry, Lord," but it was too late, the game was over.

I crawled closer to the bottom of His cross and cried out, "I love you." I felt His blood dripping on my hair and He cried as I reached for Him. In that very second

He was off the cross. The voice was gone, and I was standing back in the beautiful mansion I was first in.

Jesus was standing there, clothed in a purple garment, with a crown on His head. It was made of gold I had never inquired on earth before and there were jewels everywhere in it. They were embedded in and around it, and in the center of the crown sat a beautiful emerald.

I lay at His feet and looked at Him and wanted to say to Him what He knew I needed to say. I knew He had rescued me. I looked into His beautiful eyes. Jesus smiled at me as I moved my lips and started to speak.

"Reese, baby, wake up," Kev demanded.

I opened my eyes and smiled at Kev.

"What, babe? What you trying to say?" he asked.

I could hear the ambulance approaching the house to try to rescue me, but at this point I didn't care if they did or didn't; I had made my peace.

Kev pulled me close to his ear and said, "Say it, babe. Please just say it."

My chest heaved up and down as I began to gurgle on my own blood. One thought came to my mind before I uttered the words. I realized that whether I lived or died I was promised life eternal. So I looked up and I smiled at Kev; then I let the words fall from my lips: "I repent."

Altar Call

Jesus, come into my life. I want to be free. No more prisons, no chains, no darkness.

Jesus, I ask you to shine the light of Glory on my life, my situations, on me. Save me. Make me new. I repent of my sins. Please forgive me of my sins. I believe you are the Son of God. I confess with my mouth that You died for my sins on the cross, and I believe in my heart that God has raised You from the dead.

Romans 10:9 says that if you confess with your heart that God raised Him from the dead, you shall be saved.

> For godly sorrow produces repentances leading to salvation, not to be regretted; but the sorrow of the world produces death.
>
> –2 Corinthians 7:10

I Repent was inspired by the Holy Spirit. It was written to plead with the human race to repent unto the Lord. Reese was one young woman's testimony but there are many of stories that could be told describing the rebellious behavior that we take part in as humans.

I assure you that this story was one, but we as people live every day of our lives going on as if we have plenty of time to say sorry unto the Lord and repent.

But the truth be told, we never know when it will be too late.

We never know when the last time we say in our minds *this is the last time I'm gonna do this Jesus,* that it is indeed the last time.

Renea

From the time Jesus began to preach and to say, Repent: for the kingdom of heaven is at hand.

— Mathew 4:17

Notes

Notes

Notes